M000097855

Also by Ginny Brock:

 By Morning's Light

 ... as it is in Heaven

 Rainbow Rising

Praise for *By Morning's Light*
"I read this book in one sitting, unable to put it down... An emotionally compelling and fascinating story, beautifully written." ~J. R. Carty

"The true story of a mother connecting with her son after his sudden death is powerful and beautiful. *By Morning's Light* and its message of eternal life will capture you instantly." ~Amazon Reviewer

"Give this book to someone you know who is suffering a loss of any kind, and have them pass it along." ~Amazon Reviewer

Praise for *When the South Wind Blows*
Ginny Brock turns her glorious prose into a Civil War love story... When the last paragraph is closed, the reader is left wanting more. ~Betsy Ashton, Author of *Mad Max Mysteries* and novel *Out of the Desert.*

"Brock explores rich, deep characters, while evoking a true sense of the lush settings from Charleston to Murrells Inlet and Pawley's Island." ~K. Lamb

"A compelling mix of history and adventure with a love story so strong it crosses dimensions. A highly enjoyable read." ~Susan Coryell, Author of *A Red, Red Rose.*

"In a well-constructed, fast-moving story, Brock opens a window into the lives of intriguing characters in a tale reminiscent of Mark Twain." ~Linda Kay Simmons, Author of *Cahas Mountain* and *Lightning Shall Strike.*

When the South Wind Blows

The Untold Story of the Phantom of the Carolina Coast

A Novel by

Ginny Brock

FOR MY FAVORITE SOUTHERN BELLES

Mary Katherine Reeves Brock of South Carolina, Caroline Brock, Courtney, and Becca Kelley, of Virginia, and Karen Brock Kelley, born further south than anyone, in South Africa. And to their husbands, fathers, brothers and sons, Walter, Michael and Andrew Brock, William Randolph and Randolph Brock Kelley, James Michael and Tucker Brock.

AND TO THE LEGACY AND MEMORY OF:

William Stanley Heberden MD, born 1864 in England, grandfather, great-grandfather and great-great-grandfather, who was the inspiration for the character Doc Stanley in my book, as was William Heberden MD, born in 1767. A member of the medical aristocracy of his time, he was physician to King George III for many years and an inspiration to all his descendants.

When the South Wind Blows

The Untold Story of the Phantom of the Carolina Coast

PART 1

February 17, 1865

One

A Time to Let Go

A MIASMA OF RUMORS rose from the swamps around Charleston and, in the wake of Savannah's surrender, sunk roots into the minds of already fearful people.

The Charleston Courier reported that, following the alleged Yankee Programme, Sherman was marching on Charleston. The Charleston Mercury screamed, *"Prepare for a future of subjugation!"* And in the grip of rising panic, Charleston's population, some with bundles on their backs, fled the city.

No one doubted that the onslaught of Sherman's army would soon be upon them. That thought was further exacerbated by the latest rumor of Yankee scouts on the outskirts of town. Even now, Beauregard, the cavalier Creole general from New Orleans, was in full retreat as his lieutenants evacuated the terrified population.

Standing on the pulverized wreckage of Fort Sumter, feet planted on once five-foot-thick walls, Naval Lieutenant Ross Stanley listened to the muted sounds of the exodus from Charleston across the harbor. The screech of metal on metal was loud as locomotives steamed out of the station. He imagined the crush of soldiers loading the might of the heavily fortified city's armory onto incoming trains and crowds of panicked people pressing around the carriages, seeking passage out of Charleston.

Darkness shrouded the fort, and with it came a blessed cottony fog. A fog so dense that no one noticed the body rolling in the wake of a heavily laden barge as it pulled away from the shore.

The ghostly shapes of men moved like shadows over the rocks. Their muffled footsteps stumbled across the rubble as they hefted leaden boxes of ammunition and headed for the boat landing. A crumbling block of concrete now, the landing hardly merited its name.

Soldiers scurried across the broken terrain. A tall man cursed as his ankle turned, and two men fell heavily under the weight of guns and ordnance. A shower of rocks rattled down the slopes toward the water.

Ross walked alongside a wobbly line of wounded soldiers. All around him he heard the grunting of men moving iron-bound artillery toward the water. Some cursed the order to abandon the island. "Turnin' tail," one of them blurted. "That's my opinion."

Ross ignored the remark as a gust of wind carried it away toward the first light of dawn. He could see dark masses of clouds gathering on the horizon. He frowned. They had to keep moving.

"Shameful!" A man spat over his shoulder. "Cowardly shit, you ask me."

"Nobody asked you," an old soldier replied. "And no one gives a damn. I'm glad this war is over. Let's get this stuff outta here."

"I'm headin' home soon's I reach Charleston," a youngster murmured, his words falling softly through the early morning. "Got me a young'un I ain't never seen in Virginny."

The mood was confused. Some men were stoically somber, some wept openly. Many carried the dazed look of shellshock and tepid anticipation of the unknown. Ross sympathized with their mercurial mood changes, finding that his own feelings mirrored theirs.

He glanced across the harbor to where cumbersome barges, pulled by tugs, braced for the roughening sea, lumbered under their loads. In spite of the order to maintain silence, soldiers shouted from the boats. Ross sensed a kind of relief in their calls—relief to be moving after days of idleness, tinged with the frustration of wondering when and where Sherman might strike.

Approaching the broken landing, he took measure of his commanding officer, Major Huguenin. He noticed deep grooves furrowing the older man's brow and an uncharacteristic tightness in his jaw as he oversaw the evacuation.

"Damn!" Huguenin winced as another shout went up from one of the tugs, and low booms came from empty barges colliding at their moorings. "We'll be lucky if we don't arouse every Yankee bastard from Morris Island to Washington!" The major's sweat-soaked shirt clung to his back. He looked hot, in spite of the clammy fog.

Ross knew that the major was unhappy with the orders coming down from the high command. But a career military man, a product of The Citadel, Huguenin remained steadfast. Beauregard's abandonment order was in place, and the old soldier would, no doubt, execute it to the letter, regardless of his disdain.

Soft moans filled the air as a trickle of stretchers carried the last of the sick and wounded past the senior officer. An injured man cried out as one of the bearers tripped, jolting the stretcher. The stumbling stretcher bearer released a string of curses.

"Steady there," Huguenin said, reaching out a hand to slow the young corporal.

"Cain't see nothin' for the damned fog," the youngster grumbled.

"Get on your knees and thank God for the fog, Corporal. Without it the Feds would be bombarding the hell out of us."

"Yes, suh."

Sprawled on the stretcher at the end of the line was a man Ross recognized. "Last one," Ross called softly to Huguenin, stepping aside to let the stretcher pass. As he did so, the sick man motioned weakly for him to come closer. Ross raised his hand to halt the bearers and leaned toward the injured soldier. The now-familiar stink of gangrene rose from the stained blanket that half-draped the man's legs, disclosing the black swelling around the wound and the purple and green blotches that bruised his thigh. He imagined the scarlet streaks of poisoned blood racing upward and toward the groin. Gas gangrene was unstoppable.

"I ain't gonna make it, son," the man said, his voice barely audible. "Tell MaryAnn . . . tell MaryAnn stay strong. I cain't make it no further." Despite the fever in his eyes, he chuckled. "You remember the SS Kate, Lieutenant? Helluva ride." He tried to raise his head as a coughing spasm racked his body, and blood spewed from his nose and mouth.

"Hold on, Harry, we're going to get you home to MaryAnn." Ross put his hand on the dying man's shoulder and motioned to the stretcher bearers. "Get him on the barge."

He watched as they loaded Harry on board. He and Harry had been on board the CSS Tennessee when she was captured in Mobile Bay. The SS Kate, a Scottish blockade runner, had rescued Ross and three other sailors from the sea, finally dropping them off at Fort Sumter.

"All aboard," the coxswain called.

"Carry on." Huguenin gave the order to cast off.

Ross joined his commanding officer, and together, they watched the hospital ferry pull away from the pier.

The older man turned to Ross. "How much more is there to do, Lieutenant?"

"Almost done, sir. The Infantry has left. Soon's my men wrap up the bunker sweep we'll be on our way."

Ross straightened his shoulders, held out his hand to the man who had earned his respect over the last few months, and said, "It's time for you to leave, sir. Your barge is here."

He gestured toward the smoke-belching boat pulling into the berth just vacated, and walked the senior officer down the wooden jetty.

Huguenin rubbed his hand over his head. "It's been a long night. God dammit! God damn the high command!" His eyes dulled with the knowledge of imminent defeat. "You go to war to win. And if you can't win, you die upright and in charge, by God. What now, Lieutenant? Now what happens?"

Ross said nothing.

"God damn it to hell!" Huguenin continued. "Abandoning the fight for Sumter is Beauregard's idea, not mine. I never surrendered, son, you remember that. Major Thomas Huguenin never surrendered the fort."

"Yes, sir." Ross squared his shoulders and saluted as the officer stepped aboard his barge.

Fort Sumter's last Confederate CO stood stiffly at attention, faced the shore, and returned the salute as he left the island.

The Confederate States Army evacuation was complete. The young Lieutenant felt immeasurable relief as the barge pulled out into the roughening harbor.

Standing on the edge of the shattered landscape, Ross stared at the scene in front of him, feeling Huguenin's disgust. So many men lost. Gone forever. But in the silence, the sounds of their occupation remained. The blast of cannon fire, exploding mortar and the screams of the dying would scar this place for all time.

He shook his head, repeating the Major's words. "What now?"

He shivered. The quiet was eerily disconcerting. No bugle played reveille. The parade ground stood empty. Only the stillness of the abandoned ruin greeted the crimson sunrise over Fort Sumter.

Ross gazed at the ground. In his mind's eye he saw the bodies of a thousand men strewn in the rubble around his feet. Their eyes, glazed and dry, stared blindly at the dawn. And as he stared, a ragged line of fighting men rose from among the dead and turned away. One by one they passed before him—people he had known, like Walter Adams, Chief Petty Officer 1st Class CSS Tennessee, who stood stooped and gaunt, his empty shirt sleeve hanging loosely at his side.

"Walt!" Ross cried out. But the line moved on.

There was the Gunners Mate, unarmed now, with a deep red wound blossoming across the front of his shirt. Ross took a step forward. No one looked his way. Percy Hardy, the signalman, gazed beyond the rocks, to where a crippled warship lay abandoned, shrouded in fog.

"Percy!" Ross reached out his hand to halt the silent march, but the dead men walked on, unseeing, into the mist.

A sudden rifle shot rang out from across the bay, breaking the quiet, jolting Ross out of his reverie and back to the deserted scene in front of him. He shook his head and ran a hand through his once-black hair, now flecked with gray. Tears carved tracks through the dust and grime on his face. Hundreds and thousands of men and boys had thrown their hearts and minds into the mouths of cannons and rifle fire. Over half a generation lost for a cause they could not win.

The wind whipped the wave tops in the harbor, carrying the scent of seaweed, rusted iron and wooden ships, their hulls brined in tannin from Charleston's rivers.

A yell from one of the barges reached his ears. "We're shipping water!"

Ross turned toward the shout to see one of the barges heeling to port, waves slopping over the length of its deck. Its cargo must be shifting. "Let her go," he muttered. Hardened to the casualties of war, Ross stared at the barge, expressionless. She was going down. He was a professional navy man. His own ship, the CSS Tennessee, had been shot out from under him, a scene more catastrophic than any he'd ever witnessed. He knew they had no way to save the barge. The operation at hand had to continue. He hoped its crew could swim, but he knew that many upcountry soldiers could not.

Turning on his heel, Ross strode across the abandoned fortress toward the shaft that descended into the bunker where his seamen were still working.

They had to get out of here. Yesterday, right before their telegraph lines had been cut, the Mercury announced, in another blaring headline, that Sherman had crossed the Savannah River with his 60,000-strong force and was riding hell for leather for Charleston.

The rush to leave was on. According to all accounts, Savannah lay ruined and burning under rogue fires, and South Carolina was next. Sherman was on their heels. Around midnight Ross had seen lights on the water's edge of Charleston's deserted battery. More scouts?

So where the devil is he?

Ross turned his eyes to the only relief on the flattened landscape: A ragged Rebel flag, planted on the highest elevation of the ruin, flying above the rubble and twisted steel.

The new day was damp and strangely warm. Distant thunder rumbled in the south. The imagery of the dead seamen of his ship's company had left him shaken, and a wave of emotion threatened to choke him. In spite of the unseasonable warmth, he shivered. It wasn't the damp or the breeze. This cold came from inside, from the realization that four years of fighting had been in vain.

"But it's over," he murmured.

Reaching the ladder to the underground, he remembered how he felt when war broke out. Swept up in a wave of fighting fervor and excitement, he couldn't wait to join the battle, to lay down his life, if necessary, for the honor of the Southland and states' rights.

He'd never thought much about slavery. Had never thought of Willowgreen's blacks as slaves—they were people he had grown up with. But things changed, and in rare moments of reflection, it had become clear to Ross that there was nothing right about the enslavement of any man or woman. Not Zack, Moses, or his old Mammy Sadie Jones, or any of them at Willowgreen or anywhere else. Why hadn't he thought of that before? Somehow, God willing, he would make amends for his role in all this.

"Simeon!" he shouted down the shaft. "We gotta get out of here."

"Ten minutes, suh," came the reply.

"Make it five. I'll see you back at my boat."

"Yes, suh!"

Ross had volunteered himself and his three seamen to stay behind to secure the bunkers and make sure there was nothing left for the Yankee bastards to seize. He and his men had worked all night burning reams of documents and charts. It was time to leave, and he couldn't shake the bad feeling about what lay ahead. He turned around and trekked toward his boat mooring, on the leeward side of the island.

All he knew about what lay ahead was that the plantation life he'd known was finished. But he had a plan. And the girl he had loved since childhood stood at the center of that plan. He was going home to Katie Rose, and together, they would put this horror behind them.

He thought of his father back home at Willowgreen Plantation on the banks of the Waccamaw and felt a sudden longing to see him. The old Englishman, a doctor, had lived among the rice planters of Georgetown County for thirty-five years now. He thought of his crippled brother, Will, and yearned to be home. Would anyone remember that today was Ross's birthday? This morning he'd turned twenty-five.

Feeling much older than his years, Ross looked up at the flag drooping in the humid air and shivered. That flag would come down when he, the last man standing at Fort Sumter, left the island. He put his hands on his hips and laughed, but the sound fell flat. A navy man, the last to leave Sumter, would be the one to take down the Army's flag. What a bloody mixed-up world.

"I'll be damned if I'll take down Huguenin's flag," he said through clenched teeth. Conflict strapped his heart and mind as he walked away wondering if he was coming unhinged. Dark clouds buried the first rays of the sun, and that sense of urgency came again.

"Let's go, Simeon!" he yelled. One hell of a blow was coming in, and the sounds of the incoming storm made it difficult to hear any answering shout. He covered his right ear and grimaced. Badly damaged by the blasting of his ship's cannons over the years, little of his hearing remained in that ear.

Ross looked toward the shore, and his face softened at the thought of the warm, green refuge of the cypress woods of

Willowgreen. And of a girl as soft as moonlight: Katie Rose, his betrothed. A girl whose mind overflowed with boundless ideas and dreams, and whose heart was full of passion and, at least the last time he'd seen her, full of love for him. The greasy pall of smoke from burning cotton bales on the shore made his eyes water, and he brushed the tears away. Suddenly, the shout went up. "Bunkers secured! Ready to launch!"

"Get over here!" Ross shouted. "We've got a plan."

With any luck they could be off this pile of rubble by late morning. He stood on the rocks just above his boat, watching it pitch and roll in the waves. Spray whisked off the harbor, and he could smell the rivers in its moisture, along with the sweet aroma of yams baking in the ashes of Sadie Jones's hearth. The children, who called her Gogo, would be holding their hands out for saltwater taffy, and Sadie's cat would be sound asleep on the stool beside her rocking chair.

Ahh, Sadie. "Your boy's coming home," he said out loud, smiling for the first time that day.

Watching the sea ebb and flow, Ross seized his chance, sprang onto the sandy surface, and sprinted toward the shallop, but a rogue wave crashed behind him, sending foam and water swirling around his knees.

"Dammit!" The water chilled him to the bone as he stepped forward, and something smacked the back of his leg. Turning, he spotted a long, water-logged object and quickly realized that the body of a young boy was churning around his boots.

Stifling a yell, he caught hold of the boy's torso. Then, placing his hands under the arms, pulling against the sucking sea, he heaved the body onto the path beside the rocks.

Breathing hard, Ross turned the corpse onto its back and searched the face. It was no one he recognized. Still, something about the body bothered him, and it wasn't the pouch strapped around the dead boy's waist.

A lull in the wind allowed him to hear the sound of footsteps scrambling over the rocks behind him.

"Over here!" he yelled.

Two

Bloody Sunrise on Pawley's Island

MISS FANNIE'S INN of Southern Comfort stood silently among an outcropping of weathered oaks on the beach road. Across from it, a figure crouched beside a chestnut horse holding the reins. "Be still," he whispered softly.

Something was wrong at the Inn.

An eerie red glow from the newborn sun bathed the unusually still morning. The Inn's rooftop glistened with moisture and the promise of rain thickened the air.

No lights flickered in the windows. Everything seemed normal—but it was not like every other morning. Something was different.

There was a man slouched in a willow-cane chair on the porch and the sound of his heavy snoring carried across the crushed-shell road. Not that was there was anything strange about a man on Miss Fannie's porch, the watcher knew. This house was well-known to many a travelling man and frequented by those less-travelled as well. The comings and goings of solitary men had not gone unnoticed, and even an outcry from the island residents had failed to close the place down. And so it stood, against a backdrop of palms on this deep red early morning.

The rising wind powdered the sunrise with dust from the road. Through the eerie glow the rider could make out the shape of a wagon, roughly concealed by the shrubbery that grew wild a short distance from the Inn. The wind had flicked back the wagon's cover to expose a stack of wooden boxes.

He glanced back at the inn. If anyone had been watching from the windows of the inn they would have seen the silhouette of a youngster dressed in a woolen cap, baggy shirt and riding breeches scurrying low across the road before disappearing into a cluster of overgrown crepe myrtle near the wagon. But no one was looking.

Unseen by anyone, a head poked up over the side of the wagon and, barely breathing, the youth peered inside. A sweaty hand reached out to touch the nearest crate. In the first light of day the insignia of the Union Artillery Corps, two crossed cannons and Army of the Potomac was stenciled on its side.

Damn Yankees! There must have been twenty or more boxes stashed in the wagon. What did they hold? Breathing hard now, the youth reached in and eased the lid of the box open. It creaked. He stood motionless and listened. The sounds of the man's snoring was loud and flabby.

A ray of light glinted off the contents of the crate revealing a nest of small, metal containers that might look like toys to the casual observer. But they were not toys. There had been talk of these hand-thrown bombs. And here they were. A wagon load of grenades, they called them. Were they headed for Georgetown? To blow up the rice mills? A box of matches was tucked into a corner, buffered and covered by bricks to prevent accidental friction, he supposed. Barely breathing, the youngster took the matches, lifted out two of the grenades and stared at them. With heart pounding, and eyes wide in a young face devoid of facial hair, the task at hand became clear.

But something had changed. The early morning birds were quiet. The air seemed more oppressive. And the snoring had stopped.

The youth stood as still as a marsh heron, not daring to blink or breathe, taut with fear, before slowly disappearing like the shadow of an overhead bird into the tangle of brush.

A twig crackled underfoot as the shadowy form reappeared some fifty feet down the road, away from the Inn. He was flattened out in such a way that if someone was looking, they would have seen only a dark depression in the sand. If someone looked hard enough, they would notice that it was slowly squirming across the narrow track to where the horse stood hidden in the oaks.

But no one was watching. So no one saw the figure mount the horse and ride him silently through the trees, stopping directly across the road from the wagon. He stopped to listen. There was no sound to be heard. Fannie's male visitor could be seen facing away from the road, relieving himself off the end of the verandah. He snorted and sent a stream of spit over the railing.

It was now or never. With trembling hands, the youngster managed to light first one fuse, then the other, and with a rush of adrenaline, lobbed them strongly, in swift succession, toward the wagon.

The man on the porch was looking the other way wiping his mouth on his sleeve when the first grenade buried its nose among the boxes. He may have heard the clink of metal as it hit, but he never saw the flash of light, nor heard the explosion that shook the sandy road.

He never saw the horse and rider racing through the trees, skidding and bobbing among the out-stretched limbs, racing for the beach. He never saw them careen behind a high dune, dismount, lie low, sheltering from the next blast that detonated the wagonload of grenades.

Shards of shrapnel and splintered wood flew through the air, landing in the trees, sparking small fires in the brush. The frightened horse reared, whinnying shrilly as explosion after explosion shook the ground. "Hush, Sonny." Hanging onto the reins, with arms wrapped tightly around the animal's neck, breathing hard and fast, the rider tried to calm him. "It's alright, it's alright—you're alright. We're fine."

The chestnut snorted, tossed his head and stood still, his eyes rolling, his ears pinned flat against his skull. They waited, and as soon as the explosions ceased, they emerged from behind the dune. Looking quickly to left and right, the youth leapt into the saddle, and spurring the horse to action, took off at a gallop along the hard-packed shore. The stench of sulfur and the smell of gun powder thickened the already humid air as they tore along the deserted shore.

As the last mile disappeared under the horse's hooves, Fairhaven's tall chimneys, bright white walls and gazebo came into view behind the dunes. Dunes that protected the big beach house from high tides. Veering sharply away from the sea, they cantered toward the grassy mounds and, slowing to a walk, the horse began to climb, leaving deep hoof prints in the sand. His coat was stained dark brown with sweat, his nostrils flared from the exertion, and tiny flecks of foam streaked his mane.

Reaching the summit the rider reined in the sweating horse and turned to look back at the shore. Satisfied there was no one around, a delicate hand reached up and pulled off the woolen cap.

Katie Rose shook out her hair and ran trembling hands over her flushed face. Dismounting shakily, not at all sure her legs would hold her, she guided the horse down the other side of the dune and into the oak grove that surrounded the home.

As they reached the stables and went inside, the girl patted the animal's glistening coat and whispered in his ear. "We did it, Sonny Boy, we went to war. She removed the saddle and dumped it unceremoniously on the rack.

She had joined the fight. It was the one thing she had longed to do from the time the war began. She wanted to be a part of it. She wanted to do something for the cause, and most of all, in solidarity with her beloved Ross who was somewhere out on the high seas. And she had done it.

"I blew the whole damn wagon load to hell!" she exalted.

Exhilaration, mixed with fear and trepidation at what she had done. She leaned her head against the horse's shoulder and breathed in deeply. After a moment, she stepped away, bent over and vomited into the sand.

"We did it," she whispered, straightening up and scuffing sand over the steaming mess. She was shaking from head to toe. "I can't stay, big boy. No one must find me here. I'll be back soon to rub you down."

A smile spread across her face as she ran through the grove and silently entered the house through the beachside door. The scent of lemon oil, seashells, and sand filled the hallway as she paused on the threshold and listened. The kitchen was in darkness, and she didn't see the figure of a man step out of the shadows and watch her tiptoe down the hall.

Biting her lip, Katie Rose started up the stairs. A floorboard creaked. She winced. But there was no sound from the downstairs bedrooms. The aunts were still asleep. With her hand poised on her bedroom door at the top of the stairs, she stopped and listened, and, hearing nothing, went inside closing the door behind her.

Only then did she think of Miss Fannie. She breathed in deeply as she squeezed her eyes shut and prayed that the lady had escaped the fire.

Charles Asquith, Fairhaven's butler, had been awakened by the sound of the explosion and, dressing hurriedly, had been just in time to watch the young Miss, from the kitchen window, as she ran from the stables to the house.

Curious. There was nothing unusual about the girl coming in from an early ride. She did it regularly. But she hadn't even stopped to brush the horse down. Something didn't feel right. Leaving the shadows, he turned a lamp on and lit the wood stove to begin boiling water for the ladies early morning tea.

Had Katie Rose been anywhere near the explosion he'd heard? He rubbed his chin. She didn't look hurt. Not that you could tell much in that appalling boyish outfit she wore. She said it made her less conspicuous if anyone should see her out alone at that hour, and Charles had to agree. Certainly no one would be expecting to see a young woman cantering wildly along the road in men's trousers and an oversized plaid men's shirt at the crack of dawn.

Upstairs Katie Rose pulled the quilt up around her ears and, with pounding heart she tried to close her eyes. She clasped her hands together to stop them shaking, but she was restless and her eyelids kept flying open as the scene of the explosion played over and over through her mind. It had shaken the road and the oaks and frightened her witless, but she had helped The Cause. She had joined the fight. She had joined the battle that had kept Ross away from her for far too long.

She refused to think about Miss Fannie.

Three

The Voices of Willowgreen

"WHO DAT IS?" The old woman's reedy thin voice was soaked in sleep. "Ah heared somun callin' Sadie Jones—" She squinted into the gloom of her bedroom, a small oaken addition that was attached to the kitchen house.

The first glimmers of Sunday morning showed through the wooden slats of the windows. "De sun he up, but cain't nobody see nothin'," she grumbled. But she didn't have to see anything to know that there was no one there.

She pulled her frail body up onto the bed pillows and gazed around the room. Nothing and nobody was there. So she lay back down staring at the ceiling, waiting for the voice to call again.

"You a haint?" She used the Gullah word for ghosts. There was no reply. "Durn haints! Don' you be messin' wid me!"

Sadie lay still. Her eyes might be dim, but her senses were sharp despite the early hour. She could hear the embers ticking in the hearth from last night's fire and up in the loft, her son Zacky, made little snorting sounds in his sleep.

"You still dere, haint?" Far off in the distance, a rooster crowed, but no voices answered Sadie Jones.

Something squirrely was going on. Her right hand lay across her chest, and when she moved it, her palm felt sticky. "What dat be?" she muttered. Raising her left hand to her breast she realized that the front of her nightdress was damp. A sliver of sunrise brightened the edges of dawn as she raised herself and sat on the edge of the narrow bed. She pushed the covers aside and, as she did so, a twinge of pain rippled through both breasts making her look down at her nightdress. Sadie frowned as another twinge tightened the thin flesh of her breasts.

Then, loosened by some far off memory, a smile curled her lips. "Lawsy, I ain't felt nothing lak dat fer years." She didn't know how many years, but then she didn't know how many years she had in her anyway. Marse Doc said he thought maybe sixty-five, and that was too many for her to remember.

Her mind wandered as she shuffled her feet into her slippers, "Yes. Dat be a long time," she lifted her skirt and blouse off the peg by the bed and began to dress. "But dat don' matter none. Me and ma baby Mollie bin here all dese years since her worthless daddy done run off. Marse Doc he say I can go too, if'n I want. But he not tinking right in those days, dat's for sho," she muttered. "I gots ma baby to feed, ma sick mistress and Marse Doc, to take care of. So me and Molly we stayed raht here."

And that was a good thing, because the very next year Mistress Elizabeth gave birth to Willie boy and a few years after that, Sadie's son, Zacky boy, was born. It was not long before Mistress Elizabeth's second child, Rossie, came along. "By den Mis'tis Lilabef she so sick she like ta died, so Marse Doc he call me to feed de new baby."

Her breasts throbbed in response to the thought of Rossie and Zacky nursing together, one on each arm. She touched them in wonder as her hands again came away damp. A frown crumpled her brow as she tried to figure out why this was happening.

And then she knew.

Her lips moved almost soundlessly. "Laws God, ah don't know wat you tinkin up dere, but must be either you or ol' Sadie's goin' plum crazy!" the old woman shook her head in disbelief. "Laws, God," she smiled. Slowly, that pale brown smile began to spread from one side of her face to the other. She chuckled. "Could be ah'm plum outta ma haid, but mah milk's a rising! Yassir, mah milk's a rising, sho nuff." Her old eyes filled with tears. "Ol' Sadie's milk be coming in. And dat mean mah boy's coming home." In her mind, she could see his face. Ross Stanley, youngest son of the master, and the boy who had been like a brother to her son Zacky.

That was the first thing she thought about, and the second thought she had was that Zacky Boy must fetch him home. Sadie shuffled into the kitchen, fumbling with her apron strings.

First ting, dey gonna need is a horse, she steadied herself with one hand on the back of a chair. Sadie tossed a piece of split oak onto the embers in the fireplace and another in the stove sending the sparks flying. She dipped a cup into the water bucket and emptied it into the kettle for Marse Doc's tea then hung it from a hook inside the fireplace to boil.

She could hear Zacky moving around up in the loft and she walked over to the ladder. "Zacky, you waked up, you?" she called.

Marse Doc had told her to move Zacky up from The Street so he could be close by to help her if need be.

"Ahm up."

"Well, you c'mon down, we got tings ta do dis day," she said as she shuffled across the kitchen and tugged the outside door open.

"Lawsy, dat sky is red dis mo'nin'." She stood on the threshold sniffing the air. "Dat's some bad storm coming, dat's what dat is. Lak de storm dat blow all de folks up in de tree," Sadie stepped out onto the swept dirt yard noticing that the air was warmer than it should be this early February morning.

She could hear sounds coming from the beaten down track that lead to the quarters where the field hands lived with their families. A baby cried from one of the small houses that huddled side by side on either side of The Street, as they called it. Sadie could see the faint glow their fireplaces gave off as the workers readied themselves for the day ahead.

Picking up her skirt, she turned around and walked back to the kitchen. "Isaac Jones!" she called impatiently.

"Yas'm. Ah'm a comin!"

Grumbling to herself, she turned her attention to making breakfast. There were eggs in a sweet-grass basket on the shelf, rice in the bin and buttermilk for biscuits. She pulled a small pot down from the shelf for the doctor's eggs and a larger pot for the rice for Zacky's and Marse Willie's breakfast. "An' we gots plenty of honey," she noted with satisfaction.

Sadie Jones took pride in her honeybees and the garden where she grew all the flowers that bees liked, which is why they said her honey was some of the best in the county. And in amongst those flowers she grew herbs and spices for her kitchen and her healing potions. Some might call her a herbalist, others said she talked to her bees so she could be a witch. Of course, she talked to herself a lot these days too, so who could tell who she was talking to. Around the plantation, she was simply known as the Root Doctor.

Day was barely breaking in the southwest, when Zack came down the ladder. "Why you up so early, Mama?" he asked, rubbing his eyes.

"We got tings to do, and you got to get yo'sef down Chastin way. You goin' find Rossie boy."

"What?" he exclaimed.

"Rossie. He leaving de fighting," she turned around and smiled at him. "An' you goin' fetch him home. On dat big white horse. Da haint horse. An' don' you be looking aty me lak dat."

"Who told you Rossie's coming home?"

"Nobody. I jes knows dese tings."

Shaking his head, Zack picked up a log and some short twigs and poked them into the stove. "Shouldn't I go fetch him from the navy yard in Wilmington?" he asked.

"Chastin," she said firmly, placing the rice on top of the stove.

Doctor Stanley had bought the stove for Sadie Jones soon after they arrived from England and found that she was cooking everything in the fireplace. At first she railed against it, but as she grew accustomed to cooking on it, she guarded it jealously. Her enthusiastic polishing had worn off most of the blacking, but the brass handles shone as brightly as the day it arrived.

Zack watched her silently as she brushed her hands together and began to pat down the biscuit dough. A tiny, bent figure in her long skirt and slippers, her skin was the color of steeped tea and age clouded her eyes. She was the picture of frailty, but the picture was deceptive.

This old lady had been honed on the wheel of grueling survival, and, if her body was slowly breaking down, there was nothing the matter with her mind or her fierce will.

"That's crazy." Zack said. "How'm ah gonna find Ross in Chastin'?" He took the tray of biscuits from her and placed it in the oven.

"You'll find him. And you respect yo mama, Zacky Boy!" She gave him a swift clout on the arm and a push toward the stables.

"Fust ting you do is go get de big white saddle horse fixed up while ah fix Marse Doc he breakfast. And when you takes it to de house you ax him to give you a pass letter. Dat a bad road out dere. Bad folk looking to stop you. Dey tink you uppitty when you open yo' mouf and don't talk like no negro hardly."

She knew Zack knew that. She had told him often enough. He had been given lessons in the same plantation schoolroom as Ross and Willie and had grown up speaking as they did.

Sadie opened the cupboard, pulled out a cake of cornbread and six buttermilk biscuits left over from last night's dinner. Wrapping them in a cotton cloth, she placed them on the table. "You goin be gone 'round dinner time. No tellin' where y'all goin find sumpin to eat down Chastin way. Ah heared ain't no food an de folks is beggin' on King's St. Take dis wid you when you leave."

"Yes'm," Zack nodded and left the kitchen house.

Sadie worried about the food supply. It was tough everywhere. And getting worse with the Yankee blockade of Winyah Bay. And them wrecking the Georgetown rice mill, making it hard for the plantations to get their rice milled and shipped out. Willowgreen, a relatively small holding was still able to get a lot of their rice onto the inland trains. Everyone wondered how long that would last.

Four

Finding Ross

BUT CHARLESTON? ROSS wouldn't come ashore in Charleston, Zack knew.

The horse, Blue Boy, shuffled around in the straw as Zack walked into his stall. "Hey, big boy," he called softly, and the horse nuzzled his neck. "You ready for a ride?" He dug his hand into a sack of corn and held it out for the horse. "Mama's got us goin' fetch Ross. Don't know what she's talking about, but it's about time that boy was headed home." He ruffled the horse's mane. "Maybe she knows something, maybe she doesn't, but you and me gotta giddyup. Hey! Daniel!" he called to the stable boy who roused himself from the straw mattress in the corner of the tack room and rubbed his eyes.

"You snoozin'?" Zack rubbed the boy's wooly head. "Get Blue ready to go, y'hear me? Fill that feed bag and bring him down to the house."

"Ah brings him," the boy pushed himself up.

Zack turned on his heel and sprinted back to the kitchen through the red dawn. Sadie handed him a tray with the master of Willowgreen's breakfast keeping warm under a silver dome.

"No milk?" Zack asked, taking the tray from his mother.

"De sweet milk done turned cos o' de storm."

"What storm?"

"Cain't you smell it?"

"No, Ma'am." He headed down the breezeway to the main house. He could hear Doctor Stanley up and moving around inside as he raised his hand and knocked on the back door.

"Ah! There you are," William Stanley greeted Zack the way he did every morning.

An imposing figure, he stood six feet tall in his stockinged feet, with a head of steel-gray hair that was always combed and trimmed to the height of his winged collar. Putting his gold watch back into his vest pocket, he turned and walked over to the window where his breakfast table had been set by Tansy, the girl from The Street who helped Sadie with housework.

He sat down heavily in his chair and spread his napkin on his lap. "And what are your plans for this fine day, Zack?"

Tansy took the tray from Zack with a sweep of her eyelashes and a sassy smile.

His lips twitched as his hand brushed hers and he stepped back appreciating the way her green skirt draped over her hips as she set the silver teapot in front of the doctor.

"Mama's got the idea that Rossie's coming home and I have to go fetch him from Charleston." he said.

"What on earth is she talking about?"

"I don't know, but she's sure she's right, and she told me to ask you to write a letter of passage in case I get stopped."

"Hmmm." William Stanley poured himself a cup of tea, as Zack stood there. "The last we heard, Ross was at Fort Sumter. What the devil is she thinking? Do you want me to speak to her? This is preposterous!'"

"I have no idea what she's thinking sir. All I know is that when Mama gets something in her head nothing will change her mind."

"How well I know," William Stanley rapped the shell on the side of his boiled egg.

"Things are slack right now," Zack replied. "I've got time. Only thing I can't figure is why Charleston."

"Mmm. Don't ask me to figure out what goes on inside that head of hers," the doctor paused with his spoon in midair. "Suppose you were Ross. And you decided to leave the fort and get back to the navy. How would you do it?"

"Well, it sure wouldn't be through Charleston—if what we hear 'bout the army leaving and Yankees getting ready to swarm the place is true," he stared down at the floor. "I'd sail for Wilmington and the navy base."

"Bad choice. We hear that Wilmington's already swarming with Yankees." He straightened his napkin on his lap. "Would he perhaps leave the fort and put in to one of those coves north of Charleston and ride home somehow? Try to intercept a ship somewhere?" Without waiting for a reply William said, "Yes, by God! That's what I'd do." He picked up his spoon and gave his egg another crack. "But I'm afraid you're going on a wild goose chase, Zack."

"S'cuse me for saying so, Doc Stanley, but I hope you're wrong. That's a long way to go for nothing."

"I hope I'm wrong, too," the Doctor smiled and picked up his teacup. "Get me my pen and ink and the paper with my name and address on it. She'll drive us all mad if I don't write a letter."

"That's true, sir."

He scribbled three or four lines on the paper, folded it, dripped a spot of wax from the chunk of red sealing wax Zack handed him, and pressed his crest-engraved ring into it. "This letter says you belong to me and Willowgreen Plantation, and you're going to fetch my son. I trust you'll receive better treatment if you show it."

Zack nodded and took the letter. "Thank you, sir."

"Did Sadie tell you where she got her information about Ross?" William persisted.

"No. Just said that she knows these things."

"I've heard that before, too. Puts a neat end to any conversation that Miss Sadie Jones doesn't want to have, doesn't it."

Zack chuckled, "You know her well, Doc Stanley."

"Indeed I do. Look after yourself, lad. Bring Ross back with you," He gave Zack a conspiratorial wink and a grin, and turned back to his breakfast. "How I wish it was true. Wait. You'd better have some ferry money." He dug into his breast pocket and handed Zack a handful of notes.

"Yes, sir."

Zack closed the door behind him, wondering at the Doc's patience with Sadie. Most people would think she was plum crazy.

Fortified by a cup of buttermilk and a bowl of rice and honey in his belly, Zack mounted the white horse. His saddlebag bulged with the buttermilk biscuits and cornbread Sadie had given him.

"You ride careful, boy," she called from the kitchen doorway. "Right now, it's a fine sunshiny mo'ning, but dere's a storm a'comin."

"Don't you worry none, Mama," he laughed as he urged the tall white gelding into an easy amble down the oak-lined drive.

Sadie watched him go. How many times had she stood on this very spot watching one or another of the boys leaving for one place or another?

She was pleased. Her Gullah son would find his way to the Master's son, his childhood friend and his brother in every way but blood. No matter, blood or no blood link, Zack would find him and bring him home. Of that she was certain.

Listening to the soft tread of the horse's hooves, her old mind went back to the days when they were children. She remembered the laughter, the shouting, scuffles when things went wrong. Rolling in the dust, squealing as they pulled hair and struggled over a terrapin, a stick of sugar cane, or a new hoop.

There was the day when, mopping Zack's bloody nose following a tussle in the swept yard, the child turned to her and yelled, "Lookit him, Mama, he makin' faces at me! Why do I gotta be his friend? I hate him!"

"Hush your mouf, Isaac Jones." Sadie turned his small face to hers. "You not just his friend. Marse Doc, Willie and Rossie ain't got no family but us, chile. Dey family be far 'way. We all dey got and we gots to be better dan friends. We family, y'hear me? "

"Sorry, Zacky," Ross held out his hand with a crestfallen look on his face. "I didn't mean to fall on you."

Zack hesitated, and then took the outstretched hand and wrung it. "Can I have dat other piece of honey candy you got in your pocket?"

"No!" Rossie grinned, and digging into his pocket, he retrieved the candy, stuffed it in his mouth and ran away. They were off again.

Three months older than Ross, they were raised together from the time Ross was born. Nursed and nurtured by the same woman. And if, by an accident of birth, one was white and the other was black, neither noticed.

Zack cast a backward glance at the place that had been his home since he was born to Sadie Jones some twenty-five years ago. That strange, blood-red sunrise bathed the house and its chimneys, giving them an eerie glow.

Ahead he could see the cypress woods, their thin fronds tipped in the pale green of early springtime; the lone Live Oak by the river that had been there since before he was born. Its dipping limbs swept the bank on both sides of its massive trunk. He looked up at the tangle of branches high off the ground and chuckled.

That was the place where he and Ross crouched with their slingshots at the ready, hidden from make-believe enemy rice barges—barges that might steal all of Moses' rice and take the chickens, too. They might even kidnap all the children off The Street.

Moses was the overseer, a gentle giant of a man, who ran the small rice plantation.

"I remember the day we pelted the barges with stones," Zack told his horse. "We liked the sound they made when they hit and that skipiddy doo jump 'cross the water." He chuckled to himself. "Sadie Jones caught us and, oh Nellie, was she was fit to be tied! Chased us all the way home flicking our legs with a willow switch and us running like the devil himself was chasing us."

Narrowly skirting a deep rut in the packed clay road, Zack grinned. "That was before the time Rossie invited the barge hands back to the house. Oh Lawsy. You'd a thought we'd let a 'coon in the hen house.

"Then one day we were playing with the wooden guns that Moses whittled for us when one of those pretend enemy boats pulled up to the bank and someone yelled, 'This the place where the doctor lives?' Then a man jumped ashore and stood on the bank looking left and right.

He sure looked scary, and Rossie said, 'He's a murderer,' and I said, 'he's a murderer alright!' Then the man yelled, 'Hey! You!'"

And Ross stood up and said, real fierce, 'Hey, you, *what*?' Just as cool as you please. 'You a murderer?' "We need a doctor," the man shouted. "Got a man here who's hurt real bad."

"Then Ross, he says, 'I'm a doctor.'

Well, I was hiding behind him, and I hissed at him, 'That's a lie—you ain't no doctor. You only seven!' I pinched him on the leg, and he yelled, 'Quit that! I'm ALMOST a doctor, you idiot!' Then he tells them, 'My Pa's a doctor.'"

Zack didn't know how much of this the horse was getting, but it didn't matter. This old River Road held lots of memories.

"Then a second man appeared half-dragging his friend, saying, 'Can you take us to him?' And Rossie says 'How'd I know you aren't gonna kill us?' and points his gun at them.

'Jesus, kid!" the man said, holding up both hands. 'We're unarmed, see?'

Rossie just stared at them with his gun pointed right at their heads. The man with his hands in the air said, 'How about we walk in front of you? That way you can keep that gun on us.'

'Zackie, get your gun!' Rossie yelled, and shouted at the man, 'Start walking!'

So, we followed them down the road with our guns aimed at their backs as they hauled the man to the doctor's office, and Doc Stanley fixed him up.

Soon as they were done, Moses told 'em to git. Right Now." Moses, didn't do nothin', as I recall, just stood there lookin' like Moses, with his machete at his side, and said 'Git!'" Zacky grinned at the memory.

"That should have been the end of that, but, Lawsy! Mama and Moses started shouting their heads off about bringing strangers to the house, so loud they scared the chickens off their laying, and we beat it fast as we could back to the river."

The road was deserted at this hour, so Zack picked up the pace. "Let's go, Blue."

The games of children were one thing, Zack thought somberly. Then war broke out and things soon became deadly serious.

Recognizing the vulnerability of Georgetown and Horry Counties and their massive rice production, the Secessionist Government ordered the construction of batteries on three islands at the mouth of Winyah Bay to defend the bay and Georgetown.

For a while, these defenses effectively kept the US warships out. But things changed when a new commander ordered the removal of men and artillery for the more important defense of Charleston.

It wasn't long after that, Zack recalled, that Yankee gunboats began sailing up the Waccamaw River. Their fighters poured off the boats, ransacked homes, destroyed rice mills and captured slaves. Luckily, the shallow waters kept the warships out, sparing most of the plantations from destruction, Willowgreen among them.

Then everything changed again. With Union forces controlling the islands where the bay met the Atlantic, General PGT Beauregard replaced Lt. General Pemberton and constructed and armed two more sites further up the Bay.

But it was too little too late. The damage was done. The country's largest rice-growing region could no longer function without slaves, machinery or transportation. Georgetown, the port that the rice growers depended on, was already crippled by the blockades and its milling operation ruined.

Everything was changing. Nothing was certain for any of them, and he had lain awake some nights thinking about the next phase of his life. He would have to take care of his mother and think of ways he could help the Doc and all of them to stay on the plantation. What he really wanted to do was to teach the youngsters coming up behind him. He dreamed of one day owning a small schoolhouse like the one in Murrells Inlet, a place to teach the children who would soon be free to learn.

He ran a hand over his face. There must be a way. Somehow, they would find something to do, other than grow rice, and they would make it work. "Rossie and me will find a way," he muttered.

Settling into a steady trot, Zack patted his pocket where the letter of passage was stashed and thought of Sadie Jones. He hoped she hadn't finally taken leave of her senses, but he knew better than to dismiss her crazy-sounding whims. Nobody else was aware that Ross was coming home, but Sadie Jones knew things. He didn't know how she knew the things she did, and they mostly made no sense at the time, but he didn't doubt that she knew things that other people didn't. And if she said Ross needed him, then he and the blue-eyed horse would find him.

Zack was cautiously elated at the idea of fetching Ross. His childhood friend had been gone too long, and this time he was maybe coming home to stay. He ruffled the brown forelock on Blue's head. A blue-eyed horse with a cap of brown hair between his ears was enough to convince the Waccamaw workers, and everyone on The Street, that Big Blue was a Spirit Horse. One born with magical powers.

"Use that magic, big boy. Let's find Rossie."

Five

The Village at Murrells Inlet

FOLLOWING HIS CUSTOMARY breakfast of two boiled eggs, (three minutes and forty-five seconds in boiling water to be precise) two cups of tea, and a piece of toasted oat bread and butter, Dr. William Stanley walked outside to his buggy.

Bertie, a sturdy chestnut, was already harnessed to the small, high-wheeled vehicle with black leather canopy and seats.

Daniel, the stable boy and overseer's son, stood holding the reins waiting for the Doctor. "Mistah Bertie, he sho' acting squirrely dis day," he told William. "Every time ah tries to put him in harness, he be jumpin' around. Throwing he head."

"It's a warm morning," the doctor remarked. "Maybe he's feeling the weather change."

"Coulda bin dat 'splosion before daylight scared him."

"What explosion?" the doctor asked placing his medical bag on the floorboards. Straightening up, he lifted his chin and loosened the top button of his white, boiled shirt and winged collar. Ahh, that felt better.

Daniel handed his master the reins. "Yes. Don't know what blew up, but sumpin did."

Fanciful boy. Explosion, indeed.

The air wafting off the ocean was heavy with moisture, sticky and salty with a strong fishy smell. He wrinkled his nose and glanced at a long, low bank of clouds building in the south.

"You're off early this morning, Pa." His oldest son, Will, closed the front door of the manor behind him, and came down the wide stone steps as fast as his leg brace would allow.

"Morning, Will. I'm getting a head start on the weather," The doctor said heaving himself into the buggy. "Oomph! My legs aren't going to take much more of this. Neither is the rest of me. Old age is a damn nuisance, my boy!"

Will grinned. "You're as spry as ever, sir."

"Got to keep the blood moving, son. Remember that. If you don't, God knows what foul affliction will creep up on you."

"Yes, sir." Will chuckled.

"I know you've heard that before." He smiled at his son. It was muggy this morning. Will's dark auburn hair was damp with the effort of descending the stone steps. The brace was cumbersome, he knew, but useful considering the fact he'd been born with one leg shorter than the other.

"It's rumored that a frigate came into Murrells Inlet a couple of nights ago and landed a load of medical supplies for the troops," Will was saying. "Had you heard?"

The doctor raised his eyebrows. "No. I had not. Came in when?"

"Night before last. Jonah down on The Street told me when I stopped to check on the newborn this morning." He paused. "They pick up all the rumors. He also told me that we lost three more workers yesterday."

"The young are impatient, and the wheels of the law turn

slowly," William said. "A few more weeks, and they will be legally free," he shifted his feet on the floorboards. "I hope the rumors about a medicine drop are true. We're running low on essentials. In fact, I'm planning a stop at Jake Reynolds to see what he has, so I'll ask him about the ship. If anyone knows about a medicine drop, the druggist will. How is the baby on The Street?" The doctor changed the subject.

"Congestion's worse. His mother's burning camphor cubes in the room, but I fear there's not much we can do. I left some morphine with her."

The doctor picked up the reins and frowned. Medicine was scarce, and he had no new ideas about what to do with a baby who couldn't breathe because his heart was failing. "That's all we can do."

Will stepped back as his father snapped the reins and waved, watching the horse start off down the oak-shaded driveway. William planned to ride to River Road, which would take him to the Waccamaw loop where he would pick up the King's Highway into the village of Murrells Inlet. "I'll be stopping at the tailor's and the cobbler's," he called over his shoulder. "And the carpenter's shop to get glue for Moses." Will lifted his hand in farewell.

The doctor liked these morning rides into the village. It gave him time to think without anybody interrupting him. This morning he was thinking that the end of a bitter winter was fast approaching Carolina's coast, and thank God for that. All the chest ailments would go away and, if people would only wash their hands regularly, the contagion might stand half a chance of being contained. What in God's name was so hard about keeping your hands clean, for Heaven's sake!

The banks of the Waccamaw River were home to some of the

wealthiest rice plantations on earth. Soon, it would be springtime, and William liked the spring. He liked the stately homes surrounded by their magnolia trees. Homes that had by the grace of God, been largely untouched by a war that had destroyed thousands of other homes all over the southland.

He wondered how long it would remain so. How long would it be before Sherman's army overtook the Carolina coast. And would his beloved Willowgreen meet the same fate as its southern neighbors? He could picture it clearly. Their massive beams scorched black, consumed by 60-foot-high flames, as they thundered to the ground. Fire, malignant and avaricious, was Sherman's weapon of choice for the destruction of the South.

William shook his head. A letter from an old friend had come in the mail last week detailing the horrors of the Savannah fires. Those fires, set in the wake of Sherman's departure, by rogue elements, had burnt large sections of the city.

"God help us!" he began. *"Everywhere you look there are people running, screaming, from their homes carrying everything they own. Saw one fellow pushing his dining room table down the street. The blacks are taking everything they can find. The rules of a civil society have vanished. Blacks, who served their masters for years, are stealing left and right and some have been seen helping to set the fires. We are a country adrift. A nation in a state of collapse, such as I have never seen the likes of, my friend. If indeed we can even call ourselves a nation. We live in a place where there is no honor and no mercy.*

I've asked myself, many times, why should there be? We have not earned either."

Indeed, to date, most of the plantations of the Waccamaw had survived one of the worst of times. Soon, it would be planting time again. Even here, manpower was short. Shorter than it had been last year as slaves disappeared into the night, some of them. Others fled in broad daylight, leaving the fate of the Carolina rice crop unknown.

"But, we'll manage," he muttered. "People will still need doctors and medicines. We'll find something else to do with the land if we're forced to give up growing rice altogether."

Half an hour later, as he drove down the main street of Murells Inlet, William did a mental run-through of the list of tasks he had set himself to do. He had no planned sick calls today, just the day to day errands that he enjoyed.

A light wind whisked the tops of the reed-filled marshes, sending puffs of sand scurrying across the road, as he made his way to the tailor's shop to pick up his trousers. The shop, a small wooden building, held together by ship-lapped planks of cedar, stood a short distance off the main road in a clearing surrounded by weathered oaks.

Tying Bertie to a hitching post beside the porch, he could see the tailor sitting on a stool beside the counter, hemming his trousers. A dreadful nuisance, those trousers. They seemed to get longer every year forcing him to keep hiking them up, ruining the whole tailored cut when he did so, and bunching up around his waist. An unbearable situation.

Of course, William knew very well why they appeared to be longer and was quite sure that it had nothing to do with the cloth. Fact of the matter was that he was shrinking. An appalling thought, but the best diagnosis he could come up with, judging by the ache in his back, and the slight limp he had developed over the last few years. His blasted bones were crumbling.

He had tried explaining this to the tailor, but was quite sure that the slightly built man, with a permanently startled look on his face, hadn't a clue what he was talking about. The fellow kept pushing his spectacles up the bridge of his nose, William noticed, holding the cloth at a distance, squinting to see it better. Finally, the doctor said, "When did you last have your eyes checked?"

"Ooh! Must be years, I'd say." The tailor looked up, eyes wide, blinked, and snipped off the end of his thread.

"Stop by my office next time you're out our way, and I'll look at them."

"That's mighty kind of you, Doc," he chuckled. He wrapped the trousers in a sheet of brown paper, tied the package off with string and handed it to William. "Did you hear about the explosion this morning? Rumor is a boat load of ammunition blew up somewhere down marsh."

So Daniel did hear something.

"Yankee boat, I reckon," the tailor said. "They've got that stuff stashed all over the place."

"Dangerous stuff," William replied.

"Didn't hear anyone's bin hurt."

"Good. Anyway, stop by and we'll have a look at those eyes, shall we? Perhaps all you need is a new pair of glasses." He paid for his trousers. The tailor looked at him quizzically.

"What?" William hesitated.

"You're a good man, Doc," The man said. He watched William climb into his buggy and snap the reins.

William doffed his panama and grunted. Strange fellow. But nice to know he thought well of him.

He knew that many of the people around here thought he was odd. He supposed he was. What with his quaint, clipped speech, and starched collars. Not to mention his strange ideas about slaves. But he hoped they all knew he was a caring man, all in all. Opinionated maybe, maybe a little brusk, but he took care of people when they needed him. Even the plantation blacks who called him 'Marse Doc'. He also knew that people said he was too soft on his blacks. He had once overheard a house guest remark that he must be. *"One of those anti-slavery folks."* Well, he couldn't argue with that. Of course he was. That was just who he was. William's next stop was at the cobbler's to drop off a pair of shoes that needed re-soling, and pick up a packet of the long shoelaces he liked for his lace-up boots.

"These things are getting scarcer than frogs' teeth." The cobbler said as he handed him his last pair of laces.

He hesitated as the doctor reached for them and asked, "Doc, I was wondering if you would look at my boy?"

"What seems to be the matter?"

"Don't rightly know. His skin's done turned yellow an' his eyes too. Dangest thing I ever saw!" he stood there for a moment watching the doctors' face.

"Is the boy here?" William knew the cobbler couldn't pay for a doctor's visit.

"Yes." He hurried to the curtain in the back of the shop. *"Angie! Bring Toby out here!"*

A stout woman with a pink face appeared from behind the curtain pulling a child by the hand as he struggled to escape her grasp. She had obviously been waiting for just this moment and was breathing hard, yanking on his arm. "Hold still!" she admonished. Her hair was pinned back into a low knot at the base of her neck and the tendrils that escaped the band were sticky with perspiration.

"Mornin' Doc. This here's Toby," she gave the child's hand a jerk and then let go. Seizing the opportunity, the child raced back behind the curtain. "You get out here afore I snatch you bald-headed!" She bustled after him.

"Sounds a bit extreme," William scratched his cheek watching the woman's color rise. "What's frightened him?"

"Dang doctor up yonder in Conway put them blood-sucking leaches on him," his father said. "C'mon boy, Doc Stanley won't hurt you."

His mother reached behind the drape, dragged the whimpering child out, and stood him squarely in front of William.

"Tell the doctor good morning," she was breathing heavily from the exertion.

"That's all right." William stooped to the boy's level and held up both his hands. "See? No leaches." His eyes missed nothing, as they scanned the youngster's face. "Come here, young fella, let me look at you." He lifted the squirming child onto a stool. "Open your eyes wide and stick your tongue out." Furry white tongue, he observed. And a yellowing in the whites of his eyes. The diagnosis was easy. He turned to the mother and asked, "Has the color of his urine changed?"

She glanced at her husband, nervously brushing a strand of hair off her face, and said, "Yes. It's real dark—looks like river water."

The doctor stood on the floor and smiled. He tweaked the child's ear. "Alright, then. Off you go."

The boy scuttled out of the room, and William straightened up.

"He's got a case of jaundice," he said. "It's an inflammation of the liver."

"Can you fix him, Doc?" the mother asked.

"No," William said. "The only thing we've found that works with this sort of distemper is to change the patient's eating habits."

"His eating?"

"Yes. If you do exactly as I say, he'll make a full recovery. For the next two months—no greasy foods. Avoid cooking with lard or butter."

The woman looked perplexed. "What *can* he eat then? What do I feed him?"

"Boiled potatoes, boiled vegetables, boiled chicken, if you can find one, and fish. No pork," he looked at her to make sure she understood. She nodded. "And no milk. Give him boiled water to drink. Barley water's good if you can find it. Lightly steeped tea of Burdock root is said to cleanse the blood and reduce the inflammation. Can you remember that?"

"Yes," she appeared flustered. "Will that fix this yellow color?"

"Yes," William smiled gently. He could tell they weren't convinced. "Be diligent, and in no time he'll be well."

"But—the doctor in Conway, where we took him before, the one did them leeches, he told us that's what was needed. Said they use it all the time up north."

"Did it work?"

They shook their heads.

"Of course it didn't," he said mildly, and handed the cobbler the money for his shoelaces.

"No," the cobbler shook his head refusing the money. "We thank you kindly for taking a look at the boy."

"I'll see how he's doing next week when I pick up my shoes," William said. "Good day to you." He gave a small bow and walked outside.

Leaving his horse and buggy hitched to the black iron post, he crossed the street to the wood-working shack, a small lean-to next to the boat building yard, to pick up the glue.

William pondered the jaundiced child as he walked. It was true. There was as yet no cure for this bilious disorder. Bloodletting was still the most popular treatment of the day and was applied to everything from toothache to abdominal distempers. It was, in William Stanley's opinion, an utter waste of time. An opinion he didn't shrink from sharing with other doctors, and one that gained him few accolades from among his peers. Why couldn't they see the tomfoolery in blood-sucking? Their lack of success with that messy idea should have them beating their heads against the wall for answers years ago.

Of course, there were some who were beginning to notice the results William and others were getting with the dietary notion, and other alternative methods he sometimes used. Far-seeing men. Brilliant men of medicine. And a woman he met once in Boston. A highly intelligent woman, by the name of Dorothea Dix, who appeared to be most interested in some of his ideas and methods. Namely, the unconventional methods William had arrived at that involved combining his traditional ideas with Native Indian and Gullah medicine.

Of course, some of the Native medicine had no merit at all, but some of it did. It was also Dr. Stanley's opinion that a lot of the local traditions, using wild herbs, berries, and barks, were quite intriguing. He remembered sharing his thoughts late one evening, over several brandies, with the Confederate Surgeon General, Mr. Samuel Moore. The chap seemed quite taken with William's theories. Good fellow, that one.

As for Ben's mother, he had an opinion about her as well. But, he thought prudently, it was an opinion best kept to himself. Her high color and breathlessness, he was sure, were a direct result of the additional pounds around her hips and abdomen. The woman was begging for a calamitous cessation of the heart and instant death.

Six

The Stink of Gun Powder

FAIRHAVEN STOOD WHITE and imposing in the late winter sunlight. Shaded by the oak grove in summer and protected by tall dunes when the trade winds blew. Built by one of the renowned architects of the day, it belonged to Winifred Merriman. A spinster, and an elegant hostess who enjoyed entertaining the ladies of the island and The Strand at any time, but especially during this time of war when there was nothing else to distract them.

That morning she happened to be hosting her sister Trudy and her niece Katie Rose, who were visiting from their brother's indigo plantation on the Wando River.

Breakfast at Fairhaven was taken on the veranda when the weather was fine and in the dining room when it was not. This morning the ladies would be dining indoors, the butler Charles Asquith decided. He rubbed the wrist that always ached when the weather changed and looked out of the window. A light pall of smoke and the faint stink of gun powder still hovered over the marshes. He wrinkled his nose. The smell would absolutely ruin their blackberry preserves and oatmeal if they were to dine outside.

Katie Rose had finally dozed off, following her early morning adventure. A shaft of bright sunlight, shining through her bedroom shutters, woke her up. Lying there, the sound of people moving around downstairs, and the clink of dishes and cutlery made her open her eyes.

Millie's voice carried up the stairs. "You hear dat big bang dis mo'nin' Marse Charles?"

And that was enough to bring Katie Rose to a bolt upright position. Straining her ears she heard Charles answer but whatever he said was lost as they walked away from the stairs and into the kitchen. Footsteps could be heard walking down the hallway to the breakfast room as one of the aunts closed her downstairs bedroom door. Katie Rose swung her legs out of bed, snatched her clothes off the pegs inside the armoire, and dressed hurriedly. Another bedroom door closed, and she heard her Aunt Winifred calling to the butler.

"Have you seen my eye-glasses, Charles? I can't imagine where I left them last night."

"On your writing desk, Miss Merriman," the butler answered her as he did every morning. Again, their voices faded as they moved away.

Giving her hair a quick brush, Katie Rose slipped her feet into her house shoes and cast a glance at herself in the mirror. She stopped and stared. "Oh no!" And grabbing a cotton cloth off the wash stand, she scrubbed frantically at a dark smudge of soot on her temple. There'd be no explaining that! Charlie would be the first to spot it.

"There," she murmured. The soot, left by a flying ember, was gone leaving nothing but a red splotch from the scouring. Katie Rose pulled her hair over it, tossed the cloth onto the bed, and went downstairs.

The sister aunts, Winifred and Trudy, were already seated when she made her way down the hall.

"There's a funny smell outside," she heard Winifred remark. "What do you suppose it is, Charles? Smells like gun smoke."

Katie Rose stopped motionless in the doorway watching Winifred raise her lorgnette to one eye. Charles was pouring their tea. He didn't look up.

"Perhaps another of those paddle steamers blew up at sea," Trudy offered as she spread her napkin on her lap. She made a tutting sound as she noticed where the crocheted cuff of her bodice had been nibbled away by moths. "Ah, there's Katie Rose." She smiled as her niece came into the room and sat down.

"Your color looks a bit high this morning, dear. Are you feeling well?" Winifred asked.

"Very well, thank you," she replied, a little too quickly.

Carrying a basket of warm corn muffins from the sideboard Charles paused and cast a sidelong glance at the young woman. "I heard the explosion," he said. "In fact one of the fishermen stopped to see if we wanted any drum fish and confirmed it to me."

The girl froze.

Using his tongs the butler placed a corn muffin on Trudy's plate. "He said Fannie's Inn went up in flames. Apparently, a Yankee ammunitions wagon that was holed-up there overnight exploded."

Neither of the aunts seemed to wonder about the spontaneity of such an explosion.

"Oh, my, I know the clientele are not, shall we say—the most genteel—but was anyone hurt?" Winifred asked.

Katie Rose stared down at her plate.

"The fisherman said one of the—er—clients was killed, but

Fannie and the rest of them came flying out like bats. Quite disheveled, hysterical, but unhurt. Marmalade, m'lady?" he asked Winifred.

Katie Rose let her breath out slowly and picked up her muffin. She had no appetite. Still, she was glad to hear that there was only one dead. She hadn't wanted to actually kill anyone. She was feeling dizzy again. Oh dear. Perhaps she wasn't as ready to go to war as she had thought. And why was Charlie looking at her like that?

"Did you hear the explosion, Miss?" he asked.

"I must have been sound asleep," she answered dabbing at the corners of her mouth with her napkin. The color rose in her cheeks and she turned to look him. He looked back at her with that high and mighty look of his where he raised one eyebrow and stared down his nose.

Had the fisherman seen her? Katie Rose hurriedly brought her napkin to her lips, pushed her chair back, and excused herself. "I think I'll go and lie down," she said weakly. "Perhaps I'm not as well as I thought."

Seven

Rumors

WILLIAM REMOVED HIS time-piece from his vest pocket and frowned. It was afternoon already and he had yet to visit Jake Reynolds.

The wind kicked up a swirl of dust just as he pushed open the door to the apothecary's, slamming it behind him, setting off a jangling row of bells. Noisy contraption.

Jake finished filling a bag for one of the village matrons, looked up, and greeted him with a loud, "Howdy, Doc." Handing her the sac, he wished her good day, and looked over to where William was scrutinizing the shelves.

"There's bad weather coming up the coast," the druggist announced wrinkling his nose. "Cain't you just smell it in the air?" He sneezed. "It gets a stink of some kind or 'nother. Sort of a sulfurous smell."

"Hmmm," William grunted absently, thinking that actually, he rather liked the smell of an approaching storm. Still with his back to the apothecary, he asked, "Have you heard anything about a frigate dropping off medical supplies? Will said he'd heard a rumor that a ship dodged the blockade a couple of nights ago and came into the Inlet."

"Yes, indeedy. Caused quite a stir, she did. You know they stopped coming into these creeks back in—ohhh—'63, wasn't it? 'Tween the US Navy and the pirates it got too dangerous and they finally just quit running. But, yes. A frigate, she was. Came in so silent no one but the fishes knew she was there!" Jake told him excitedly. "Just hugged the marshes real close with no lights showing, dropped her load on the wharf, and was gone in the blink of an eye." He leaned across the counter, his eyes gleaming. "Next thing we knew, two o' the troops from Will Hardee's column come beating on my door, scaring the Missus half to death, and unloaded two big crates of stuff we ain't seen in months. And just in the knick of time, I'm thinking, what with this storm coming in." Jake grimaced as he bent over to retrieve a pencil from the floor.

William raised his eyebrows, looking pointedly at the man's thigh.

"Got this ol' wound in Vicksburg," the chemist said straightening up. "The one that got me sent home. And I'll be damned if the durn thing don't start acting up whenever there's heavy weather brewing." He rubbed the place near the femoral artery where a bayonet slash had almost ended his life.

"Maybe the damp getting to you in your old age," the doctor smiled. He turned a small bottle of liquid upside down, shook it, put it back on the shelf, and walked over to the counter. "Far be it from me to presume to tell an apothecary what to take for it. However, a fusion tea made with willow bark sometimes helps."

"So I've heard," Jake said.

Sadie Jones told William that a long time ago, and having tried it himself at the end of a long day, he could vouch for it. It eased the aches and pains that came with creeping old age. Indeed, the willow remedy made perfect sense judging by what he had read in his medical books.

"You look bedeviled, Doc. What's on your mind?"

"Bothersome encounter with a patient who still believes in leeches and blood-letting. Some doctor from Conway had them convinced of its miraculous powers."

"I know the one," Jake said. "He's a moron, one of many who still hold with Rush's ideas."

"I met the good Doctor Benjamin Rush at a convention in Philadelphia once." William put a bag of sulfur on the counter. "Humorless fellow. Self-righteous man who didn't hear a damn word I said to him."

"Well, soon's he and his ilk quit teaching blood-letting at the Medical College in Columbia, maybe we can make some progress."

William snorted and changed the subject. "What did the ship bring in?"

Jake reached under the counter and produced two cloth bags full of supplies. "I filled these for you. Real mixed bag, you might say. Heh, heh. Figured you'd be needing these if Charleston falls. They say our soldiers are all over the countryside, some of them wounded. There's also rumors that Columbia's in flames. Don't know how true that is, but, if it's true it must mean Sherman's in the capital."

William's eyes lit up as he pulled the contraband toward him. "Is that so?" He ran his hands down the sides of the bags in anticipation of what might be inside. "Doctors are always the last to hear the news," he said. "The last I heard was that Sherman had been ordered to march on Richmond."

"Maybe he did. And maybe the devil stopped by the capital to teach the rebels another bloody lesson on how to burn women and children out of their homes."

"The fellow's almost certainly mad," William said. "In fact, I wouldn't hesitate to render a diagnosis of pyromania."

"I heard tell that Hardee and his troops, being as badly outnumbered as they are, are getting the hell out." Jake offered. "Getting the armory and the horses upcountry to keep them out of Yankee hands. Bound to be wounded men out there and some of them headed home." He rubbed his thigh. "Then there was that explosion not far from here before sunup. Did you folks hear it? Fair shook the north end of the Island."

The doctor raised his eyebrows trying to make out the name on a bottle he'd seen on the counter. "I didn't hear it. What happened?"

"Yankee wagon load of ammo passing through blew up, they said."

"That's what happens when you transport an unstable load of gun powder," William opined. He actually knew nothing about gun powder transportation. "I imagine that stuff just needs a good bump, a pothole or something, to set it off."

"Another cache went up in Conway yesterday." Jake leaned on the counter taking the weight off his thigh.

"Good. Less of the stuff to blow us up," William lifted the bags off the counter. "These will be most useful."

"Got more opiates—bandages and salves too, if you run short. Why in the world they want to send bandages to a place that grows more cotton than the all of the rest of the world put together, I don't know."

"Addled thinking," the doctor agreed. He paid for the supplies and took his leave. "Thanks, old man. Stop by when you have a chance, while I've still got a bottle of that good Napoleon brandy."

He smiled at Jake with a twinkle in his eye. "And in the meantime, make yourself a tisane of willow tea." He gave a small bow and headed out into the street.

The afternoon sun was high, and it was time he was getting home. The wind gusted off the marshes and the sea beyond, and William had to hold onto his hat as he approached the buggy. His horse snorted softly as William stashed his precious cargo on the seat and unhitched the chestnut from the post.

Settling himself into his seat, he flicked the reins. He could see the river wharf beyond the store, and beyond it, the brightly painted hull and high stacks of the once proud, ocean-going paddle steamer and gambling boat, 'Marietta'. Moored between two fishing boats, she was one of the few survivors of her kind. Most of which had exploded due to overly combustible engines. The doctor nodded to a couple of people he could swear he recognized, but couldn't remember their names. Damned embarrassing.

The horse settled into a slow gait, and he headed for the store and the post office, which occupied the same building. His last stop would be the paddle steamer for a mug of Jenny, the bartender's, ginger beer.

A pretty lass with a sassy turn of phrase, he enjoyed Jenny's company for the length of time it took her to retrieve the ginger beer from the cool room and pound the mint and sugar together in a stone bowl. Truth be told, he enjoyed her flirtatious repartee. He also liked the way she held her skirts off the dusty wooden deck as she bustled about, making it hard to ignore the occasional glimpse of her plump stockinged calf.

Of course, he was quite beyond that sort of thing now, but still, he could remember. Good God! He still had most of his faculties intact, didn't he? He could still appreciate the soft curve of a woman's breast or the milk-white flash of a slender ankle in summertime.

The aging postmaster, still dapper with his waxed handle-bar mustache, stepped out from behind his counter in the back of the store as William entered the building.

"Aft'noon Doc!"

"Afternoon! Is there any mail for me?"

The man swiveled on worn-down heels with his thumbs hooked in his vest pockets and glanced at the row of pigeon holes behind him. "Nope, box is empty. Not much getting through these days. Only one mail drop last week. This week there's been nothing. Reckon the drivers have been robbed too many times lately. It's a lawless time, I say."

The postmaster's daughter stopped dusting the counter in front of her. "Why! Just yesterday, on my way home from catching crabs, two stray Yankees walked down the main street just as bold as you please. Sent me running for the store, I was so scared! But Biddy O'Neil saw them, snatched up her shotgun and fired through her bedroom window, killing one of them dead."

"Good God!" William muttered.

She picked up her duster. "Lordy! The wind's blowing all kinds of dust in here," she said. "They fed him to the 'gators I heard. What d'ya need, Doc?" She waved her hand over the almost empty shelves. Shelves that used to be laden with canned preserves, peaches, jellies and syrups. "It's time this war was over," she grumbled. "That way the mail could run the way it used to, and we could get the goods we've run out of." She sneezed. "Sugar's scarce, and we're entirely dependent on local folks for things like soap and salt—that sort of thing. And we haven't seen any wheat flour, coffee or cider for weeks."

William picked up a bag of salt. "What happened to the second Yankee? Did Mrs. O'Neil get him, too?"

"No. Someone saw him running for his life through the piney woods with Tommy Nelson chasing him. But Tommy came back saying, no one in his right mind oughta be running through that swampy place. He turned back and left him to the snakes and gators."

The doctor chuckled. With Mrs. O'Neil defending the cause from her bedroom window, and the Inlet full of angry villagers, the swamps must be a damn site safer place to be. He paid his bill, and, with a smile and a wave, he walked outside onto the sagging porch.

"Hmmph," he waved to the postmaster, making a mental note to send Moses down to fix his porch, and drove down the wharf

The choppy water rocked the paddle steamer at her mooring making William stagger as climbed on board. Overhead, her flags flapped and snapped in the stiffening breeze, and the marsh slapped up against her barnacle covered hull.

"Howdy, Doc!" Jenny stood with her hands on her hips behind the bar, smiling. "Saw you leavin' the store and figured you'd be here looking for your ginger beer and mint." She cocked her head to one side and ran her fingertip up the side of the glass where it had overflowed. She licked it and handed him the mug.

William smiled. "Thank you." The girl's reddish-brown braids reminded him of his dead wife Elizabeth's, auburn curls. Ah yes. Curls she brushed to a shine as she sat before her mirror every night before bed.

He took a swallow from his mug and set it down beside a pair of tall candle sticks coated with dribbles of old wax. "Do you remember the candlelight dinners on board this boat? The music, the minstrels?" His voice trailed off. "A lot's changed since then."

"Damn shame!" Jenny sauntered to the end of the bar. "No men, no parties. Nobody's travellin' these days, neither. Only the robbers. And the dad-blamed bull frogs in the marsh makin' the only music. 'Course there's damn Yankees roamin' around blowin' things up everywhere. The one this morning rocked this old boat so hard I thought it might crack wide open." She sighed. "Yes, this ship musta bin something in her day." She leaned her elbows on the counter. "Heard tell of dark-eyed gamblers throwing the dice 'till dawn—their ladies in scarlet silk and feathers." Her eyes had a dreamy look in them. "Pirates too, I heard."

He chuckled at her outburst feeling a pang of pity for her at the same time. He was quite sure every woman in the county would agree with her—if not in the same colorful way. "Cutthroats," he said. "No one you'd want to meet, I assure you, dear girl."

"Anything'd be better than this God-forsaken life of deprivation!" she flounced. "Heard tell the negras are leavin' in bands, stealing everyone's horses and mules. And the damn Yankees are fixin' to march through here and burn us all out of house and home."

"Let's hope that doesn't happen." William said. He finished his ginger beer in silence, listening to the water lapping against the sides of the old ship, thinking of the way it had been. A gathering place for old friends—some of them long-gone. Others who had lost everything they owned. Some were probably still out there fighting for a lost cause.

The smell of frying fish wafted through the ship's bar reminding him of Friday nights at the Hot & Hot Fish Club. He missed those days. Missed the nights he and his planter friends gathered for a tumbler of rum and lime and conversation. And the grilled sheep's head fish freshly caught off the wharf.

"What happened to the old Hot & Hot Fish Club?" he asked, standing up to pay.

"Oh, that's been closed awhile now," Jenny answered. "The Planter's Club, too. People miss that old club."

What was to become of them all? William left the ship feeling dejected, climbed into his buggy and headed for home. He had hoped there would be a letter from Ross. He wished he knew where he was. With all the rumors of troop movements flying around, and fort evacuations, he had no idea. Now Sadie Jones had the whole household in a flap, talking like a crackpot about Ross coming home.

He drove in silence, switching his thoughts to the Frigate that had made the perilous run from Cuba, to drop off precious European medical supplies, and was suddenly in a hurry to get home. "Pick 'em up Bertie," he called. "Let's go and see what's inside these bags."

Had Ross really been gone four years? First at the Academy, then with the United States Navy, before transferring as a ranked officer to the Confederate States Navy. "I wish this bloody war would end," he said out loud. "As crazy as it sounds, I hope Sadie's right."

Tomorrow morning his youngest son would be twenty-five.

Eight

The Body on the Shore

TWO OF ROSS'S seamen came on the run, sure-footed as goats, they jumped from rock to rock and jerked to a stop, staring at the body lying across the path.

"Holy shee-it!" the short one with the black pigtail exclaimed.

"It ain't one of ours," the seaman from Norfolk, with long hair flying around his face, said.

"How can you tell?" The first man moved in to get a better look.

"Ain't got no uniform for one thing."

"That don' mean nothing. Lookit us, son! This look like a uniform to you?" He plucked at his torn jacket, looking up as the Bo'sun joined them. "Hey, Simeon. You ever seen this man?"

Simeon stood with one foot on a low rock beside the corpse's head staring down at the body. "No. One thing I can say for sho, he ain't kin to none of y'all white boys," the men roared with laughter.

"He a Geechee boy like me," Simeon used the word the Gullah people used for each other. Squatting down beside the dead boy he pointed at a ragged hole in the cap just above the ear. "He ketched a bullet raht hear."

The Norfolk boy raised an eyebrow. "Ha! Hard to find a dead body with no bullet hole in him 'round these parts." They laughed again, slapping hands.

Ross fixed them with a cold stare. "That's enough, he's just a boy. What d'ya think? Twelve years old?"

The seamen shuffled awkwardly. "Could be, suh." Simeon said.

"He hasn't been dead long."

"No, suh."

The man with the pig tail shifted uneasily. "He a Yankee?"

"Could be." The officer leaned in for a closer look. Something wasn't right.

"Lawsy! If dat so, Ah want to know why he wid de Yankee folk. An' how'd he get here."

Nobody answered. Seabirds cried above the broken turrets of the fort.

"Is Sherman here?" the first man asked.

"Not yet. Look at this," the officer said. He crouched down beside the body and detached a buckskin purse from the boy's hip and as he did so, the woolen cap that was pulled down over the ears, toppled to the ground. Nobody spoke.

"Whoa!" The youngest of the seamen took a step backwards. "That's a girl!"

"Ain't you de smart one," Simeon taunted.

Long curly braids, and the small mounds on her chest, barely noticeable under her thin, cotton shirt gave her away. The small-boned build hadn't seemed right to Ross at first glance.

"Stop gawking," he said gruffly. "So it's a girl. That doesn't change anything. Look at this," he held up the sack.

"A dispatch pouch."

Ross tore the stitches open, reached inside and removed a power horn, inside of which was a folded piece of paper. It fluttered damply in the wind as he opened it. "She was a carrier," he looked southward as if expecting something to appear on the horizon. "Of course! She came from one of the slave groups that joined the Yankee armies down south of here," he muttered. Ross stood up with the sheet of paper in his hand. "This girl was a spy."

"Suh?"

He waved the piece of paper in front of them. "A spy. She fought for the South. This note must have been given to her by another spy, most likely posing as a Yankee soldier—just as she posed as a boy— Jeese! A spy, by God!"

"Not a Yankee soldier," Simeon said.

"Nah, she's one of ours."

"Wheew! If'n he came from down yonder, Ah'm tinking for sho she musta jumped a train. Ain't no way a girl can run dat far—not even da debil hisself be chas'n her! Dis Geechee girl, he know how to jump de train and ride to Chastin," Simeon laughed. "Heh! Heh! Geechee chilluns knows 'bout jumping trains." The black seaman's eyes darkened, and he asked somberly, "Who shoot dis chile?"

"Could've been anyone." Ross glanced back at the paper in his hand and shrugged. "Someone who saw her running from the camp? On a train? Maybe she jumped into the sea to escape. Who knows?" That was the most likely thing. A girl would not want to be caught by a band of soldiers. The body hadn't been in the water that long, so it was likely that she'd been shot running into the sea. Last night, perhaps.

He looked at the note again. "It says, *"Sherman by-passing Charleston. By the time you get this, Columbia will most likely be in Union hands. We estimate the Yankee force at about 89,000 strong.'"* He paused. "So that means Charleston is safe and so is Sumter, at least for now. But the bastards will be here, make no mistake.

He crinkled his eyes and looked toward Charleston. It was rumored that Sherman had a score to settle; that he wouldn't rest until he'd destroyed the first southern state to secede. They said it worked on him like a burr in his saddle.

"What we gonna do wid her, suh?" Simeon pointed at the girl.

"Bury her at sea." Ross knew what had to be done. He looked from one to the other of them. "Our orders are to go into the city and round up stragglers. We'll follow them—with one change. I will not be accompanying you to Charleston." He placed the empty pouch back on the child's body. "When the three of you reach Charleston, Simeon will leave two of you there to help clear the city, and he will take this note, ride out to join Beauregard's forces and deliver it into the hands of an officer. We don't know if the General knows anything about this yet, but no matter—he needs to see it." He handed the note to Simeon.

"I'll sail from here with the girl's body, bury her and, when that's done, I'll go ashore and ride to Wilmington to see what's left of our navy."

In the meantime, because there was no urgency, Ross could still make the detour he had planned. He would head for the north end of All Saint's Parish, Willowgreen, and Pawley's Island, before riding for North Carolina.

"Here! Give me a hand." He pulled a square of cloth out of his back pocket and spread it on the ground beside the body.

Nobody moved. "What?" He looked at their blank, silent faces.

"You cain't bury no nigger in that!" One of the men spluttered pointing in disbelief at the thin, silk Confederate flag the officer had taken from his pocket. "Pardon me, suh, but don't you be wrapping no niggah in that flag!"

Simeon looked away. Ross felt the heat rising up the back of his neck and into his hairline. It was a personal flag that bore, on its bottom left hand corner, the embroidered crest of Willowgreen Plantation.

"Stand down, man," he said quietly. "This girl was a Confederate soldier. I don't give a damn what color she was." His face was pale with anger. "We'll bury her with honor. Now, wrap her up, dammit!"

He clenched his teeth and turned away. "And while you're about it, you will remember how many men went into battle under this flag. Black and white, they fought and died for the cause. So did she."

"Yes, suh." The men lifted the girl's body and laid it in the center of the flag.

When they finished folding and tucking the fabric, Ross said "Put her in my boat." He watched as they lifted the body off the path and deposited it carefully inside the small sailing craft.

"Now, get going. Simeon, you're in charge. When you get ashore, see the other two on their way, then find a horse and head north to the column."

He dug into his inside breast pocket. "Here's most of the money I have left. Use it to buy horses, mules—whatever you can find. It'll be worthless when this bloody war ends, so spend it." The wind fluttered the notes in his hand. "The rest of you follow Simeon's orders. Search the place, and when you're done, go home to your women and children."

"Home?" The long-haired seamen from Norfolk looked shocked. "We going home?"

"And be quick about it. Not only is there a storm coming in, but you're white. You'll find no mercy at the hands of Yankee soldiers when they arrive." Ross clapped a hand on the seaman's shoulder, "Go home, son. This war's over."

"Some wouldn't agree with you, suh. Nor 'bout the girl," the sailor with the pigtail muttered.

"You're right. But if you've learned nothing else from this war, remember this; sometimes you have to think for yourself. You've got a brain so use it. Don't worry about what someone less smart than you might think. Do what's right."

He stared at them. "Remember this, we are Southerners. Born and bred. By the grace or damnation of God, we are Southerners. So is she. Don't ever forget that. We're all in this mess together."

As if to emphasize his words, thunder rolled across the horizon. The first drops of rain hit the rocks and a shiver ran down Ross's spine. If this war went on, he may face court martial for his decision.

He had known, on that day in 1861 when he'd written to his father informing him of his decision to join the Confederate States Navy that this war would not end kindly for the South. But his allegiance lay, then and now and through whatever lay ahead, with the Confederacy. He had little doubt at that time that his father would accept his decision. William Stanley didn't like war and he despised slavery. But he would understand his Southern-born son's need to finish something he'd started.

It was a confusing time. He walked to his boat then turned and looked at the men who had been rescued with him the night the Tennessee was captured—three sailors of the Confederacy. Two white fishermen and an ex-slave. Their clothes were torn, their shoes were falling apart. Their once dark blue uniforms—the pride of the Confederate Navy, had worn out—replaced by drab gray as the Carolina plantations ran out of indigo dye.

"Get me off the beach," Ross said gruffly. "Turn her bow into the wind."

"Yes suh!" The Bo'sun grabbed the line and yelled at one of the seaman to stand ready to untie the boat.

Ross felt a rush of emotion as he stepped into the small wooden boat and the men got their combined weight behind it ready to launch him into deep water. Steadying himself, he raised the reefed mainsail and paused. "Simeon!" he called to the Gullah sailor who came from one of the southernmost Waccamaw plantations. "If you don't find your people, follow the river north until you get to Willowgreen, and, if I'm not there, ask for Sadie Jones. They'll be needing help." Rain pelted his boat as he prepared to leave, coming down hard now, as the fog swirled across the island.

The sailor's voice broke as he called back, "Yassir!"

"And men! Take whatever supplies you need in Charleston before the Yankees ransack the place." His voice was gruff. "Now get outta here! And God Speed."

"Yassrr!" the deep-throated shout came back in unison as they gave the boat a mighty shove and jumped back, splashing through the spray of the incoming tide.

Standing at ragged attention in the rain, they saluted as Ross, pulling strongly on the oars, with his bow pointing into the wind, heaved himself and the boat into the swells.

"*Miss* Sadie Jones!" He yelled over his shoulder, "Remember that name, Simeon."

Nine

Willowgreen Plantation

IT WAS EARLY afternoon along the Waccamaw, the river that ran parallel to the coastline from Conway to Winyah Bay. With the sun beating down on its banks, it was hard to believe that summertime was still two months away.

Willowgreen Plantation thrived and prospered on the deepest curve of this part of the river. The Stanley manor, built on a high mound back from the water, rose elegantly from its skirt of sweeping lawns that rolled to the water's edge. Shaded by a grove of sprawling oaks in summer, the home was somewhat protected from swarms of mosquitoes by swaying willows that grew in clusters on the banks. Knobby-kneed cypress, on the edges of the rice fields, where the insects bred, helped keep them at bay with their misty green foliage that picked up every breath of air.

This was Sadie Jones's home, and as housekeeper, she made sure things ran smoothly from the eaves to the wraparound verandas of the house. It was also her job to know where the next meal was coming from.

"And wid all de fighting, dat ain't easy," the old Gullah woman thought. She stood by the wood stove stirring a cup of last spring's cane syrup into a black cauldron of sweet potatoes. "Dey gotta stop dis fightin' mess. Lawsy. Too many fields burned and people kilt. And I cain't get no wheat flour."

Her small form, bent with age, and wrapped in a snowy white apron, leaned over to breathe in the flavors of sweet potatoes, cane syrup and tender wild onion shoots. A blue and white piece of gingham cotton was wrapped around her head. It kept slipping down her forehead, coming to rest on a set of tangled eyebrows. Small rings of tightly curled grey hair escaped from underneath it. She pushed it back in irritation and turned her attention to the pot on the stove. She cackled. "Hmm, hmm, dat was good fixins."

She talked to herself a lot these days. "Yes, we lucky to eat dis good." Sadie put down the spoon and wiped her hands on her apron. A hunk of dark red venison stood on a plate on the table. She poked it with her forefinger and grunted.

"Dat Willie boy cain't walk real good, but dere ain't nuttin wrong wid he eyes. Dat chile can spot a deer from 'cross da rivah."

There would be plenty of meat for everyone tonight.

She let her mind go to Zack riding through Georgetown, and her thoughts made her uneasy. She had heard tales of the dangers that could befall a body on the King's Highway. He was a big man but still no match for a band of hooligans.

Pushing those thoughts aside, Sadie Jones looked at the venison lying on the table satisfied that as long as there was meat in the woods, and potatoes and greens in the vegetable garden, no one was going to starve at Willowgreen.

"How in de world folks in de city feed deyself I jes don' know," she mumbled. But that was something she didn't like to think about because it made her think of her girl child Mollie. Her eyes clouded.

"Hardheaded like her daddy. What for she want to run off?"

Whatever it was, Sadie didn't want to know. Someone said they'd seen her, soon after she left, down in the Charleston marketplace with a man. Sadie Jones could only hope he was a good man, but somehow she didn't think so. So she didn't think about it.

She took her mixing bowl down from a low shelf and scooped a cup of cornmeal out of the bin to begin mixing the corn bread. "Un, unh. We done good here. 'Cept for some lost Yankee soldiers dat came, we ain't seen no fightin' here." All she knew was that they were "Hungry as wild dogs in winter." But a bowl of rice and grilled catfish took care of them. And, not one of them Yankees wanted to tangle with Moses, who had them roped and tied up in the barn before they even knew he was there. And there they stayed until it was time for them get gone.

"Heh, heh," Sadie chuckled. "No suh! Ain't no Yankee boys gonna mess wid Big Moses. He gots his machete and his rope and dat all he need."

Sadie looked at the kitchen shelves that used to be filled with field peas and peaches and took down a sealed crock of runner beans. She took the job of cooking for the household seriously. It was a job that had, from time to time, involved her in an altercation or two with the doctor. One such disagreement, a boisterous difference of opinion, occurred when he walked into the kitchen house unannounced one day, to find his cook frying up large, fat caterpillars for the noon day meal.

"Good God!" His voice could be heard clear across the courtyard and then some, the gossip on The Street went. "What the devil are you feeding us?"

Sadie tried to explain that caterpillars made strong bones and good blood. "For sho you goin' lak 'em!"

He would have none of it and ordered the hapless creatures fed to the chickens, an action which created a din of joyful barnyard clucking, and a lot of irate muttering from the cook.

Striding down the breezeway away from the kitchen that day, the doctor made up his mind to keep a closer eye on what Sadie threw into the pot in future.

"What in the name of God was she thinking," he muttered as he pushed open the back door to the manor. Weren't some of those things poisonous? At times like these he missed Elizabeth fiercely. She would have been much better at dealing with Sadie Jones than he was.

Before long, there was a knock on the back door as he made his way into the library planning to look up the properties of caterpillars, and others of their ilk, poisonous or otherwise. "Come in," he bellowed over his shoulder.

"Ah brings you sumting dat make you feel better," Sadie Jones stood in the doorway with a small silver tray that held a steaming mug of mint tea.

"There's nothing the matter with me." he glowered at her over his steel-rimmed glasses. But, seeing the crest-fallen look on her face, he relented, holding out his hand for the tray. "How do I know what you've brewed up in this?" he asked holding the mug to his lips, inhaling the steam.

"No cat'pillys." She gave him a tight little smile. "Jest green mint leaf wid honey." She paused, "You likes dat."

"Yes, I do," he said grudgingly. "Thank you." He nodded to her and Sadie picked up her skirts and left him with his tea before the conversation could deteriorate.

Setting the mug down on his desk, William selected a book from the bookcase on butterflies, moths and other creatures that turned into caterpillars, and settled into his chair.

After a few sips of the mint tea, he began to calm down. He shouldn't have blasted off like that. After all, he reasoned, none of Sadie Jones's meals had killed any of them yet. In fact, if the cooking had been up to him, they would have all have gladly succumbed to starvation.

From then on, Sadie Jones made it her mission to educate the doctor on the edible offerings of the Carolina countryside. And William took up the study of plant and animal life in the Carolinas.

The old cook began by giving him small samples of delicacies, telling him where they grew and whether they made strong blood, cured constipation or fixed the more persistent problems of getting rid of stomach demons.

So they reached an uneasy truce. William took each of Sadie's offerings seriously, studied them, and made some interesting discoveries—including her cure for tape worms or, as she called them, "Long flat debil snakes."

Over the years, although she'd served up a number of unidentifiable morsels he'd wondered about. Some he had liked. In fact, the frog legs that she rolled in cornmeal and fried for their dinner sometimes, he enjoyed and they happened to be the only thing he vaguely recognized from her repertoire of island recipes. He didn't much want to think about the unfortunate creatures that had been stripped of life and limb, but he'd gone along with Sadie's offering, and, truth be told, developed quite a taste for them.

He also liked the wild okra pods she picked from the star-leaved plants that grew on the sandy banks near the river. They too got rolled in corn meal before frying, as did the fish, and anything else Sadie could get her hands on now that she knew he liked things cooked that way. One day that even included an experiment with his prize figs he'd grown with such care. And although edible, that too, had to be addressed, and he taught her how to preserve them in jars of syrup instead.

Thinking of frog legs, there were no sounds coming from the bullfrogs yet. Too early in the year, he supposed, but it wouldn't be long before their muddy nests, washed by the ebb and flow of the river tides, would be filled with their nighttime operatics.

Soon the curving lines of the rice trenches would need sowing. And soon after that their tender green shoots would be waving above the glassy surface of the water.

Born and bred in the rice fields of Africa and the West Indies, there was little Moses and Sadie Jones didn't know about rice planting, and harvesting. And William was thankful for that. He had never imagined himself the master of a rice plantation and had no training in the matter whatsoever.

Outside, the air was damp and warm. Bright sunshine made Sadie Jones shield her eyes as she stepped into the swept yard. Already, the branches of the wild lilac that grew beside the tall brick manor bubbled with buds and soon their scent would fill the air.

Down by the river, two snowy egrets tiptoed through the reeds, their harsh squawking breaking the quiet afternoon stillness, and in the distance she could hear children's voices drifting from The Street.

She squinted down river. "Deez ol' eyes cain't see much o' nuttin' no more," she grumbled. She raised her hand to adjust her head wrap, and stopped abruptly. There was that tingling in her breast again.

Her hand went to her chest. A flock of seagulls swooped low

over the river as she stood there. Sadie watched them as they rose on high wind currents and flew noisily over the tops of the willows, making their way inland ahead of the storm. Dense cataracts clouded most of her vision these days, making bright circles around the orb of the sun, making it hard for her to tell one thing from another. Hardly any breeze rippled the marshes today, and the only sound on the river was the occasional splash of a fish.

Sadie ran a hand over her face. It came away sticky with perspiration. She sniffed the air to see if she could smell the earth, dampened by raindrops falling far away. She couldn't, but as she shuffled back toward the kitchen house, the ache in her joints assured her rain was coming.

She cocked her head to one side. Someone was calling her.

Standing very still, she turned toward the place the sound had come from. "Who dat somebody saying *Sadie Jones?*" She squinted into the southwest sun. "Who dat out dere shoutin? *Dat's Miss Sadie Jones!*" She waited a moment then continued her walk back to the kitchen. "Might be nobody dere, but somun be calling mah name."

She stopped just inside the doorway, listening. The voice had stopped. "Haints!"

Lowering herself with difficulty into her chair beside the fireplace, Sadie groaned, and pulled the ginger cat up onto her lap. "Marse Doc best get hissef home afore de rain," she told him.

She rubbed her elbow, jostling the cat who lifted an eyebrow and said "brrrp." He stretched one long ginger and white striped foreleg out in front of him with claws extended, and yawned.

"Yayss," Sadie said. "Ah knows who dat callin me from o'er yonder! Dat mah boy, Rossie." She scratched the stripy cat's head. "You and me knows he comin home. But ah cain't be sittin here a talkin wid you when dere's tings to be done." They had to get ready for Ross's homecoming.

"Next ting is we gots ta get word to Miss Katie Rose."

Ten

The Wind and the Angry Sea

AT HIS FEET lay the body of an unknown soldier wrapped in his personal flag. As Ross stashed the oars and lowered the port lea board his sails captured the wind, and, aided by a strong offshore current, he pulled away from the fort.

The red oak planks of the bow met the sea with a resounding crash as the boat forged forward. Minutes offshore, rain pelted his sails. He set his course southwards and sailed on a fast beam reach toward Morris Island to avoid the obstruction ropes that lay across the harbor. Just off shore at Cummings Point, he would turn into the shipping channel and head for the Atlantic.

The southeasterly winds were getting stronger, and the challenge of sailing the boat through the channel loomed ahead. The lea boards would hold her steady through the rough water ahead, but it would take all his skill to manage the boards, sails and the tiller as he entered the channel and began the tack toward the Atlantic.

For now, all Ross's attention was fixed on the bay waters, swelling three feet high on either side of the boat, and the rising wind hurling spray in his face. Foam-crested waves rolled off the bow.

Dark mist rising from the rain, all but obliterated his view of the land, allowing the small, gray-painted craft to sail undetected by enemy lookouts.

In the distance lightning shimmered above the sea and thunder growled as he left the land shadow, the full force of the south easterlies met him broadside sending the boat heeling to port. The wind ripped across his bow as he let out the sails and, with the boat on the rails, Ross centered his sights and sailed hard. Exhilaration lifted his spirits making him feel one with the ocean and the storm.

"YeeHAW!" His yell melted into the sound of the squall. He was on his way again, filled with the excitement of the sea, and the sound of the water slapping the hull as his boat threw herself forward hugging the edge of the wind.

He sailed, unafraid, and shouted into the wind. "I won't be caught, by God!" He raised a fist at the glowering sky. "Not by any damn Yankee, nor by the storm!" The bastards were too far offshore by now, headed for Wilmington, and no rogue storm had out-smarted him yet. He had sailed far worse seas than this, and, hidden by the rain, Ross felt no fear of detection.

It had been too long since he had felt the adrenal rush of being at sea in heavy weather. The thrill of high water, and the screaming wind in his sails, filled his veins. His purpose was clear, and his plan was in place.

His only concern was in staying clear of the blockading shoals of granite that had been dropped by the ancient vessels of the Yankee Stone fleet before they sank. But Ross knew where he was going. The precisely updated charts on the "SS Kate" had shown the exact location and positioning of every obstruction in the bay. Again, he thanked God for that ship.

Sailing fast now, keeping his eyes skinned for the channel

markers, he knew that soon he would have to make the left turn into the strait. When he reached the Atlantic shelf, he would lower the girl's body into the deep water, and, moving fast to avoid being swamped, he would turn the boat around and head for the north shore of Charleston Bay and Mount Pleasant. There, God willing, he'd find shelter from the storm.

Later, he would need transportation. Finding a train still running would be a miracle. Failing that, it would have to be a horse, and a long, stormy ride through Georgetown County. First, he had to find a place to land and a beach to run the boat up on.

Ross vaguely remembered a fisherman's shack on the point that belonged to a family he had known as a boy. It used to be part of the old Ramsey place, as tall summer home built on the hill at the top of a path that wound its way up from the beach.

Bringing his attention back to the task at hand, with the channel markers directly in front of him now, Ross turned toward the wind, to begin the long series of tacks that would carry him out to the open ocean. And whatever lay beyond.

Eleven

The Medicine Drop

THE DARK GREEN canopies of the oaks, that lined Willowgreen's driveway, swayed overhead as William Stanley drove his horse and buggy up to the house. Strands of Spanish moss, clinging misty grey in the tree limbs, fluttered in the wind. The smell of the ocean was strong today.

It was late afternoon and the sky had been darkening steadily as he drew closer to home. To the south, banks of clouds rolled above the trees pressing down on the heat, stifling any wayward breeze. William's face and neck glistened with perspiration.

Zack was usually waiting to take the horse and buggy from William when he got home. But today there was no sign of him. God only knew where the boy was. Somewhere between here and Charleston, obeying his mother's cockamamie notion of finding Ross, William supposed.

Bringing the buggy to a halt in front of the house, he stretched, and holding onto the side of the vehicle, he climbed down onto the brick pavement. At sixty-two years old, the doctor was tired from the ride. His hips ached. So did his shoulders. The air felt like damp cotton making it harder to breathe. Why he put up with Sadie's nonsense he didn't know.

He stood still for a moment, looking at his boots in distaste. Their black sheen was covered with dust. He stamped his feet to shake it, placed both hands in the small of his back and stretched again.

"Daniel!" he shouted for Moses' son.

In minutes, the boy came running from The Street carrying an armful of firewood.

"I'm comin' directly, Marse Doc," he called and disappeared into the kitchen house with the wood.

The doctor turned his attention to Will who was making his way through the oak grove, walking as fast as his leg braces would allow. A lifetime ago, he had jokingly named his young son 'Assistant Overseer' of the small plantation that had been given to the Stanley family by his friend and sponsor, Jeb Ainsley, when they arrived from England. And when William said, "Someone in this family better learn how to grow rice because he, William, didn't have a clue," the youngster had responded to the call with childish enthusiasm.

That enthusiasm continued until he was old enough to attend school and, eventually, the Medical College in Charleston. The boy spent his afternoons working alongside Moses, the overseer He dogged the big Gullah man's footsteps everywhere he went. He learned how to build canals and embankments, and how to plant rice, tamping the seeds down with his bare feet. Moses had lived on this plantation since he had been sold off by a slave trader from Georgia many years ago. He taught Will everything his people knew about growing rice. Eventually the boy could read the river tides and thresh rice with the best of them.

"Evening, Pa."

William smiled. The young man had inherited his mother's same quirky little grin and her auburn hair. It always surprised him how much he resembled Elizabeth at the same age.

"Hello, Will. Ah, here comes Daniel." Moses' son came running toward them and took the reins from William. "Before you deal with the horses, please take those bags inside for me."

The doctor turned back to his son. "These are from Jake. He confirmed the story about the mid-night medicine drop in the Inlet and managed to save some of it for us."

"Good man. We need them," Will took the reins from Daniel. "Here, Daniel, get these inside. Be careful. This stuff's more precious than gold."

William grunted and watched as the youngster lifted the two cloth bags full of medicines and carried them around to the side door of the house, calling for Tansy to let him in.

He turned to Will. "Sadie told you that she's sent Zack to find Ross?"

"Yup." Will grinned. "Let's hope this latest whim of hers is right." He unhitched the horse from the buggy. "I'll take him around to the trough."

Standing with one foot on the wide steps, William said, "I can't understand her at all." He turned to go indoors. "After dinner let's look through those bags and see what we've got."

"Alright. I'm off to the Georgetown plantations in the morning and our supplies are low." A full-fledged doctor now, Will had taken over most of the house calls and travelling chores from his father. "Whatever you've got will come in handy."

The doctor watched Will lead the horse to the water trough, his crippled foot leaving deep grooves in the dirt.

Moses had been fashioning wooden braces for him from the time Will was a small boy, lengthening the apparatus, adjusting it to fit, as he grew.

"If'n Marse Willie going be a ov'seer one day, he best be gittin 'round good," Moses used to say with a chuckle, and proceeded to carve him a wooden clog with an elevated heel.

William walked slowly up the stairs, thinking how fast the years had gone. It seemed like yesterday when Will was just a tot. Before he was big enough to ride, Moses had built him a wooden cart to ride in when he got tired, and wherever Moses went he would pull the little fellow along. "One day you be a mighty fine ov'seer, Marse Willie. Dat fo sho." He would tell him.

The heavy oak door creaked as William let himself into the house. The smell of cedar that greeted him was one of the things he liked best about this house. He breathed deeply as the faint scent drifted from two cedar closets and a cedar chest that Moses had built for Elizabeth a long time ago. The smell reminded him of how much he missed her; especially when it came to dealing with Sadie Jones. He was damned if he knew what went on in that head of hers. Clearly he was too soft on her and it was time he put a stop to her nonsense.

He missed Zack. As damp as it was, they might need a fire tonight. Especially if the temperature dropped. He unbuttoned his collar and placed it on the hall table as a gust of wind blew the front door shut behind him.

William walked into his library, sat down heavily in his favorite chair, and removed his boots. He was glad of the high ceilings that helped keep the room cool in summer, letting in whatever breeze there was, airing the books. Books involving everything Doctor Stanley had thought prudent to haul all the way from England. Yes, indeed, everything from expert opinions on disease prevention, to surgical procedures, to beekeeping.

It was stuffy in here today. He suspected that the shutters had been closed all day. Sadie Jones had been instructed time and again to air the room out at least three times a week, to keep the damp from taking over, mildewing everything from the drapes to the books and walnut paneling.

He resolved to have another chat with her. For whatever good that would do, he thought wryly. He had learned long ago that Sadie Jones did precisely what she wanted to do, and gave short shrift to his suggestions and thoughtful diatribes on healthy living.

William would have preferred her to be more obliging, but in the scheme of things, he couldn't complain. In the wake of Elizabeth's demise, she had brought up both his sons and had done it well in her odd way. Both boys were alive and well, and for that, the doctor was extremely thankful.

He frowned and rubbed the sole of his foot. God knows what she had filled their heads with as youngsters, and how many of her potions had been stirred into their oatmeal, but they had thrived in spite of her ministrations, so all was well.

Pushing himself up from his armchair, William walked over to the shutters and pushed them open. The curtains billowed out into sultry afternoon, flapping against the window frame. He could feel the stale inside air churning with the windborne smell of the ocean. He breathed in deeply. Far away, he thought he heard a rumble of thunder.

Twelve

SS Kate Blockade Runner

R OSS SAILED FAST toward the open sea thinking that the last time he had been at sea was aboard the *SS Kate*, the Scottish blockade runner, as smooth and swift a ship as he had ever seen.

He remembered the night that his ship, the *CSS Tennessee*, was captured in Mobile Bay in one of the worst sea battles of the war. The chaotic memory ensuing from the bombardment of his warship was tattooed on his mind. The stink of oil, the sight of powder kegs rolling across the decks on fire, sails burning and her masts blackening, stayed with him. And, finally, the sound of her armed canons exploding had left him deaf in one ear.

When the cry went up from the bridge to *"Save yourselves!"* with his throat scorched, and stinging from the smoke, Ross yelled at his sailors to "Swim for your lives!" Simeon picked up the command, as one after the other the men launched themselves over the side.

The two men, the Lieutenant Commander and his Bo'sun waited until the ship was boarded, then followed them into the roiling waters and swam for all they were worth.

Hearing the shots fired in their wake, pinging the water, the screams of men who were hit, Ross yelled "Make for that raft!" A sturdy piece of decking that had been blasted free of the ship, miraculously floated upright, and within reach of the sailors. Flames lit the water, and swimming through swathes of golden silk and breaking waves, Ross was the last to make it to the floating wreckage.

As night fell, they clambered aboard the planks, and lying on their stomachs, not waiting to catch their breath, hand-paddled as fast as they could away from the ship.

The cries of wounded men drifting from the captured ship had never left Ross, and he could only hope they were treated with compassion. He remembered the smoke-filled sky turning blood orange from the fires burning on the water and the stench of oil.

And then, Lord have mercy—a ship! From out of nowhere, long and gray, a sloop glided through the water, cutting through Mobile Bay toward them. Calloused hands hauled them roughly aboard, dumping them one by one onto her decks, before the ship veered hard and steamed with all she had into the Gulf of Mexico.

"Snatched 'em right out of all that busted wood and shit and fire, right under those bloody Yankee noses, we did!" The captain shouted, his muscles rippling, as he gripped the helm.

Ross could still hear the mate bark the order for "Full speed ahead!" and the sailor's cries taking up the holler the length of the ship, breaking into loud and boisterous song as they steamed eastward. Disappearing into the safety of the dark ocean, with her side-wheels churning, and funnels belching steam, he estimated the *SS Kate* was cracking well over eighteen knots—faster than any ship he'd served on.

"They'll ne'er catch us noo! Not this ship, not Bonny Kate, by God!" the Scottish captain yelled, taking a drag from his rum bottle, handing the helm to his mate who changed the course to due south.

"Aye, ye can relax a bit, noo!" he boomed over the sound of the wind, "We'll slow her doon in a wee bit and catch our breath." He slapped his hand on the wheel, letting out a roar that became a loud spluttering cough as the rum scorched his throat. "Kate did it agin, by God! Gi' her a fair wind and she'll tak' the challenge every time. As fine and furious a racehorse as ye can find, is no match fer Kate! And ye canna find another ship like her in these waters."

Simeon, white-knuckling the rail, his lips clenched, and his skin getting grayer by the minute, said, "Lawsy! Dey sho don' sail dis wild in Ca'lina! We goin' be sleepin' wid da fishes dis night, fo sho."

Ross roared with laughter, born of relief, "I've a feeling this is just the beginning."

Bonny Kate, indeed. Unable to contain his grin, his thoughts turned to a girl as spunky and as full of vigor and purpose as this ship named Kate. Katie Rose, the girl he'd make his wife as soon as this bloody war ended, or before if he could.

Now, a long way from Mobile Bay, sailing close to the wind, the young sailor shouted into the gathering storm "I'm on my way, Katie Rose." All alone, out here on the edge of the Atlantic, Ross couldn't stop the grin that spread from one side of his face to the other.

He took a deep breath, steadying the boat on course. Outward bound through the channel, he thought back to those days and nights on the *SS Kate*. The narrow escapes, the gut-twisting arms drops made under volleys of rifle fire, treacherous shoals, and high winds as they made their way north. Finally, easing alongside Fort Sumter one moonless night, with no lights showing, the sloop dropped anchor with barely a splash and unloaded the sailors and her cargo onto a landing of broken concrete.

Ross recalled the willing hands scrambling down over the rocks in silence to receive the contraband and the rescued sailors. In short order, the drop complete, the ship heaved anchor and, skimming the tops of the waves, she raced silently for the ocean.

Thirteen

Friendly Persuasion

WITH ONE LAST glance at his bags of medicines, the doctor smiled to himself, rubbing his hands together. *"As excited as a wee boy at Christmastime!"* Elizabeth had once remarked, when his first supplies finally arrived from England all those years ago.

William thought back to the day he had first arrived on these shores in 1834. Was it thirty-one years ago? he marveled. Walking over to the tall windows he stood with his hands clasped behind his back, staring at the shadows dappling the ground cast by the filtered sunlight in the oaks.

Like a young hare, the young doctor had sprung off the ship that'd carried them from South Hampton. He remembered standing on Georgetown's wharf beside Elizabeth as she gazed, in undisguised horror, at a line of slaves being loaded onto a nearby rice barge.

Separated families waved to each other, watching their loved ones being crammed on board. On the wharf, children cried, some screamed, reaching for their parents as relatives and friends restrained them, trying to comfort them. One child squirmed out of crowd and ran for the gangplank calling for his mother. Another distraught child raced behind him, and Elizabeth turned just in time to see a big lout of a man grab one of the boys by the arm and fling him squealing across the concrete.

"Oh no!" she cried, "William! Did you see that? Help that child." She couldn't watch, and he took her by the arm just as the big mulatto backhanded the second child with his ham-like hand, sending him sprawling toward the edge of the wharf.

"Hey, you!" William yelled letting go of Elizabeth's arm.

The barefoot child's nose was bleeding, and the rough concrete had scraped his legs and arms raw.

"What do you think you're doing?"

The brute turned toward William. His thick arms hung menacingly at his sides, his eyes were bloodshot, and sweat ran in rivulets down his bare torso.

William pointed to the child. "Pick him up. You have no right to treat a child like that."

Someone shouted from behind him. "Dubois! Get the hell off my dock before I powder your ass with 'gator shot!" A burly middle-aged man in uniform walked out of one of the warehouses carrying a multi-stranded whip in one hand and a long gun in the other.

The man placed his hands on his hips, spat on the ground and ambled insolently toward the street without a backward glance.

Two women broke from the crowd to reach the child still lying on the edge of the dock.

The man in uniform turned toward William and his distraught wife. "Mornin' Ma'am!" He removed his hat, causing his perspiration-soaked hair to stand on end. "I'm the Harbor Master, John Mason." He held out his hand to William. "You must be the new doctor Jeb Ainsley's bin 'specting."

William lifted the first trembling child off the ground and set him on his feet. "Where can he get these cuts washed off?" he asked.

"Joshua!" the man signaled to one of the dock workers.

"Get this kid to the pump and 'tend to him. T'other 'un too." John Mason shouldered his gun.

"Yassir!" The slave ran across the wharf, picked up the small boy and scurried back toward the street. Two women carrying the other child followed him. "He bleedin' bad fom he nose!" one woman cried.

People shouted from the barge. The captain started the engines easing the over-crowded craft away from the dock. The wood around the wheel house was splitting, and the ropes were bleached white by the sun. It creaked in protest as the nose swung away from Georgetown.

The barge pulled out into the stream. Some of the slaves were singing, and others crying. People could be heard calling to each other as the vessel turned upriver. "Where are they going, William?" Elizabeth whispered.

"They've been sold to a plantation upstream, Ma'am." The Harbor Master answered her. "Those are their folk come to say goodbye." He waved his hat in the direction of the crowd that was beginning to dissipate as the vessel moved out of sight. "And that bully you had the misfortune to witness, is Marcel Dubois, the foreman of one of the rice plantations in Horry County. Bad to the bone."

A black man, pulling a cartload of supplies, stopped for a moment, staring at the boat leaving Georgetown, and said, "Folks is scairt of Dooby. He no good bastid. Unh, unh. Dat man is de Debil." He adjusted his burlap head wrap and moved on in the blistering sun. The cloth harness over his shoulder had left permanent indentations in his flesh.

"There's Ainsley now," the Harbor Master pointed to a man stepping down from his carriage on Front Street.

William looked at his wife. Her fair Scottish skin was turning pink in the unrelenting heat of June on the southeast coast, and her eyes brimmed with tears. He should have known then that this country would be the death of her. He remembered too, the frightened look on four-year-old Will's face, pink and speckled with perspiration, as he stood at Elizabeth's side, holding tightly to her hand.

"Why are those children crying, Mama?" he asked.

"Hush, Will," she said dabbing at his face with a damp handkerchief that smelled of lavender.

William remembered escorting his young family to the street where his old Cambridge University friend waited. Now an important politician and wealthy landowner, it was Jeb who had persuaded William to come to America, citing the need for a doctor on the plantations. It was a warm reunion, he remembered, as the two men embraced and clapped each other on the shoulders.

But William never forgot what Elizabeth said as they lay together in the heat of their first night in Carolina.

"Those people were driven onto that boat like cattle."

It wasn't the first time the doctor questioned his decision to leave his practice in England and head for America. But Jeb had been persuasive, insisting that he was sorely needed here. Doctors were scarce, and few had the time or inclination to treat the sick on far flung plantations.

That and the excitement of living in America would have been enough to bring him out, but Jeb had promised the young doctor land and slaves to work it, and a house worthy of his profession for his family.

True to his word, the house he gave to William and Elizabeth Stanley was a magnificent manor, worthy of any country squire's estate anywhere in England. Built in the Queen Anne style, so popular at the time, it went a long way toward calming Elizabeth's fears about living in America.

The first thing the doctor did after moving his family into their new home was to discount the gift of twenty slaves.

Elizabeth pleaded with him to free them. But in 1834, as they soon found out, there was no fast or easy way to emancipate slaves in South Carolina. So, knowing that they would eventually be free, the Stanleys devised a plan. While emancipation was still a long way into the future, he would pay them for the work they did on the plantation out of his family money.

He promised the men and women that this was their home. They would never be sold or their families separated. He solidified his promise by allotting each family a small piece of the Stanley land, and encouraged them to plant vegetables and berries to sell at the surrounding markets. Some wove baskets made from bulrushes and saw-palmetto from the swamps. Others sold crude paintings they sketched on weathered pieces of wood they found in the marshes, and some tended their own beehives and sold the honey. Moses, the overseer, and part-time carpenter, hired himself out to work when the plantation work was done. And Sadie, under the doctor's watchful eye, gathered medicinal herbs and vegetables to sell.

Over the years, Elizabeth diligently put the slaves' earnings into the bank for safe keeping. She never lost hope that one day slavery would be abolished and their savings could be used to help establish them as free men and women, land owners in their own right.

William wasn't the only landowner who paid his slaves. Nor was he alone in allowing them to work outside the plantations. Many of the merchants and plantation owners, at least those that were so inclined, paid their people a small stipend for their labor.

Looking back, William was pleased with the way things had turned out. They responded well to the hope of being free one day and worked hard for their money.

And then there was Sadie Jones, getting bossier by the day. Which didn't surprise him. During his wife's long illness and at her subsequent death, Sadie took over the running of the place and had, over the years, become increasingly opinionated and downright aggravating at times.

That thought brought William's attention back to the here and now. And right now he wanted to know why, for God's sake, had she sent Zack off on a fool's errand. And what was this babble about Ross? So he put his slippers on and walked purposefully to the back door.

"Sadie!" he called.

"Ah's a comin', Marse Doc." The old woman's voice, carrying the sing-song lilt of the islands, answered him from the breezeway.

"Why did you send Zack off with that ridiculous story about Ross?" he asked gruffly. "We're going to need a fire tonight if it turns cold."

"I done seen to dat." She pursed her lips. "How long Sadie Jones bin takin care of you, Marse Doc? You tell me dat! I ain't goin' fergit to set no fire." Grumbling loudly, the old woman trundled over to the tall open fireplace and drew back the mesh curtain that kept the sparks from flying.

Noticing the way she was limping the doctor frowned. She should not be lugging fire logs about.

"Why didn't you ask Moses or Daniel to do it? And where's Tansy?"

"Don't need dem. Ah seen to it."

"You're a stubborn old woman." William took the tongs from her and winced as he shuffled a big log to the back of the grate. "Get one of the youngsters from the quarters to help you while Zack's gone."

"He be back t'morrow he," she said cheerily.

"No, he won't. He won't be back for days. You sent him to Charleston." William put the tongs down and fixed her with an unwavering stare.

She looked away and dropped her head. "Alright den—you wants to know, den I tells you, but you sho is fidgety dis day. Yassir!" She stuck out her chin. "Ah tol him get his self down Cha'stin way, go find Rossie, and dat's where he gone. Him and de white horse."

"Absurd!"

"Not a'surd. He goin' fetch Rossie and give him da horse to ride home. Rossie he comin' home he. Mebbe t'morrow, mebbe soon." She frowned, turned around, and headed for the door.

"Stay here, Sadie Jones," he raised his voice. "You're going to tell me what's going on. You know Ross's with the troops on Sumter island."

"Nossir. Not no more." She shook her head vigorously. "Unh,uh. He be comin' home." She pulled a piece of willow bark out of her apron pocket and began to chew it. "An ma laig's hurtin, and I gots ta tell Katie Rose her man be comin' home."

In other words, she has no intention of speaking to me. He sighed and ran his hand through his hair. *We'll see about that.*

"Ma laig sho is hurtin'," she repeated. "Yassir, Marse Doc. It hurtin sumpin bad." She stopped her rolling trek to the kitchen house and turned to look at him sadly.

He gave in as she knew he would. "I'll give you something to help it," he said. "Then you're going to tell me what's going on." He would ease her pain in exchange for information. He chuckled inwardly, his conscience prickling him only slightly at his unconcealed use of bribery. Sadie followed him into his dispensary. "And another thing, you'd best be careful about what you tell Katie Rose. She's a high-strung girl."

"I knows dat. I ain't fergot how dat chile come a ridin in here one day wid no seat on her horse, to see Rossie, hair flyin, dress flyin and no shoes on he feet! She a wild chile. Yassir."

"She needs a firm hand," William agreed sternly. *But then, so did her mother, he thought.*

The Stanleys had been friends with the Merrimans, from the indigo plantations, since their arrival in the Carolinas. Violet Merriman, Katie Rose's mother, and Elizabeth's best friend, had been quite a handful for her patient husband. In William's opinion, the man was a saint in the way that he tolerated her unabashed ways, and her inappropriate spontaneity, with the utmost composure.

Of course, the doctor reasoned, she could not be blamed entirely, possessed as she was of a disposition that could not, and did not, end well for any of them.

Suffering from a strange affliction, not unknown or rare by any means, Violet's emotions fluctuated between high mania that had her laughing wildly one minute, and sinking into suicidal melancholy the next. A devilish affliction.

In fact, over a few glasses of whisky one evening, William had strongly recommended to her understandably intoxicated husband, that he take her to the mineral springs in the mountains. They were said to have stabilizing effects on this disorder. In the meantime, William treated her with high doses of chamomile tea for hysteria, and caffeine for the melancholia. And poured his friend another drink.

He walked down the two steps into his office with Sadie close on his heels. A small room, set up as an annex to the main house, its white-washed walls and scrubbed pine floor gave an impression of cleanliness not often found in doctor's offices. Cotton towels were neatly folded on a shelf alongside steel basins, and beside them, instruments lay neatly on a white cloth on the marble countertop. A set of curved scissors, a scalpel, straight forceps, a probe and a bullet extractor lay side by side next to a tourniquet; all within easy reach for rapid selection. On the shelf above, there were rows of labeled, brown glass bottles. And, beside them, a cubby hole where three cloth surgical masks were stacked, next to a tall bottle of chloroform. Rolled cotton bandages were placed under the cubbyhole.

William Stanley's attention to cleanliness had been his focus in his medical training under some of the most innovative and forward-thinking men of his time. In keeping with that thinking his office shutters were opened every day to allow the cleansing air in. He was happy to find that, even here, the community put much stock in the curative powers of the sea air. Holidays by the sea were widely prescribed for whatever might be ailing a person. And in the hot summer months when the mosquitoes were at their worst, those that could, left the plantations for their beach houses.

Sadie stood quietly by, watching as he removed a small sachet of white powder from a box of opiates and shook it into a glass of water. She accepted the cloudy liquid the doctor handed her, swallowing it in one gulp. Handing back the glass, she wiped her hand across her mouth making a sound of deep disgust at the bitter taste of the morphine.

"Oooh, dat so bad!" she sputtered.

"It'll help you rest."

"Cain't rest none til ah gits de message to Katie Rose bout Rossie. An ah's tinking bout Zacky. What if dat bad man, Marcel Dooby, find Zacky?"

She turned to leave, and then stopped and looked at William. "Dat stuff you got, Marse Doc, sho helps dis ol' laig. Yassir. But I gots ta tell you, dat whisky you gots in da book room," she pointed toward the library, "Dat sho is fine hoodoo." Sadie cackled and shuffled toward the outside door.

William had noticed the level in his prized bottle of single malt Scotch whisky going down, and her remark didn't surprise him. His lip curled in a half smile.

"What's Marcel Dubois got to do with the conversation?" The very name of the overseer on the plantation that Sadie had been shipped from made his stomach recoil. Middle-aged now, the big Jamaican slave, the same man they'd first seen on the Georgetown wharf, was the cruelest man he had ever had the misfortune to lay eyes on. A thug with a big bullet head, bulbous bloodshot eyes, a result of high blood pressure, he guessed, and overindulgence in everything he did from vicious whippings to shooting those who defied him. First making them run, he would hunt them down like hogs, William had heard, so he could say he'd killed a runaway. And his appetite for prepubescent boys and girls was apparently well-known. "What's Zack got to do with Dubois?

"Ah's scairt Dooby goin' hurt him," she said. "Heard tell he bin lookin fer ma boy. Cos he heared ah's planning put a powfull spell on he black hide!"

"I told you about putting spells on people," William folded his arms across his chest.

"Dat debil-man need a spell an he gonna git one from Sadie Jones."

"Spells sometimes come back on the one that uses them. Remember? I want to know who told you Ross's coming home?"

She muttered something under her breath.

"Ah knows dese tings." She pursed her lips. "You member dat time ah tells you Rossie he ain't on de ship no more?"

"Yes, I remember."

"An' den I tol' you he in de water and he swimmin'."

"Hmm."

"And next week some chile come a riding to tell us em seen Marse Rossie on de island."

Yes, he remembered. He hadn't known what to make of her rambling at the time. He supposed that the slaves had some sort of network that carried news of everything that was happening in the County. Then a letter came from Ross about two weeks later to say that he had escaped his captured ship and was at Fort Sumter. He had no idea how Sadie or anyone else could have known that.

"And you think Ross is coming home."

"Yassir. I knows dese tings."

And that was that. "Maybe you do, Sadie," he said tiredly. "Maybe you do." He could hear her cackling as she closed the door behind her.

Sadie walked slowly back to the kitchen house. There was a tight knot in her stomach when she thought of her children. She thought of the dangers she had sent Zack into to find Ross. And she thought of her girl child, Mollie who, as a five-year-old, had been raped, beaten and left for dead on the river bank by the man she called Dooby.

"Dat's what changed dat chile," Sadie muttered. "Dat what make her run away, and he goin' pay one day." She opened the kitchen door and went inside. "Yassir, he goin' pay."

Fourteen

Fairhaven on Pawley's Island

KATIE ROSE SPUN around in front of her bedroom mirror watching the girl who smiled back at her. She hugged the indigo shawl around her shoulders admiring the way it swirled into the pale lavender folds of her dress as she turned, and how her eyes went from blue to light gray when she held it to her face.

The shawl had arrived that day, a gift from her father who was at Riverbend, their home on an indigo plantation near Charleston. There had been a note in the box that said, "To my lovely daughter on her birthday."

She wondered whether or not Papa actually knew which birthday it was, but it didn't matter. "In one week I turn eighteen. Ancient!" she told the girl in the mirror, hugging her shoulders and pouting. "And what good is 'lovely' I ask, when there's not a man around for a hundred miles to see it!" She wheeled around. "Tell me Aunt Trudy, what am I supposed to do with 'lovely'?"

"Be grateful, Katie Rose," Trudy Merriman chided as she patiently picked up a corset and a pair of patched silk stockings from the floor, and folded them neatly. "Be modestly grateful. And speaking of modesty, it's high time you were wearing stockings—and a corset. Those short silky drawers you wear with bare legs are an abomination."

"Oh, Tru Pru, you're so old fashioned." She stared dolefully at her aunt in her green and white striped taffeta dress. The green stripes were faded now, and the hem was frayed, like so many of their clothes these days. And no matter how often Trudy showed up with those old patched stockings and corset, Katie Rose refused to put them on.

"Someone should have thrown away all those things years ago," she said. "It's no wonder everyone's fainting all over the place. I would be too in all that long underwear, ribs and laces." She picked up the hem of her skirt and fanned her bare legs. "Those whale bones poke my sides. I hate them!"

"We must suffer to be beautiful, dear girl," Trudy said, patting the small white bow she always pinned into the coil of her hair.

"I'm already beautiful."

The girl was impossible. But then, nobody should be surprised. She was Violet's daughter. And Violet's lack of respect for the more delicate graces of society had been the talk of Charleston.

Trudy pursed her lips as an image of her brother's wife drifted across her mind. What with her bunch of black curls pinned to the crown of her head, sprinkled with gold-tinted power to match the gold-painted sandals she loved.

Trudy knew of no other lady who indulged in that sort of *vulgarity*! She blinked rapidly. It had been too much for the sensitive nature of the ladies of Charleston.

But Violet was a beauty. No one could deny that. And an alternately volatile and adoring mother to Katie Rose.

Katie Rose twirled the shawl over her head of pale blond hair, pulling the tasseled corner over her face. She ran both hands along the curve of her waist. "Should I hide all this? Cover it up with drapes and petticoats? And from whom, pray? There's not a man in sight!" The girl picked up the corset that her aunt had just folded and tossed it in the air with a peal of laughter. "As for these—maybe I'll light a bonfire on the beach and burn them. Somebody should have done that years ago."

"Over my dead body," Trudy said calmly, catching the corset in mid-air and sticking it behind her back. "You'd better behave, missy. Winn and I have friends coming for supper and quilting, and I don't want them upset." She turned away from her charge with her hand pressed to her forehead. "Oh, how I wish your father was here! Why did he leave, anyway?"

"He didn't want to be the only rooster in the hen house, that's why."

"Don't be vulgar, Katie Rose. I don't know where you come up with such things." She brought her hand to her cheek. God knows she had done her best to raise this child in a manner befitting her station.

"It's what Papa said. 'A rooster in the —"

"Stop that right now! You shouldn't repeat the things men say."

"What, like, 'What's good for the goose is good for the gander?' Papa said that too, and I agree with him. The other way around, I mean—and what's more, if men can say whatever they like, why can't I?" The look on her aunt's face made her giggle.

Stung by the defiance in her niece's eyes, Trudy resolved to talk to her brother, James Merriman.

And sensing that Trudy was about to pop her cork, as papa would say, the girl relented with a mischievous smile. "I'm sorry, Aunt Trudy, but just imagine! A crackling, bright fire that smells of seaweed and pine! I wonder if corsets flame scarlet? Or green and blue like pinecones?" Katie Rose twirled across the room, picked up the offending garment and placed it on her head laughing. "Look at me! Young bucks of Georgetown County! Gather 'round the queen of the corset-less damsels!"

She stamped her foot. "I knew I should have gone with Ross!"

"Stop it, immediately. You are behaving like a—like a *gypsy*! Ohh! In a fashion quite unbecoming to a young woman of your breeding. Stop it at once! And what do you mean you should have gone with Ross?"

"I wanted him to take me to war, but he said 'no'. And I don't understand that, either. Other women get to go, and I can shoot as well as any man out there. And I can blow things up, too." Katie Rose snapped her mouth shut realizing she had gone too far. Following her early morning foray into the war zone around Miss Fannie's, she had definitely gone too far.

Trudy was silent and her face had turned a kind of blue-ish white.

The girl waited a moment. When she could bear it no longer, she feigned a shame-faced look, snatched the corset off her head and grabbed her distressed relative in a hug so tight it was a wonder the poor lady didn't succumb to a loss of her vapors.

"Don't worry, Tru-Pru. I didn't go with Ross, did I? And I won't embarrass you tonight," she said planting a gentle kiss on Trudy's cheek. "I'll be nice to your friends. I promise." And with that, she whirled off and swirled through the doorway in a fluff of petticoats and lavender eyelet.

She stopped suddenly and turned around. There were tears in her eyes as she stood there and said, "Oh, Aunt Trudy . . . Where's Ross? When will he be home?"

"I don't know, child.

"Sometimes I wonder if my heart will burst with love. And then I think that maybe that wouldn't be so bad, and I'll just die."

"Don't say such things, Katie Rose." Trudy shuddered. "It's rumored that this loathsome war will be over soon. Let's pray that they're right."

"No, it won't! I know it won't! I'll die an old maid with a broken heart—just waiting to drop from the vine," she leaned against the door frame with one arm across her eyes. "Into a river of tears. Goodnight, sweet prince," she sighed theatrically. That would have been a great line for the book she planned to write one day. Too bad someone else had already thought of it. Katie Rose turned and went down the stairs trailing a limp wrist along the banister behind her.

Trudy rolled her eyes. So like Violet. She shook her head as memories of her troubled sister-in-law tumbled unbidden into her mind. Full of life one minute and gone the next. She was either swinging from the top of the world or falling into the depths of an abysmal depression. There was little peace in her life. But how Trudy had loved her.

Images bloomed in front of her eyes of Violet climbing a tree to reach for Trudy's bonnet. Violet teaching the younger girl how to hold a fan—just so! And how to ride sidesaddle. *"Bound to knock a man dead,"* she declared. *"And Trudy, if you really want him to follow you, you lower your eyes like this—and slowly, very slowly, you cut them to the side, holding his for only a second. And don't forget to wet your lips—like so."*

Trudy had practiced diligently in front of her mirror, but somehow, all the gesture managed to produce was a pair of temporarily crossed eyes and a headache. She even tried her moves and flutters at Riverbend during a race week ball, to no avail. Only to watch the target of her advances cut a beeline across the floor to where her brother's beautiful wife held court.

Sometimes she heard Violet's silvery laughter in her dreams. The laughter was gone now, carried away on an outgoing river tide. A tide that took her life all those years ago, following an unspeakable tantrum with James, who had had his fill of her flirtations with other men.

Trudy had tried to erase the memory, but it still ran through her mind, carried on Violet's screams as she ran across the lawns of Riverbend. With her hair blowing wildly in the wind, her skirts billowing out behind her, crying out, "I'll kill myself before I let any man rule me!"

It was the last time she saw Violet. Her body had been found downriver in the mud, caught by her bright blue satin skirt in the reeds that lined the banks.

Trudy shook the images away as she bent to retrieve the unwanted corset. Placing it slowly in a drawer she shut it firmly and walked briskly down the hall to her room to change for dinner, praying to God that Katie Rose behaved in front of the ladies.

Fifteen

Miss Sadie Jones of Willowgreen

SADIE JONES WAS an odd duck if ever he saw one, William mused as he sorted through the bags from Jake's. He handled each small packet, each glass bottle as though it was gold, as well it might have been.

"Here, Will," he said, handing him a small brown bottle. "This stuff kept your mother alive for a long time after she contracted malaria."

Will held the bottle up to the light. "Quinine powder."

William nodded. "You probably don't remember much, but after Ross was born your mother contracted malaria and become too ill to feed him. That's when Sadie took over his care."

"I remember that. I sat beside her while she nursed both Ross and Zack at the same time," he smiled.

"And before Elizabeth could recover from childbirth, milk fever set in."

"I've seen it in one of The Street mothers. Painful. And the fevers that come with it are fierce." Will stood up. "Speaking of The Street, I've got a child with a throat infection down there that I must get to him before dark." He prepared to take his leave.

"We'll go through these later," William replied and turned his attention back to the bag he was holding.

"Yes, indeed," he said to himself as Will left. He had stayed with Elizabeth, night and day, treating her with willow and dogwood tea, giving her laudanum to calm her when she began to rave. Sadie made poultice after poultice to relieve the redness and pain in her swollen breasts and came up with an endless supply of damp cloths with which to bathe Elizabeth's body in an effort to break the fevers. Only to start all over again as her temperature returned with hardly any respite.

Too tired to think and at his wits end to know what to do about his wife and newborn son, he moved Sadie into the nursery to nurse and care for the infant.

Ross was a wee scrap of a thing. "Wouldn't have given tuppence for his chances of survival," William murmured. But Sadie took over the child's full-time care, and within days, she had him sucking strongly beside her own three month old son, Zack. Within a week or two the baby they named Ross Stanley had actually gained a half a pound, while Elizabeth lay close to death.

Days became weeks, but finally the fevers ran their course. When they abated, she was able to take some chicken broth and a thin gruel of warm grits. The doctor was exhausted, but seeing his young wife beginning to rally, he began to hope that at least the milk fever was under control.

The malarial infection was something quite different. He knew how it could become chronic, lying dormant for months, sometimes years, then raise its head throughout a patient's life, bringing on virulent chills and fevers. In extreme cases, even death.

Sitting in his library, he picked up the bottle of quinine powder and stared at it. Native to the high mountains of Peru, it came from the quina-quina trees. They kept it on hand at Willowgreen at all times these days.

Ah, yes, he remembered. They dealt with each on-set of the malarial fevers as they happened, but the disease gradually stole Elizabeth's strength. He recalled how pale she became. And how shocked her nurse had been when he ordered all the windows thrown open, and the bed sheets changed on a regular basis.

"She'll catch her death," the nurse wailed.

"No, she won't." William shot back. "Fresh air. And clean sheets. And wash your hands in the bowl in the hallway when you arrive every day and every time you enter the sick room."

Elizabeth's recovery was slow and, in spite of his and Sadie's best efforts, it looked to William as though she was destined to be an invalid for the rest of her life. All the chicken broths and barley waters they came up with did little for her strength. Indeed, most of her food was returned to the kitchen house barely touched.

"I'm so tired all the time," she told William. Her usually fair skin was now a translucent white, and she was so thin he could trace the blue tangle of veins along her neck and arms.

Her best time of day was late afternoon when she took her afternoon tea, sitting in a high back chair that Moses had placed beside the window. The East Indian tea she liked perked her up, and this was when Sadie brought the baby in to see his mother.

Over the weeks that followed, William watched, with something approaching awe, as the Gullah woman took over the running of the household while caring for two babies, himself, and Will. She was like someone possessed. When she wasn't ordering her battalion of servants around, cleaning every corner of the manor, she would be out in the fields directing berry picking. Or sending a child up a tree for bark, or across the fields digging for roots.

Her evenings were spent in the kitchen house concocting root cures for her mistress over the black wood stove. She mumbled incantations while she worked, which came close to driving the doctor to distraction. What was worse, he was forced to watch as she spooned her unlikely brews gently into Elizabeth's mouth before every meal. He knew what was in the brews so wasn't concerned that they would have any ill effect on his sick wife—or any effect at all, for that matter. And, some of the things she came up with made a sort of *raw* common sense.

That was when William began to study plant medicines, and spent many afternoons, talking to Jake at the apothecary, who welcomed his visits and enjoyed sharing his knowledge. Jake also enjoyed sharing the odd glass of William's rare Scotch whiskey And on days that he closed the shop early, he rode out to Willowgreen to deliver some new drug or gadget he knew the doctor would appreciate.

One afternoon, Elizabeth called William to share her afternoon tea because, she said, "I have something to talk to you about."

Pulling up a chair he sat down beside her and took her hand. "What is it, my love?"

From her seat at the window, and still very frail, she raised a hand to his cheek. "You're looking tired, William," she said, putting her hand up to stop the protest that was bound to follow. "You've been so good to me all through this wretched sickness, dear, you've exhausted yourself. I am so lucky to have you."

"No, no." He shook his head. Overcome by fatigue and her concern for him, he put his head in his hands. "I should never have brought you here."

She put a finger to his lips to stop him. "Don't say that, dearest. I've had a lovely life with you. More than any woman could ask for. And as for Sadie, she's been like a mother to us. And I want to do something for her."

"What is that, dear heart?"

"I want to give her a new name."

He looked perplexed.

"You know, a *real* name. Oh, William, I would like to give her my mother's name—that is, if she would like it. She could be Sadie Jones! Isn't that a wonderful idea, dearest? She's done as much and more for me than any mother could have. Don't you agree?" Her eyes were pleading with him.

William smiled at her. "Your mother was a good woman, and I think it's the greatest compliment you could pay Sadie. We'll ask her if she would like that." He said softly kissing the palms of his wife's hands. "But you know what she's like—she'll probably want a name of her own choosing." He raised his eyebrows.

"Oh." Elizabeth was quiet for a moment. "I hadn't thought of that. Then she shall have whatever name she wants." Her face lit up. "Oh, William, I'm so glad you agree. Will you tell her or shall I?"

"We both will," he said. He walked to the back door and called her. "*Sadie!* Come on in here! We've got something to ask you."

With Elizabeth's bequest of the new name, Sadie Jones took over the running of practically everything in a way that George Washington himself would have envied. She ran things with precision, and, William thought privately, with an electrifying gusto that would have been utterly unbecoming in any woman, let alone a slave. She lorded it over the workers on The Street, and with her already esteemed place in their society as a root doctor, she became unbearably domineering. She might have taken over the boss man's job in the fields if Moses hadn't come to him complaining loudly about her interference, and begging for her to be taken down a peg or two.

"Lawsy, Marse Doc," Moses said, holding his hat in his hands on the doorstep of William's dispensary. "She worse dan any ah ever seen! And now she sayin' we has to call her *Miss* Sadie Jones!"

"Miss Sadie Jones, huh?" William stroked his chin. He should have known. He turned away from Moses, walked into the breezeway and bellowed, "MISS Sadie Jones! Would you do me the honor of presenting yourself in my study, forthwith? That means now!"

But his thoughts were wandering. The back door was open and he could hear noises coming from the kitchen house as Sadie trundled around making supper. The aroma of stewing apples wafted through the breezeway and wood smoke from The Street's cooking fires wound through the cypress. The field workers would soon be coming in, he mused.

William wished he knew where Ross was. Did Sadie know something no one else did? Or was she raving mad?

Sixteen

Burial at Sea

THE LAND WAS a long way behind Ross, hidden behind clouds and encased in a mist so thick that no one but the highflying gulls could spot it. He was approaching the Atlantic.

Stinging raindrops slammed his sails, soaking his coat and the woolen cap pulled down over his ears as he tacked one last time.

Casting his memory back to the smeared wall charts on SS Kate, he estimated his distance from the shore and his timing, and pinpointed the spot in his mind. It was here. This was where he would bury the girl.

With waves pounding the hull, Ross turned the boat into the wind, bringing it to a virtual stop. Its speed fell off immediately as he eased the main and locked it down. Using all his skill, he back-winded the jib, and, almost simultaneously, pushed the tiller far to starboard and secured it.

He was sweating and dripping wet, but satisfied. In spite of the wind and the current, with the jib and the rudder counter-acting each other, the boat was at a near standstill. The young officer could now move around and do the job he'd come to do.

Here, the deep water would hold the girl's body until an outgoing tide, reaching far below the unsettled surface, carried it out to a much deeper resting place. Ross stepped over the oars that lay in the bottom of the boat and moved toward the corpse.

The thunder was louder now. The wind tugged at his coat as he made his way to the bow and sat heavily on the bench. Moving fast, using the anchor rope, he bound the anchor around the ankles. He raised his head as lightning flashed, pulsed, and died over the southeast ocean. Then, breathing heavily with the effort, cold and wet, he grasped the weighted body and lowered it, feet first, over the side.

A wave broadsided him as he let go, sending him staggering backwards, clinging to the mast. Sadly, he knew the words of a burial at sea by heart, but there wasn't time. So, staring into the water where the body spiraled toward the ocean floor, he said quietly, "Rest well, young woman."

Wasting no time, Ross unlocked the tiller, and freed both sails, allowing the storm to swing the bow toward the harbor.

It was a long haul, and it was cold, but he kept telling himself that every roll of the waves, every blast of wind, carried him closer to Willowgreen and Katie Rose. And with the wind at his back, he lifted his boat into the swells and rode the sea homeward.

On a straight run now, with a following sea and the wind holding its direction, he let his thoughts wander. The war was over, the future lay ahead, and there were plans to be made as he faced the next phase of his life.

The heady days of plantation life were numbered. The slaves were deserting in droves, and soon there would be no one left to hoe the fields or plant the crops. The rice growing trade and a way of life would be gone. But, on this stormy day, Ross was back at sea with a plan and thoughts of home and Katie Rose filling his mind.

The sweeping lawns of Willowgreen where he and his sweetheart walked hand in hand seemed very far away. He remembered the feel of her hand in his and the way she swayed toward him brushing his arm as they walked. His eyes misted at the thought of the sparkle in her eyes when she raised her lips to his for a kiss.

A sudden cold wave slammed into the bow, chasing his memories and sending him scrambling for the stays. The weather was worsening. He could feel it building in the thrust of the sea that carried him down the channel.

And carried on the wind, strangely, Ross could swear he smelled apples cooking. He shook his head and grinned at his foolishness. But the strong scent of hot syrup and baking apples lingered. He could almost see the fire blackened tongs hanging on a hook beside the fireplace in Sadie's kitchen, and feel the warmth of the kitchen house envelop him.

There would be no need for him at Willowgreen once the rice was gone. The men and women who worked for William Stanley would move on to better things, and Will and their father would keep on practicing medicine.

But with all the hardship and loss caused by the war, opportunities would be opening up everywhere in the South, and Ross planned to seize them.

First, he would buy up all the land he could in Charleston and restore the old buildings to their former glory. Developers would buy them, and builders would buy his surplus land for new town homes for new arrivals to the new South. And next year, or the year after that, Charleston's festivity-filled Race Week would return, bringing back the old days to the fine old city.

He would find a choice piece of land, and there he would build a smart hotel and, one night in May, he would open its doors to the sound of brass bands playing as the dancers arrived. On opening night, he and his bride would open the ball with the first dance. Definitely a waltz, he mused. Katie Rose would like that. His fearless Kate would love being held close against his chest in the scandalous mode of the waltz. He grinned, picturing her radiant in satin and lace as she danced with him in his dress blues of long ago—if he could find them. And the sound of music would carry across the harbor, chasing the memories of cannon fire, mortar, and dying.

What a wonderful night it would be.

A cold blast of wind buffeted the boat, sending it surfing down the slope of a high swell. Elated and with the channel behind him, Ross began to sing with all the gusto he had and after a moment all the tension of the night left his body. Lifting his voice, he let it be carried loud and clear, soaring ahead of him on the fast running sea.

It was an old song, one his Scottish mother used to sing to him and Will when they were children. A song from the Scottish isles of her youth, his older brother said. Wild places that gave birth to wild songs, full of the sounds and fury of the North Sea, filled with the sailor's cries, carrying Bonnie Prince Charlie to the Isle of Skye. *Speed, bonny boat, like a bird on the wing.* It was a brave song full of hope and courage that warmed Ross, sending adrenaline coursing through his body, as it had generations of sailors before him.

His sails, filled with wind, carrying the boat on a fast run toward Fort Sumter. At this speed, he calculated, they would reach the rock in no time. He strained his eyes for a glimpse of land. And at last, there it was. Rounding the western end of the deserted Fort Sumter, he set his sites on Sullivan's Island rising out of the mist, and sailed on. Avoiding the obstruction ropes and steering clear of Rattle Snake shoals, he headed for the crumbling mass of Fort Moultrie and the old fisherman's shack he remembered so well from his boyhood had better be there. For that was where he planned to leave the boat. He had no rope with which to moor her, not even if he could find a post or a tree, so he would have to surf the breakers, allowing them to carry the boat far enough up the cove and wedge it into the sand.

He wondered about the Ramsey house and if it was still standing. There might be a horse in the stable. There might even be people there to give him dry clothes and a bowl of hot grits.

"But, holy God if you can hear me—a horse will do, for I must get home to Katie Rose," he whispered.

The storm was getting louder. He would take shelter tonight and head out at first light. He might follow The King's Highway, he mused. Or stick to the woods if it was unsafe to travel. The old mail route would take him within a short distance of Willowgreen. But if there was no horse to be found—well, he'd worry about that later.

His thoughts went to Katie Rose. And just as he was imagining her hair running through his fingers, the soft curve of her breast cupped beneath his hand, and the flush in her cheeks as she came into his arms, a massive explosion blasted across the harbor.

It was followed by flames roaring through a column of black smoke, towering above the buildings huddled around Charleston's wharf. The metallic stench of gun powder swirled through the wind stinging his nostrils, making his eyes water.

The arms depot was on fire. An intentional fire, perhaps, he hoped. With his eyes glued to the inferno on shore he hoped that Simeon and his seamen were nowhere near it. It was an awesome sight as blast after blast rocked the wharf, sending billowing clouds of smoke into the air as each new stash of ammunition blew up.

But he couldn't stay. The sea was quickening and his boat was fair skimming the wave tops as she gathered speed. Sullivan's Island was clearly visible now, receding into the mist only to appear again as the winds blew the smoke and fog in swirling chaos across the land. He could just make out the ruin that was Fort Moultrie. There were no lights on the island. Straining his eyes he looked for signs of life but could see nothing in the fast-falling dusk as he rounded the point and left the island behind.

Easing the bow across the current, the boat heeled, continuing to turn almost directly into the wind. Ross dropped his mainsail, reducing his speed, and let the jib carry him toward the shore.

Lightning trembled in the grip of thunder that rumbled above the coast. Then, as he had hoped, a wave caught his stern, thrusting the boat forward. Thrown from one wave to the next, Ross grappled for control and then, from out of nowhere, a long, low swell rose up beneath the boat. And, as though guided by some angelic hand, it carried him gently toward the shore. "A miracle," he whispered in wonder as he raised the lea boards and surfed the wave. "A bloody miracle!"

The mist cleared. The rain had stopped, and there was the fisherman's shack he remembered. Right where it always been, behind the high tide mark of seaweed and broken shells. And beside it, the old rutted path that led to the Ramsey home on the cliff. Still standing.

The boat glided from the sea on the dying swell and ground to a stop on the sandy beach. Ross leapt leaped ashore, waited for the next wave, then, heaving with all his might, he hauled the craft up, wedging its bow between two dead tree trunks.

There was no time to think about the weakness in his legs, as he prayed to whatever God in Heaven had delivered him. He stood with his hands on his hips staring at the clouds. The storm was coming fast. Ross stashed the oars, retrieved his sword, and with pistol in hand, ran up the beach toward the shack.

Derelict now, it lurched to one side, its cedar boards showing wide gaps, the slope of its roof touched the sand that had piled up against it. But it was the prettiest sight his eyes had seen in months. A quick look around the inside showed only a rotting fishing net and a splintered buoy in one corner.

Backing out of the door, leaving it swinging on one hinge, Ross spun around and strode up the rocky pathway to where the house stood gleaming whitely against the dark sky that swallowed the lemony rays of twilight.

He had no idea what he would find. Had the Ramseys fled as so many others had? Was there food in the house? In the field? His stomach growled at the thought. It had been days since he'd eaten anything but the barest of rations.

Ross held his breath as he drew closer, noticing the paint peeling off the woodwork. Mist swirled eerily through the oaks and a wrought iron balustrade on an upstairs balcony had separated from the wall. No smoke coiled from the chimneys.

The house was dark. Strands of Spanish moss whisked ghostly shadows on the walls, and Ross felt the hairs prickle the back of his neck. He shivered.

Slowly, he withdrew his pistol from his belt and walking around the side of the house, staying low, he made his way to the back door.

Seventeen

The Beach
(I never know what day it is here)

ﾠA S SHE USUALLY did when she was sad, Katie Rose left the
house with her journal under her arm and walked through the
oak grove to the gazebo perched on top of the dune she called Big
Sandy. It was the highest dune on this part of the beach, and from
here she could see the length of the strand—and a hundred miles out
to sea. Curled up on a cushioned chair, she could watch the ships
sailing across the horizon and wonder if Ross was on one of them.

And she wrote in her journal. The words, flowing from her pen
like honey, coming from deep within her, calmed her. Sometimes she
just gazed down the beach and pretended he would come to her if she
waited just a little longer. Sometimes she tried to lose herself in the
mists that rolled over the dunes in winter, or in the spray of a breaking
summer wave.

The seasons roll by, she wrote, *and if he is on one of those
spectral vessels on the horizons, he doesn't come. It's not as though I
want him to have to swim for the shore because of a shipwreck or
anything . . . but if only I could see him again. I should have gone with
him.*

Katie Rose pulled her shawl around her shoulders. One day, she would write this story of the devastation of war and, above all, its stupidity. She would take her writings to New York City where, it was said, the best writers lived. And she would dare them to turn her down. One day when this foolishness was over, she would take her place beside Miss Louisa May Alcott and the Bronte sisters. And her favorite, Jane Austin.

A cool breeze blew through the open-sided gazebo. It swept through the leaves on the boardwalk making tiny dust devils that danced on the wooden planks, dipping and swaying to the unwritten music of the wind.

Everyone's spreading rumors. They're saying that the war will soon be over. Well, all I can say is that it's about time, dammit. We would have been married by now if not for this senseless war that just goes on and on. What's wrong with men anyhow that they have to fight like dogs over just about everything!

Tears blurred her vision. As she looked toward the oaks with their solid trunks and sweeping limbs, she felt their mystical energy envelop her. The forest was lovely. Katie Rose blinked the tears away, tracing the line of her upper lip with her pencil and wrote.

Here I am sitting on this island, getting older by the second! Dammit. That's the word Ross used when he left the last time. He didn't think I heard it, but I did and what's more, it's exactly the right word for him being gone. Dammit.

She gazed absently at a gull racing along the shore trying to catch an almost invisible ghost crab before it blended into the foam that ruffled the edges of the sea. The horizon was dark today, and the clouds above that dark line of lumpy water, as black as ripe plums.

She chewed the end of her pencil. *There aren't many birds out today. Just a couple of sandpipers racing along the shore. The waves*

are breaking high up the beach, leaving mounds of foam behind that
the wind blows helter-skelter, tumbling down the beach . . .

She cocked her head to one side, liking the sound of the words,
'helter skelter.' It was easy to picture her skinny, black-inked words
scattering helter-skelter across the pages of her journal, racing in
every direction. As free as the foam.

Closing the book, she stood up, turned around, and placed it on a
white cushion with scarlet cherries embroidered across its middle.
Then, dropping her shawl, she ran to the top of the dune, kicking off
her slippers as she climbed.

She stood there poised for a moment enjoying the feel of the cold
sand under her feet and the taste of spray speckling her lips. Then,
with an unexpected surge of joy, skirts flying behind her, Katie Rose
ran down the mound, feet flying, reveling in the embrace of the
elements all around her.

Maybe this is how you learn to fly, she thought. "Look at me!
I'm flying!" She called breathlessly into the wind, and, feeling as
light as sea smoke, she skipped over a clump of grasses, caught her
foot in the hem of her dress and went tumbling down to the hard-
packed sand of the beach.

That wasn't the way her flight was supposed to end. Lying on the
cold, damp surface, she caught her breath and blinked rapidly. She
wiggled her toes and sat up, pleased that there had been no one on the
beach to see her. Better still, there were no broken bones for Tru Pru
to get hysterical about.

She jumped up, flapping her skirt and shaking the sand out of her
hair. Retrieving her shawl, she twirled it over her head and ran toward
the ocean. It was invigorating to be out on the deserted beach away
from the stuffy houseful of old maids. And with the wind blowing
around her bare legs, she picked up her skirts and ran into the

shallows.

"Where are you, Rossie?" she shouted into the spray flying off the waves that were higher today than she had ever seen them. "Where are you?"

The only answer she got came from the high-pitched piping of a sea bird scurrying up the beach as it escaped the incoming tide.

Eighteen

A Message from Sadie Jones

WILLIAM COULD HEAR Sadie shouting across the courtyard for one of the youngsters who was in the middle of a game. "Drop dat hoop! Get you down here. You gots to take mah message to Edenton," she yelled.

Edenton, with its Ionic columns and white archways, belonged to Winston Perry, a crippled war hero, now confined to his home in a wheelchair and the owner of one of the newfangled telegraph machines that William so admired.

"You hear me, boy?" Sadie called out again.

William knew what she was doing. It was Tuesday evening and, because everyone on the plantations knew everybody's business, Sadie knew that on Tuesday evenings the mistress of Edenton, Leah Perry, visited Fairhaven on Pawley's Island for her weekly quilting bee.

Sadie was going to ask 'The Duchess', as William called her, to deliver a note to Katie Rose. He grinned. There wasn't another person, black or white, who would dare ask a favor of the imposing Leah Perry. A large woman with a commanding presence, she was a veritable dowager of the realm of Southern coastal aristocracy. She claimed to know all the right people, and never hesitated to let others, of lesser estate, know who was who along the southeastern Atlantic Coast. And God help anyone who crossed her.

"You put dis note raht in Mis'tis Leah's hand and aks huh nice to give it to Miss Katie Rose." William heard Sadie saying. "Lemme see dose hands. Dey clean?"

"Yas'm Gogo," the boy replied, hopping from foot to foot. "Dey clean. Sho are." And with that, the child's bare feet could be heard scampering across the hard-packed clay of the courtyard to run the mile and a half to Edenton.

"And you tell Mist'is Leah, Miss Sadie Jones done sent you." she called after him.

William shook his head. Will and Ross had taught Sadie to write simple sentences, a practice that was downright forbidden in most places, and she took great pride in sending notes to everyone— including those who couldn't read them.

He chuckled. Sadie Jones had been with the Stanley's so long, he couldn't imagine life on the plantation without her. *Miss* Sadie Jones.

Where other women tiptoed around Leah Perry, Sadie did no such thing. And, for her part, the Mistress of Edenton appeared to be intrigued by Sadie, and probably didn't know quite what to do with the tiny, outspoken Gullah woman. Or her apparent reign over Willowgreen Plantation. William had no doubt that she would not only agree to take Sadie's message to Katie Rose but would make absolutely certain that she got it.

He pulled a dark blue bottle with a tight glass stopper out of the sack and turned it over to read the label. Chloroform. Ah, ha! He was down to his last whiff of the stuff.

Of course, it probably didn't hurt Sadie's quest that Leah had a soft spot for the handsome doctor and was not averse to an occasional flirtatious flutter from behind her gloved hand. If truth be told, this terrified him. Especially when, after three glasses of Spanish sherry, the lady's flutter became a stirring invitation to a rendezvous in her town home in Charleston. William had felt himself redden to the color of the Persian carpet under his feet, while desperately hoping to be swallowed up by the same.

She was a handsome woman, to be sure. And while the idea of a playful frolic beneath the sheets with the perfumed and formidable Leah, wife of his respected neighbor, was titillating, it was utterly unthinkable.

There were two more bottles of chloroform in the bag and underneath them, one precious bottle of ether. His face lit up with pleasure. Developed by a certain Mr. Morton in Massachusetts, ether was considered to be safer than chloroform and was fast becoming the anesthetic of choice.

William cleared his throat, carried the precious anesthetics into his office and deposited them in the locked box that held his supply of morphine.

No, he thought, more to reassure himself than anything else. He had no need for the intrigue and secret meetings offered by Mrs. Perry. The pretty Widow Anderson in Georgetown had satisfied his masculine needs quite well for some time. And, quite apart from that, Winston Perry was an old friend, and so it would remain.

The wind blew and he felt a cool draft coming from under one of the outside doors. William shivered, and walked across the old Wilton carpet to close the windows. He wondered what Sadie had said in her note to Katie Rose. He hoped that her ramblings about Ross wouldn't send the young woman into a whirlwind of fantasy.

The war may be nearing its end, but it would take months for everything and everyone to calm down and for the men to get home.

It was also true that Katie Rose was high-spirited and excitable. William knew the Merriman family well. Violet and her daughter, Katie Rose, had been guests at Willowgreen many times, but in his opinion, she showed no signs of developing her mother's unfortunate clinical disposition. She was overindulged, perhaps. Horribly spoiled to be exact. And whereas she could be head-strong, it was not in the manner of anything approaching the mania of Violet Merriman. For which he was mightily thankful, given Ross's fondness for her.

Indeed, Katie Rose had grown into a lovely lass. Unpredictable at times and a pain in the neck to her aunt Trudy Merriman who had moved into her brother's home to care for the girl and her father when Violet died.

A very patient woman, who had taken on a job that would have brought on a rash of hysterical fainting spells in most other women of her class. A strong woman. William shuddered to think of where the family would be without Trudy's watchful eye.

Yes. Katie Rose was a loving child. A charming girl in many ways. With a considerable talent for getting her own way every time. And, used to being given everything her heart desired, Ross fell squarely into the category of something, or some*one* in this case, that Katie Rose's heart desired.

William cleared his throat. His son, a Naval officer, was a man who would brook no nonsense from a young woman and her wiles, a man in every sense of the word to be sure. He was exactly what the tiresome child needed.

Again, he wondered, with some trepidation, what Sadie had said in her note.

Nineteen

Katie Rose

GLANCING AT THE setting sun, she supposed she ought to go back to the house before someone came looking for her. Katie Rose gazed out at the far horizon shrouded in rain now, remembering the first time she met Ross Stanley.

It had happened right here at Fairhaven on the day he had ridden from Willowgreen with a basket of vegetables and a bag of rice for Aunt Winn.

She was five. He was nearly eleven and seemed very grown up. She hung on his every word and followed him unmercifully around the house, skipping behind him, talking non-stop as he placed his basket on the kitchen table. She remembered how he handed her the vegetables to put in the airing cupboard and the eggs into a wire basket that was shaped like a hen. When they were done, he gave his young admirer a stick of sugar cane.

Sometimes he would linger, and they would go to the beach and watch the ships sail across the horizon. And sometimes they ran out over the top of the marsh, along the boardwalk that stretched halfway to the mainland. When they had run as far as they could go, they would sit in the sunshine panting and watching the turtles that came out to lie in the sun on shiny black rocks. And tiny green ribbon snakes that squiggled through the grasses.

Their childish friendship blossomed. She liked the figs and strawberries he brought from Willowgreen, and he never forgot the stick of sugar cane.

When she was twelve, and he was almost eighteen, Katie Rose turned suddenly shy around him, blushing whenever he spoke to her. But that didn't last long.

She picked up a broken shell. A gull shrieked and plunged into the white crest of a wave. The girl turned away from the sea and made her way over the big dune to the gazebo.

She sat there remembering the times when all the Merrimans were invited to Willowgreen. Those were the best times of all. She remembered how excited she became when one of those invitations arrived, so excited that she couldn't sleep a wink the night before. She remembered the day she just couldn't wait for the household to ready themselves, and she jumped onto one of Fairhaven's horses, and cantered bare foot and without a saddle all the way to the Stanley plantation.

The thought made Katie Rose smile. Lord have mercy! Tru-Pru got so red in the face, she almost blew up. Katie Rose thought her ears would fall off from the scolding she had to endure, and the yelling from Sadie Jones about what a wild child she was.

But what was she supposed to do? It would have taken the women forever to get all the pies wrapped in clothes and put in baskets. Let alone pack the marsh crabs for boiling, and the smoked sea bass they had saved for the occasion. It would be nightfall before they got there. And she just couldn't wait that long.

When the summers were over, she and Trudy went home to Riverbend on the Wando River to be with Papa through the winter. She saw little of Ross over the winter, but, as he got older, he sometimes rode the train or horses to Riverbend with Will to deliver medicines to the indigo plantations.

Sometimes, she begged to be taken along with them, when the boys ran their errands. And when Ross said, "This was man's business," it was Will who said, "Let her come, she can learn how to be a nurse." Which made her wrinkle her nose in distaste, but she went anyway, and Will let her carry the medicine bag.

At other times, the boys came with their father when the doctor ran his week-long clinics for the surrounding plantations and their slaves. Will spent most of the time at his father's side, learning how to be a doctor, but she and Ross found other things to do. Sometimes, they drove the carriage into town and went to the Gullah market with a list from Riverbend's cook, and, sometimes, they went fishing or galloped out to meet the mail coach.

The Stanleys always stayed at Riverbend when on their medical errands in Georgetown. Katie Rose vividly remembered her mother churning the household into a chaotic froth of readiness for their guests. The shutters had to be re-painted and new drapes had to be hung in the guest bedrooms, why, Katie Rose could never figure out. The old drapes looked fine to her. The cook was sent to Charleston to scour the markets for new spices, dried fruits, fragrant oils and other delicacies that, for some reason, all of a sudden they couldn't do without.

Violet said she did it for her best friend, Elizabeth, who sometimes travelled with the doctor.

It was an exciting time. As a child, Katie Rose would sit in the drawing room at their feet for hours watching the ladies sip lemonade, listening to them swapping stories about Charleston society and the latest fashions from Europe.

"I've heard that the color indigo is all the rage in London town," Mistress Elizabeth said.

"It's rumored that Queen Victoria herself has ordered hundreds of yards of indigo-dyed cotton in the wake of Prince Albert's untimely death," her mother remarked. "She's inconsolable, I hear," Violet reported solemnly, "and it's thought that the purple sheets from Carolina will be used to drape the balconies and public rooms of Buckingham Palace."

Katie Rose had no idea what or where Buckingham palace might be, but wherever it was, it sounded very grand.

As she got older, she spent less time at her mother's knee, and grew closer to Ross and Will.

During their visits to Willowgreen, Ross taught her to hunt for frogs at the water's edge and how to keep her eyes skinned for water moccasins. They moved, he said, with the stealth of an attacking Indian and struck with the speed of lightning. And that was enough to keep Katie Rose's eyes glued to the riverbank.

He showed her how to test the skinny vines that dangled from the trees for sturdiness, and how to make a knot that could hold a person's weight and swing you across the river. But, he warned, "You better hold on because there are alligators below waiting to eat you if you fall."

The first and last time the little girl's knot came unraveled she went flying off the end of the vine and landed in the tall grasses at the water's edge. The shock sent her scrambling up the bank crying hysterically, sure there was a congregation of alligators behind her waiting to chomp down on her ankles. The next thing she knew, Ross swooped down toward her on his own vine, grabbed her around the waist and hauled her squalling little person to dry land.

It was getting cold in the gazebo. Katie Rose rubbed her arms remembering how her mama threw the biggest hissy fit anyone had ever seen when they got back to the house. And Ross's mama fainted clear away at the sight of the mud-caked children.

She could still see Violet falling at Mistress Elizabeth's side, yelling for Sadie, in a most unladylike way, to "Fetch smelling salts, for the love of God! And for Pete's sake, hurry!" Katie Rose never could understand what God's love had to do with it. And who was Pete? Whatever was in those smelly things brought mistress Elizabeth around long enough to drink a cup of chamomile tea to calm her nerves.

But she never forgot it, or the worst that was yet to come, as she was dragged off by Sadie Jones and scrubbed, none too gently, under the pump.

"Ow!" she wailed as Sadie pulled her muddy dress over her head, leaving her standing in her shift, while she washed her legs and arms with an evil smelling bar of creosote soap. "Stop it!" the little girl yelled, spitting soapy water, much to the delight of the children from The Street who danced around them laughing and pointing until Sadie picked up her broom, and they all fled.

"No, Gogo, No!" they shrieked with laughter, using the African name for Grandmother.

"Next time Ah'll take a switch to all a y'all!" she cried after them.

"Where's Rossie?" Katie Rose had cried out.

"Don' you worry none bout Rossie." Sadie said, trying to avoid the child's flailing arms. "Moses he got Rossie, and be tellin' him a ting or two bout learning you such stuff as swinging cross da rivah. What next, I aks!"

So, being forbidden to indulge in anymore "boy tings", as Sadie called them, she began to watch Will when he sat in his father's office learning to mix medicines. He let her mix some once, and another time, he took her to a place in the fields where they found some fat leaves that he said could be used on burns. "You just slice a thin piece off the leaf and lay it right on the burn," he said.

Ross's mama died the summer he was twelve, and Will was fifteen. Malaria finally carried her away on a devastating case of chills and fevers that not even Doctor Stanley could fix. No matter how much of the quinine powders he gave her, no matter how many cups of willow branch infusions Sadie fed her, "And God knows what else," as Doctor Stanley said. Nothing worked.

Violet came from Riverbend to help Mistress Elizabeth. The women spend days bathing her with wet cloths, for the fevers, and wrapping her in blankets against chills that shook her wasted body. Within a short time, Elizabeth succumbed to the ravaging her body could no longer endure.

Five years later, when Katie Rose was eleven, Violet died. That was when Aunt Trudy came to stay with them at Riverbend. No one talked much about her mama's tragic demise, but Katie Rose thought of her every day for a long time. Sometimes she would sit all by herself near the riverbank and talk to her. And sometimes, even now, she had vivid dreams of her beautiful mother.

When she was fourteen, Katie Rose fell in love with Ross. That was in the summer of 1860. Before the country went to war. It was a tender summer, filled with hot, sultry days perfumed by the honeysuckle that clung to the thorny branches of wild roses that grew along the banks of the Waccamaw.

She and Ross would sit together in the long tree swing holding hands. Gone were the days when he would scamper up onto the thick round limbs of the giant oak, dragging her up behind him.

And sometime during that year, on her fifteenth birthday, he opened the door to the beach house for her, lifted her hand to his lips, and kissed it.

"Why! Aunt Tru! I almost died of love right there and then!" she exclaimed.

There was the time in the gazebo when, with his arm around her, he had leaned forward and kissed her on the lips for the very first time.

She found herself living in a cloud of euphoria. But it couldn't last.

A few months after that first kiss, South Carolina seceded from the Union, and suddenly, the whole country was at war. Ross left the Naval School in Virginia and rode for Wilmington to join a ship that would take him into battle for a very long time.

Katie Rose cried herself to sleep the night he left and many nights after that.

Will, with his crippled leg, stayed behind working with his father, making house calls and tending to those left on the surrounding plantations.

"What's going to happen to Ross," she asked him one day.

"Ross is the bravest man I know," he said. "And the smartest, so don't worry. If any damn Yankee gets in his way, he'll shoot him dead."

The next time Katie Rose saw Ross, she thought she would die of love at the sight of him. In full dress uniform, more ruggedly handsome than she remembered, she knew with all her heart that there had never been a man more striking than he.

Her eyes followed him as he walked toward her. The lamplight winked off the gold buttons on his navy-blue coat, and a sword shone at his side. Their eyes met, and Katie Rose felt herself dissolve into a pool of tenderness. The light scent of Bay Rhum cologne made her want to reach for him and melt into the same desire she felt in him.

His mouth curled upwards, filling her with a fire that sent the heat rising up the back of her neck and flushing her cheeks, as Katie Rose remembered the next thing she did.

Staring into his eyes she said, "Will you marry me, Ross?"

Aunt Trudy spluttered when she told her about it. "You did WHAT?" she said, reaching for the side of the settee before she slid to the floor.

Katie Rose remembered yelling for Millie to bring smelling salts as her aunt's eyes rolled back in her head, and, kneeling beside Trudy, she said, "And do you know what he did?"

"Lord help us, no." Trudy murmured with her eyes closed.

"He threw back his head and laughed, till I thought he was as crazy as a loon, and he said, 'Katie Rose, my love,' And burst out laughing again."

"And then what?" Trudy whispered.

"Well! I told him that his display of merriment was the most ungentlemanly thing I'd ever seen! And just as I was about to smack him, he caught me in his arms and kissed me on the lips."

"Ohhhh, no!"

"*Millie!*" Katie Rose yelled again. Where was that housekeeper with the salts? "Oh, yes! And then he said, "I would marry you this very night if could." She paused. "And then guess what happened!"

"Don't tell me." Tru Pru's hands got all fluttery the way they did when she came across spiders and such. "I can't take any more!"

"Well, as soon as he said, 'this very night if I could' the bells from All Saints chapel began to ring." She watched a small smile creep across her aunt's lips. "Isn't that the most romantic thing you've ever heard?"

"You silly child." Trudy said weakly, shaking her head, as Millie arrived and began waving the salts around.

In spite of her protests, Katie Rose knew that Trudy loved hearing these tales. Well, most of them, anyway. She left out the part about Ross's hot, moist breath on her neck, and how her body grew moist in response. It was sweet and scary at the same time. And sometimes she thought there must be something wrong with her that this hunger in her rose so intensely, so fast.

Tru Pru would definitely not want to hear *that*.

Katie Rose remembered that night as if it were yesterday. That kiss was burned into her lips forever.

Of course, he couldn't marry her that very night because he was sailing out of Georgetown in the morning. So, she asked him to take her with him.

"Absolutely NOT!" he had exploded. "But soon," he promised, holding her close. "I'll be home soon, and we'll be wed."

Sitting here on this misty afternoon, the memory came back to pierce her heart. "Where are you, Rossie? Please come home," she whispered, as tears filled her eyes. It had been nearly a year since that night.

Slowly she became aware of someone calling her name. She turned toward the house.

"Miss Katie Rose? You come in afore you ketch your def out dere! Miss Toody be lookin' for you," Millie cried.

"Coming," she called, dashing away the tears.

"You get in dis house right now," Millie cried again.

The light was fading fast as she walked barefoot along the boardwalk to where the housekeeper waited.

She stopped suddenly. Who was that lurking around the corner of the house? She looked again. There was no one there but someone, a man, had been there. He must have pulled himself back into the shadows.

"You come on inside," Millie's voice rose impatiently. "Mistis Leah done brung a letter for you from Sadie Jones, an' Miss Toody she fit to be tied, you bin gone so long."

A letter? From Sadie? Katie Rose forgot about the shadowy figure in the bushes, picked up her skirts, and ran into the house.

Twenty

Mount Pleasant

R OSS PICKED HIS way gingerly through the camellias growing in untended profusion below the windows of the summer house. He trod carefully so as not to make a sound. Not that anyone could hear anything above the clamor of the wind.

Holding his pistol in front of him, he made his way around the side of the darkened building, looking for a door. The outside kitchen stood behind the main house with its door wide open and creaking on its hinges.

Bent over double, Ross ran toward it and flattening himself against the outside wall, he peered through the doorway into the gloom. There was no one there. Turning from the kitchen, he could see the back door of the big house. He sprinted across the yard and backed himself into the shadows of an overgrown wisteria clinging to a trellis on the side wall of the house. He listened for any sounds coming from the other side of the door, silently cursing his damaged hearing. Shifting his weight, Ross kicked open the door and entered the house with his pistol cocked, ready to shoot anyone or anything he found there.

There was nothing and no one.

It was a funny thing, Ross thought. Along with his damaged hearing, his sense of smell and awareness of his surroundings had sharpened to the point of being almost feral. The house felt empty. He could smell cold candle wax mixed with the smell of charred firewood. And there was a chill in the air that would not have been there if a person or an animal had been present. He would have picked up the stink of stale sweat, dirt and urine on the unwashed body of a soldier, a half mile away. And the smell of wood smoke on his clothing would be strong, along with the tangy scent of pine resin and swamp mud on his feet.

Ross tucked his pistol back into its holster and listened to the crepe myrtle tapping on the windowpanes. A branch cracked and fell close to the house causing him to pivot. He peered through the windows. A dead limb lay against the side of the house, near the casing, still trembling from its fall. He took a deep breath.

Memories of summers spent at the Ramsey house filtered through his mind. He remembered the morning sun beaming through the bay windows and a table always loaded with food for an assortment of guests who streamed in and out.

His stomach growled. Clearly, the people who lived here had fled. The hall closet door was wide open and most of the coats were gone, their pegs empty. Shoes had been hastily pulled off racks and thrown aside. Small ladies' shoes and soft indoor shoes were scattered everywhere, but there was no sign of a sturdy boot or solid shoe anywhere. There were no hats or bonnets left either, but soft Irish linen shirts and silk blouses lay in a heap at the foot of the stairs. They had simply grabbed what they needed and left.

Walking over to the fireplace, Ross held his hand on the inside brick casing. The bricks felt cool.

He walked back out to the kitchen house feeling sure that the occupants would have taken all they could carry. The smell of rancid grease and spilled, baked-on food emanating from the stovetop was strong, and a pan of corn breadcrumbs and a saucepan of beans had been left untouched. He held his hand to the side of the pan. It was cold.

Pulling the stove door open he saw a mound of cold ashes and turned away. He opened the latch on an airing cupboard with a wire mesh front, peered inside, and found a basket of onions and potatoes on the top shelf. Lying beside them, tied with a piece of twine was a wilted bunch of greens and a small bunch of carrots. Squatting, he peered at the bottom shelf seeing a bag of lumpy salt, a half-empty jar of honey and an open bag of cornmeal lying on its side.

He stood up. There were two bins standing against the wall, and he lifted the lid off one of them to find a cupful of rice sprinkled in the bottom. The next bin revealed a thin layer of dried beans. It wasn't much, but it was enough for a meal and something to eat along the way. He prodded one of the potatoes. It was hard with a small green leaf still clinging to it. There must be more of these in the field, but there was no time to look for them.

Returning to the house, Ross took off his wet coat and sprinted up the staircase to the bedrooms. More discarded clothing was draped over a chair and a hairbrush still bristling with hair lay abandoned on one of the dressers.

A shiver shook Ross's shoulders. He needed dry clothes, ammunition and a Mackintosh. Outside the window gathering clouds looked as though they could burst wide open by morning.

There were candles on the nightstands and when he yanked open the drawers below them he found matches. "Good," he breathed. With matches he could light a fire and the stove.

Buried in a stack of clothes on the bed he found a pair of long underwear, pants and a flannel shirt that looked as though they'd fit. Ross threw off his wet clothes, climbed into them and headed for the staircase.

With one hand on the banister, an armful of candles and the box of matches, he took the stairs two at a time, strode into the drawing room and placed the candles on an ornately decorated mahogany desk. It was getting dark, so he stood them in conveniently placed holders and lit them. The effect was instantly gratifying. He stood still for a moment watching the wicks cast a flickering glow on the wall behind them, giving off the illusion of warmth in the cool damp.

The drawing room reminded him of the wide, high-ceilinged room at Willowgreen where his parents entertained visitors before the war. That was when money and food were plentiful, and no expense was spared in the preparation of lavish dinner parties. He remembered the nuts and cheeses laid out for the after-dinner poker players in the study, and bowls of fruit and small tarts for the ladies playing whist in the library. Tarts that inevitably found their way into Ross's pockets to share with Zackie.

That was before the men went off to war, when everyone had friends and neighbors to entertain, Ross thought wryly. He wondered how future generations would view the decision to go to war and doubted that history's judgment would be kind to either side.

He also wondered what Zack was doing on this blustery night. Ross imagined him sitting on the rug in the kitchen house, surrounded by three or four of the children from the slave quarters, teaching them to read and write.

Twigs snapped overhead, leaves rattled, and thunder rumbled across the water, as Ross loaded an armful of logs from the woodpile onto a wheelbarrow. Emptying it near the back steps he hurried back to the pile to reload and carried the second load into the drawing room for the grate. The wood was dry, and in no time he had a crackling fire going.

He was anxious to be on his way, but he would have to wait until first light. The Old Kings Highway went straight through the forests and swamplands of Georgetown County. It was bad enough during daylight hours, crawling with brigands and robbers, but in the dark it would be foolhardy. And he had yet to find a horse.

Leaving the warmth of the fire, he loped across the courtyard toward the horse paddock with scant hope of finding any horses. As he opened a rusty gate that lead into the field where the stables stood, lightning struck close by. His scalp tingled as it struck the ground, and a clap of thunder shook the point, sending Ross racing down the same pathway he and Luke had raced along as children.

He could hardly see where he was going in the gathering dark but, remembering the potholes and ankle twisting vines that stretched across the path, made him keep his eyes on the ground.

His friend, Luke, had suffered a broken ankle one summer that had to be set by a doctor from Charleston. He remembered his friend howling as it took two house slaves to hold him still so that the broken bones could be clamped in place. Ross shuddered at the thought and made it through the stable door just as a second lightning bolt forked into the bay behind him. The storm had arrived.

There were no horses. Just a lot of scuffed straw on the floor and a few spare reins, horseshoes and bridles hanging on the walls. He stared at them for a moment, then raised his hand and fingered the leather in the reins. One set was badly frayed, the other looked better, and the bridles were strong. He unhooked two sets of each knowing he would need them if he found a stray, or runaway, horse.

Looking around he saw no saddles and wasn't surprised. Saddles would have been taken as currency. His eyes scanned the almost empty hooks and shelves in the tack room. A rope caught his eye. He may have to rope a horse wandering in the open. "Yeehaw, Ross!" He muttered, grinning as he snapped the rope testing its worthiness.

Slinging the coiled hemp over his shoulder, he walked slowly down the row of stalls. They were empty so he walked back through the gloom toward the stable doors. A barrel stood on a concrete slab just inside the entrance. Lifting the lid he found it was half-full of oats, and above it, hanging on the wall, was a feed bag. Feeling his spirits rise, he stuffed the bag with grain hoping to God he would find a horse to feed, and jogged back to the house.

A gust of wind slammed the back door behind him, making the candlelight flicker and dart on the walls. The fire blazing in the grate warmed the room, sending tongues of orange flame racing up the chimney.

Ross picked up his navy coat and slung it over the back of a chair to dry. The damp wool smelled like a wet puppy, he thought. He flopped into another chair across from the fireplace and leaned his head back.

Forgetting he had been up all night the night before, he hadn't realized how tired he was, or how cold his hands and feet were, until now. Leaning forward, he held them out close to the fire. Soon its warmth began to curl through his veins, warming his face, drying the salty dampness in his hair and relaxing the tension in his muscles. He wanted to stay here, never to leave the aura of the burning logs, but his stomach was growling, and he knew that if he was going to eat, he'd better get moving.

Carrying one of the candles into the kitchen house, he placed it on a high shelf and went outside to bring in more wood. In seconds, he had a fire going in the stove.

Putting his hands on his hips Ross stared at the ingredients in front of him wondering what to do with them. "I have no damned idea," he muttered. Grabbing a bucket he went outside to the water pump he'd seen earlier, filled the pail and carried it back inside.

His eyes searched the shelves and he reached for a cooking pot, found a knife in one of the drawers and hacked off a piece of smoked ham he found hanging on a hook in a pantry. He tossed it into the pot and watched the fat begin melt. The smell of hot meat frying filled the kitchen house, making his mouth water. Next, he went into action chopping the onions, and the potatoes, and pretty soon he had a pile ready to throw on top of the sizzling meat. Casting an eye over the rest of his ingredients he grabbed the wilted greens, cut the bunch roughly in two and tossed them into the cooking pot followed by the rice, and listened to the grains pop as he stirred them all together with his knife.

Reaching back into the airing cupboard, Ross pulled out the bag of salt, sprinkled some of it into the pot, topped the whole concoction off with a metal cupful of water and let it cook. Sadie Jones would be proud. He grinned, rubbing his hands together thinking that right now he was so hungry he could have eaten a piece of matted cotton fried up in the pan.

Then he remembered the jar of honey on the shelf. Honey and cornmeal. He had an idea.

Rifling through the drawers he found a spoon, dipped it into the honey jar and scooped a spoonful of the gooey stuff into his mouth. He poured the yellow cornmeal into a bowl, added salt to the meal, and water to dampen it, then rolled the putty-like stuff into dumplings. Yup! Sadie Jones would be mighty proud, he thought scooping up another spoonful of honey, which got his stomach rumbling again. Oh man, that was good! He couldn't remember the last time he'd had honey, and he couldn't remember anything ever tasting as good as this did at this moment. He was surprised there was any honey in the place at all. A couple of years ago a new recruit had come aboard the ship with stories of the pillaging and destruction that was going on all over the country. He told of soldiers seizing homes, taking everything edible then salting the grain fields. He painted pictures of them stomping vineyards into the ground, stripping orchards, and overturning and smashing beehives.

Apparently none of the marauders had ventured through here. Which is why the old house was still standing, he mused.

Leaving his stew to simmer, Ross went back into the house. He wondered where the battles were raging tonight and hoped no deserters from either side were headed this way. His gun was loaded and at the ready if they did.

Twenty-One

The Wind in the Willows

THE LAMPLIGHT CAST a circle of light on the burled maple desk in the corner, throwing tall shadows on the walnut paneling in the library as William continued to delve through the bags he'd brought back from Murrells Inlet

He rubbed his hands gleefully, especially pleased to see several bottles of carbolic acid and rubbing alcohol. It was a fact that boiling water with a pinch of the acid would kill anything lurking in the joints and on the blades and handles of his surgical instruments. A rubdown with alcohol, as they lay on a clean white cloth drying, did the rest.

It was a mystery to the doctor that so many others of his profession hadn't figured that out yet. Why, he had once had the unthinkable misfortune, on a trip to the mountains, to have been stuck with an upcountry doctor to attend to a cut on Ross's arm. "Doctor, my foot!" William grunted out loud, as the memory came back. Unwashed instruments scattered on a filthy counter and a basin of bloody water he used to rinse them in.

Much to the man's surprise, William had snatched the crusty needle with its dangling thread of cat gut out of his hand just as he was about to begin stitching Ross's arm. "Hand me that, man!" he had shouted. "And put some water on to boil! Have you got any salt?"

The startled doctor nodded, reached into a drawer and pulled out a bag of coarse salt.

"Soap!" William said. "And look at that!" He pointed to an enamel cabinet that was streaked with so much dried blood and muck that William couldn't begin to describe what he was looking at.

"Now, look here, you!" the doctor found his voice at last and pushed his spectacles up onto the bridge of his nose with a dirty fingernail.

"No! You look here," William said. "Find me some soap. Have you any idea what havoc this filthy needle can cause in a person's blood stream? Have you ever seen a case of blood poisoning? Have you ever wondered how many microbes are clustered on this tiny piece of steel?" He waved the offending needle under the medic's nose. "BILLIONS! Billions of death-causing microbes." William exploded and began sweeping all the instruments off the counter and throwing them into the pot of steaming salt water. "Let them boil for at least ten minutes. I need soap. And so do you." He stabbed a finger at the doctor's grimy hands.

He held out his hand, and the perplexed doctor slapped a bar of dirty soap into William's hand and watched him as he scrubbed his wrists and hands and proceed to wash the area around Ross's wound.

"What are you doing that for?"

"I learned it from a man named Joseph Lister." William replied.

The doctor smiled. He lined up his new purchases on the shelves and in the cubby holes of his dispensary before standing back to admire them. What a difference it made to have what you needed when you needed it.

From where he stood, he could see Sadie Jones shuffling around in the kitchen house. Smoke coiled out of the chimney before being born away by the wind and flung in ragged swathes among the strands of moss that hung from the tall oak beside the house. William watched the tree's great canopy shudder under each assault from the northbound wind.

The children's hoops, which had been leaning up against the gate to the rice fields, rolled and skittered across the grove and the dinner bell outside the kitchen rang crazily, as it was tossed this way and that.

Irritated, he looked around for something to stuff it with and picked up an old *South Carolina Gazette & Country Journal.* Crumpling up the pages, he strode the short distance to the kitchen and wedged the pages inside the bell, effectively silencing the offender.

"Hmmph," he snorted and went back into the house.

Sadie looked up. "Yassir. Marse Doc he mighty squirrely dis night," she murmured as she spied the doctor making a dash through the breezeway to his office. "Wat he tinkin'? Wind's gonna mess wid dat bell no matter wat."

But Doc Stanley wasn't the only squirrely one. The wind unsettled Sadie, too. It especially unsettled her knowing that Zack was on his way to Charleston. "Dat wind up to no good," she muttered. "Ain't no tellin' wat gonna happen when da south wind blows."

Sadie walked slowly over to the window, watching the Carolina night creep across the yard like wood smoke. She became quite still, holding on to the sill, and her lips began to move. "Now, you hear me, Lawsy, and I hope you lis'ning where you at over yonder, cos mah boys is out dere and I don't want dem scairt none. So you git yo your wings, I heared talk about, and bring dem chilluns home."

Sadie's biblical knowledge of who was who and what was what among the hierarchy over yonder may have been sketchy, but her intent was clear.

She placed her hands on her hips and glared menacingly out of the window. "An Lawsy, if you be needin' some hep, Sadie Jones got pow'ful hoodoo kin send you. You tell me where you live, and Ah'll get it to you."

A smile spread across her face and folding a towel on the counter, she addressed the deity once more. "Maybe Lawsy ken hear old Sadie, maybe not, but Ah knows Rossie ken hear me. So, you and Zackie get yousef home y'hear? It's dinner time."

She went over to the pot of sweet potato and legume stew and moved it off the stove. The roast was done, and she had it out on a wooden board cooling enough for her to slice it. The corn bread had risen to a warm, golden brown. Not that she could see it, but its nutty aroma told her it was done. Reaching inside with a towel wrapped around her hand she seized the iron skillet handle and hefted the cornbread atop the stove away from the heat.

Ginger cat wailed as she picked up a carving knife and sliced off the end of the roast.

"Dis for you and me," she told the cat, as he sauntered over from his place by the fire and rubbed up against her skirts. She placed the piece of meat in an enamel bowl and scooped a helping of the potatoes and greens down beside it. "Dere. Now we let dat cool." She pushed the plate to the back of the stove, picked up a dish cloth and wiped her hands. "An' Lawsy, while ah be feeding dese folk, you best be lookin' out for my mah boys. Dere's bad stuff out on de road." She pursed her lips and remembering her manners, added "If you please."

Twenty-Two

Safe Harbor

SITTING IN THE chair up close to the fire, Ross brought the bowl up to his lips and drained the last of the stew's broth. It was a fine dinner. Maybe not quite up to Sadie Jones standards, but here on the hill, in this big empty house, with a storm bearing down, and the candles flickering, it was a fine dinner indeed.

He had even found a bottle of French brandy that someone had overlooked in their hasty departure, and proceeded to pour himself a snifter before replacing it in its cabinet.

"To the next traveler. Whoever you are!" He raised his glass, swirled the golden-brown liquid around and took a sip.

"Ahhh!" He took another sip and set it down on a piecrust table top beside his chair. He thought of his father and a smile touched his lips. He was an old man now, who still enjoyed his single-malt Scotch whisky, which, Ross thought, must be scarce as frog's teeth, these days. Perhaps he knew someone in the know who was able to get him a bottle from a blockade runner in the Inlet. He hoped so.

His thoughts went to Will, crippled from birth, helping to hold the plantation together while studying medicine. He'd heard he was a doctor now, and as such, his brother was probably riding out with Pa, learning the role of a country doctor.

Soon Ross would be home with them. One quick stop at Willowgreen on his way to Wilmington wouldn't take much time—and the next morning he would head for Pawley's Island and Katie Rose of the deep blue eyes and petal soft lips.

Had she changed while they'd been apart? He remembered the last time he'd seen her after a long absence, and how astonished he'd been when he saw her. The childish grin and tangled hair were gone. The bony elbows and knees, replaced with the graceful limbs of a woman. His Katie Rose had blossomed into the full promise of womanhood while he was away. Only the freckles remained, barely concealed by the pink flush of her face. A face delicately chiseled now, into the loveliness of the grown-up woman who stood before him. He closed his eyes and remembered the graceful arch of her neck above bare shoulders and the mischievous sparkle in her eyes that flamed with desire as they gazed at each other in wonder.

That was the night she asked him to marry her. A broad grin spread across Ross's face as he remembered how incensed she became when he laughed. Oh, Katie Rose—nothing had changed on the inside.

Ross swirled the brandy in his glass, deep in thought. He'd been gone a long time. Was she still waiting for him? His hand touched his breast pocket where he kept her letter. He knew the words by heart so there was no need to take it out. "*. . . I'm longing for your return! Oh, Ross, I miss you so.*"

"I'm going home," he said to the shadows on the wall and raised his glass.

His thoughts turned to images of Willowgreen, and the thought of his old mammy lit up the corners of his mind. Sadie Jones would have dinner bubbling on the stove about now, and perhaps a creamy rice pudding full of raisins and cinnamon keeping warm on the hearth.

Ross was starting to feel the effects of the brandy. "I'll be there soon, Sadie," he whispered. "First, I have to find a horse." A small frown crinkled his brow. There must be one somewhere.

Pulling his socks off, he hung them on the fireplace hobs to dry and threw another log on the grate. He dragged an overcoat he'd found in the pile of clothes, around his shoulders, leaned back in his chair, and closed his eyes. His eyelids grew heavy, and his head nodded onto his chest as his body relaxed into the warmth of the cushiony chair that smelled vaguely of mildew. The fire danced and crackled in the grate.

Before long, giant waves of tiredness overtook him, and he didn't hear the first raindrops plinking on the windows. Nor did he hear the gust of wind that toppled the wheelbarrow by the back door and lifted the tiles on the roof, sending them skidding toward the guttering.

The last thing he remembered, before he disappeared into the deep gullies of sleep, was an image of two boys, one black, one white, racing along the riverbanks, and the sound of Sadie Jones's voice calling them home for dinner.

The sound of hoof beats, charging through the storm, were still too far away for him to hear.

Twenty-Three

Dinner for Two

THE DINING ROOM was set for the evening meal. Two places were laid, one at each end of the long rosewood table. Two Irish crystal goblets stood beside Elizabeth's cream-colored china and French silver. In summer there were flowers in small vases beside his and Will's plates but, flowers being scarce, they had to do away with that nicety in winter. Silver rings held white cotton napkins, frayed and a little threadbare in places, but pressed and neatly rolled. A candelabra missing half its candles, hung over the center of the table, its light glinting off the polished wood surface. This was the way it was every night.

Sadie Jones placed the venison roast on a thick wooden carving board in front of the doctor's place. A silver tureen of sweet potatoes sat on a woven grass trivet to the right, and a platter of greens was beside it. The tureen was missing one of its handles, but there was nothing to be done about it until the silversmith got back from wherever the army had sent him.

She set the cornbread, still wrapped in a white cotton cloth to keep it warm, in front of Will's chair and, on her way back to the kitchen, she picked up a small silver bell from the side board and jangled it three times to let them know dinner was ready.

Soon, the master of Willowgreen would come down the broad stairway in his dinner jacket and striped cravat. His dark gray trousers, a little shiny at the knees and the seat, would be neatly pressed, his shoes polished and buttoned at the ankle. The buttons didn't match anymore, but this was the best the cobbler could do these days.

William Stanley and his oldest son might be dining alone, but, as he had taught both sons, there were standards, by God! Even in wartime. "Man loses sight of his standards, he may as well pitch a tent in the wilderness and learn the ways of wolves."

Every night he lit the candles in the candelabra. It was part of his ritual and he enjoyed it, reasoning that Sadie Jones would fall off a chair if she tried to reach them, "Most likely setting us all on fire," he said.

And every night, Will held his father's chair out for him and waited until he was seated before taking his own place at the other end of the table.

Sadie watched as they settled themselves at the table. "We gots custard puddin' dis night," she announced knowing it was the doctor's favorite. It used to be lemon custard, but lemons were hard to find since the ships took them all for the sailors. "Miss Leah done sent us some eggies dis mo'ning."

"Hooray! Presumably the hens were undisturbed by this morning's explosion." William grinned as she turned to leave. "Thank you, Miss Jones. This roast looks delicious."

Her old face crinkled with pleasure as she closed the door behind her.

William set about carving the venison and suddenly began to

chuckle. "Will, do you remember the night the Perrys came to dinner with the Merrimans and the Ainsleys and God knows who else, and Ross had arranged with Sadie to surprise us by making the dessert himself?"

"I remember the disaster in the kitchen after Sadie gave us our first cooking lesson when Ross was about nine." Will grinned. "And after the second lesson, he thought he could cook."

"Well, he made us a lemon custard pudding that night, if you recall, and he did quite well, under Sadie's instruction, but she must have turned her head when it came to the part about adding the eggs."

"And the next thing we knew, everyone began to crunch down on the custard when they got the first mouthful of eggshells." Will finished.

William laughed. "Ah, yes. Made perfect sense to Ross. Add three eggs. Trouble was, no one told him to take them out of their shells."

Will walked to the end of the table grinning and the doctor forked a slice of venison onto his plate. "What made you think of that?"

"Oh, I don't know. The pudding, I suppose." He helped himself, straightened his napkin on his lap and frowned. "It's Ross's 25th birthday today."

"To Ross," Will raised his glass.

William smiled. Will missed Ross as much as he did. He picked up his glass. "To both my sons, and to Ross on his birthday," he frowned. "It seems such a long time ago that he wrote to me from Virginia of his decision to fight for the Confederate States in this God forsaken war."

"1861," Will said, "I would have given anything to have gone."

William folded his napkin beside his plate. "You know your mother and I loathed the idea of slavery. It was abolished in

England—and practically everywhere else in the world, and I was sure it was only a matter of time before it was abolished here too. But they waged war instead."

"I knew you didn't want Ross to go."

"Quite. But I knew his allegiance was to the South. Can't argue with loyalty, son. I was proud of him for that, but," William shook his head. "it's been a most terrible war. On so many levels. I'm glad you had to stay here." He smiled at his son and helped himself to a second glass of wine from a cellar that was looking sparse these days. "You have the makings of a fine doctor, Will."

"Speaking of the explosion on Pawley's Island," Will said. "There's some speculation that it was a local job. Someone from the island, they say."

"Oh?"

"Apparently, a fisherman saw a youngster galloping away from the scene."

"Then we can assume that it wasn't the Ladies Guild of Pawley's Island." William chuckled.

Sadie was uneasy. She sat in her chair with a bowl of sweet potatoes in her lap, unable to shake the fear she felt blowing in the windy night. She couldn't read the kitchen clock, and she couldn't see the sun anymore, but Zack had been gone a long time. She hoped he had found Ross by now.

"Wid dis storm coming in, ain't no tellin'." She tapped her chin staring blindly through the window. She had a sense that he was close to getting there. "He got a good horse," she said to reassure herself. "An' dat boy know a ting or two 'bout finding de road through the woods. He not goin' get lost."

She would never forget the day after Mistress Elizabeth died when she went out to look for Rossie, who, filled with grief, had run away from the manor house and all the people who had come to mourn his mother's passing. No one knew where he was. But Sadie had an idea.

It was evening time and dusky in the heavily wooded far end of the property, as she made her way down to a dried-up creek bed where he and Zacky liked to dig in the sand and catch lizards.

And there they were. Rossie, still dressed up for company, sat on the sandy bank with his head between his knees, scratching in the sand and sobbing. Zacky had his arm around his friend, talking softly to him.

Sadie stood very still, listening, and heard Zacky say, "Don' cry, please don' cry no more—Ah'd do anything if it'd stop you hurtin. Ah'd die for you, Rossie boy, if I had to."

The old woman shook her head. She thought about the days the two little boys spent running the woodland trails, climbing trees, fishing with bent pins for hooks, and pieces of salt ham for bait. And how Moses showed them how to thread the fish they caught on a skinny vine so they could carry them home when she called them for dinner.

She sat there rocking for a minute, remembering the quiet times, too. Her memory might be fuzzy these days, but Sadie clearly remembered those rainy days with both of them sitting on the rag rug in the kitchen house, eating the honey candy that she made for them. And the steamy afternoons when they sat with Moses under the oaks whittling wooden toys and flutes.

The mornings were spent with Miss Ellie, a schoolteacher from Murrells Inlet, who came in to teach Ross the alphabet and how to count from one to a hundred. And when she left the house, he would yell for Zack, and with pencil and paper, Ross would show Zack how to form his letters, and how to make words with them, and how to count.

"Heh, heh!" Sadie chuckled as she thought about it. "Dose chilluns! Rossie boy dint know much 'bout teaching and such, but Zack sho got him a egecayshun! Yes." Between Rossie and Miss Ellie, who sent for him one day and told him to sit himself down next to Rossie and pick up a pencil, "Zack got him a good egecayshun!"

And it wasn't long before Sadie was hurrying to get through the morning chores, and lunch time meal, so she could sit at the long table with them and follow along.

Sometimes, she remembered, Willie boy came in, too, and taught all three of them what he had learned from his schooling at the Waccamaw School House. And when Rossie outgrew Miss Ellie's teachings and went to the School House, then both he and Willie would come home and teach them. By then, Sadie had her own pencil and paper.

After a while, Willie went to the Medical College in Charleston. "Dat's where he got schooled in da ways of helping Marse Doc," Sadie Jones would tell the others in the quarters, with undisguised importance.

When Katie Rose visited with her mama, she would join in their lessons. She liked the words, she said, but not the numbers, so when the boys did their counting and such, Sadie taught the little girl to sew. And sometimes they made saltwater taffy or a sweet grass basket full of pralines.

Sadie also remembered Willie sitting on the floor with Katie Rose long after their lessons were over, helping her to recite her numbers. "See, Katie Rose? You can make them fun sounding. Like a song," and he sang them with her until she learned.

"Yes. Dose were da good times," Sadie's old eyes clouded, as she let her mind wander. She lifted her bowl to her lips. "My, but dose taters taste good."

When she had finished, she put the bowl down on the hearth and leaned back in her rocking chair. She closed her eyes thinking back over her life and how soon Rossie's turn came to leave home.

"Yes," she muttered. "And off he goes ta 'tend da navy school on account he goin' be a sailboat cap'n." She knew nothing about any of that, but it sounded very grand. And before long, Katie Rose got old enough to go to the Girl's School in Charleston, and she was gone, too.

It had started to rain. And as it pelted the wooden shingles of the small house, Sadie dosed off for a moment. When she opened her eyes she was surrounded by a misty light that filled the room.

Scrunching her eyes and squinting into the light, she saw Miss Violet standing in the middle of the rag rug dressed all in white. Her dark curls lay on her shoulders the way they used to. There was a tear under her eye, but her voice was clear when she spoke. "Take care of Katie Rose, Sadie. Remember the dream."

The old woman awoke with a start. "Well," she shook her head and stared at the rug. There was no one there. "She done gone!" Sadie blinked. "But she was dere, sho nuff. Ah seen her." She stared at the floor where the apparition had been. "She a haint," she rubbed her eyes. "An' I heared her say sumpin 'bout a dream."

Slowly the fog cleared from Sadie's mind, and a long-forgotten memory came drifting back in wisps. "Dat da dream I heared her telling Miss Lillibef! About Rossie riding along da sand to see Katie Rose. Lawsy, dat was long ago." That was the dream she was meant to remember. She just couldn't remember why.

Just then, the kitchen house door blew open to reveal Moses

standing on the doorstep with a note in his hand.

"What you got dere, Boy?" she asked, rubbing her eyes.

"Note fom Marse Perry over at Edenton for Marse Doc."

"What's it say?"

"How'd Ah know? Is all sealed up, but you s'posed to get it to da Doc raht now."

Sadie got up slowly, holding out her hand for the folded piece of paper with the sealing wax ring print holding the flap shut. She dismissed the overseer with a small wave and trundled off into the Manor.

William had just pushed his chair back from the table when she shuffled into the dining room.

"Moses done brung us a letter from Marse Pelly." She handed him the note.

"Ah, ha. Let's see what my old friend has to say." He took it from her and broke the seal. Monocle in hand, he unfolded the piece of paper.

"News of Ross?" Will walked around from the other end of the table and stood beside his father. Sadie stood there quietly with her hands clasped in front of her, not moving.

"Thank you, Sadie, you may go now," William looked at her over the top of his eye glass.

"Ah's wonderin' what Marse Pelly saying."

"I'm sure you are. What have I told you about curiosity killing the cat?"

She gave him a wounded look and made her way slowly to the door. "Ah's wondering if Mis'tis Leah Pelly given mah letter to Katie Rose," she muttered.

"I'm sure she did, Sadie Jones. I'm sure she did," he adjusted his monocle and began to read.

"A'raht, den. Ah goes now."

"Good idea," he said as he scanned the spider-like script.

"Ah goes now," she said again standing with her hand on the door looking doleful.

"Good *night,* Sadie Jones."

He heard the door shut behind her, but not before she said, just loudly enough for him to hear, "You sho is squirrely dis night."

William turned his attention back to the message. His neighbor, Winston Perry spent most of his waking hours confined to a wheel chair on the top floor of his mansion. He could be found at any time during the day or night sitting in front of a wide bay window with his Italian binoculars, relaying messages to the Confederate forces on his telegraph machine. He was one of several coastal spotters and messengers who filled in the gaps in the Navy's chain of land and sea communication, and appeared to have a whale of a time conducting his own brand of warfare. Doing his part, he said with undisguised pride.

William chuckled. He was thinking that if, God forbid, in some drunken moment he had found himself joined in holy matrimony with the fair Leah, he might well have found the seclusion of the top floor a most welcome refuge. Both from her incessant demands on his bank account, and from the unrelenting committees she headed up. Committees that spent their time cooking up torturous events for the rest of the population, they rode up in their carriages every week to hold their meetings at Edenton.

Yes, indeed. He could see how the top floor must have become an oasis of calm for Winston.

During daylight hours, Perry could watch for flag signals, and at night he could scan the ocean for flashing lights. And not give a hoot about the never-ending line of battle-axes beating down the front door.

William held his note closer to the lamp and squinted. Bloody nuisance not being able to see. And this monocle was a diabolical invention guaranteed to fall into your soup when you were least expecting it.

"Apparently, Winston's message machine picked up flashes from a ship at sea earlier this evening saying that the abandonment of the forts off Carolina's coast was complete." The message didn't specify which forts, but wasn't Ross stationed at Sumter? Perry wanted to know.

Yes, he was. William hadn't heard that he had left. No matter what Sadie Jones thought. He read the note again and put it down on the table.

In light of what he'd heard from Jake Reynolds this morning, he supposed it was likely that as a last resort they would abandon the forts. So where was Ross? And with the defenses crumbling, was Carolina done for? With no one left to fight, the abandonment of the forts did not bode well for the rest of the state. He thought of his pair of matched pistols lying in his desk drawer. Lot of good they would do.

He would go over and visit his neighbor in the morning to see what else he could find out. Perry was a damn good soldier he'd heard, before he was hit by a bullet in the spine that had paralyzed him for life. A brave chap! A stellar fellow! And it had been too long since the doctor had stopped by to pay his respects.

He turned to leave the dining room, and as he did, so another thought struck him. Maybe this was what Sadie's mutterings were about. It was Will's turn to shrug. "But Sadie Jones can't read Morse code, so how could she know any of this?"

Twenty-Four

Pawley's Island: The Note

"THE NOTE FROM Sadie Jones will wait," Trudy said as Katie Rose ran through the outside door. "Look at your shoes—and your ankles! They're covered with sand. And your hands! She picked up one of the girl's hands and rubbed it. "Why, you're freezing."

"But the note from Sadie—"

"It's probably just another one of her recipes, so hurry upstairs and get changed. Winn says dinner's in half an hour."

"Is my gown pressed?"

"Of course it is. It's on your bed. I'll ask Millie to bring a pail of hot water up for your bath. It'll warm you up."

Katie Rose spun around, blowing a kiss over her shoulder with a grin at her aunt. "Thank you, Tru Pru!" She raced up the stairs,

Trudy shook her head. Always racing. She wished her niece would use the stairs in a more ladylike way. Speaking of ladies, they were all gathered in the parlor, partaking of Winn's homemade cherry brandy before dinner. Which sounded like an excellent idea. She'd better join them.

Leaving a trail of sand behind her on the carpet runner on the stairs, Katie Rose flung her bedroom door open, pulling off her shoes as she went. And stopped dead in her tracks, with one shoe in her hand, staring at the dress her aunt had spread out on the bed.
"Oh, no!" she cried.

How on earth was she supposed to button that thing up? The pale pink silk gown had once belonged to her mother. "Mama was ten times smaller than me," she wailed "Tru Pru'ss gone mad. Or has she? Is this her way of forcing me into a corset? The trickery of it! *"Ohhh!"*

The young woman walked around the bed. And then turned and walked back the other way, assessing the situation. She was nothing if not practical, and if she didn't wear this, because of the limited wardrobe she had with her, she would be left with two miserable choices.

She opened the armoire, pulled the other two dresses off their hangers and threw them onto the bed. One of them was that poisonous yellow taffeta that Aunt Winn had given her, and the other, the navy linen with a sailor's collar which was entirely unsuitable. It made her look ten years old.

Fine! She'd put mama's dress on and with any luck the buttons would pop, pop, pop—one by one until she stood in the living room in a puddle of pink silk and tears! She would not wear that corset.

There was a knock on the door. "Miss Katie Rose? Open dis door. Ah's got da baff water and ah cain't be standin here all night." Millie called.

Katie Rose pulled the door open and Millie walked past her into the bathroom and placed the steaming tub of water on the wooden rack that stretched across one end of the claw-footed tub.

"What chu lookin' mad as a rattlesnake for?" the housekeeper asked.

The girl flung an arm toward the dresses lying on the bed, pursed her lips and said nothing.

"So which one you gonna wear?"

"How can I wear any of them? They're all wrong!"

"I cain't see nuttin' wrong wid none o' dem," Millie said walking over to the bed and fingering the material on the sailor dress. "Dis one's real purty. Dey all purty, but Ah's you, Ah be wearin da pink dat b'longed to Miss Violet. Wass wrong wid dat?"

"Millie! How will I *evah* get into it? It'll take all night to button all those tiny pearl buttons—even if I could get them to meet in the middle!"

"Go git yo baff and den ah'll hep you."

Katie Rose rolled her eyes. "You're as crazy as Aunt Tru. You're coming back, Millie?"

"Soon's you git outta yo' baf," Millie said as she closed the door firmly behind her.

Under Millie's strong hands, with much pushing and shoving and yelping, Katie Rose was finally buttoned into her mother's gown.

"Well! I hope everyone's happy," she said to the girl in the mirror. "I can hardly move. And I can't breathe. I shall probably turn blue and die before the night's over."

Then she smiled. Somehow Millie had squashed her into the thing without the corset. And that was that. Tru Pru's trickery had failed.

Slipping her feet into a pair of scuffed silver slippers she took one more look at herself in the mirror secretly pleased with the way the dress clung to her waist and hung in soft folds around her legs. She cocked her head to one side. Standing there in the pink silk, she had to admit it made her feel beautiful. The dress was ancient. But that couldn't be helped. No one had worn new clothes in years. She tilted her head to one side, admiring the long, smooth lines that hung like gossamer from a time before the crinoline. She liked its high Empire waist and low-cut neckline. Katie Rose smiled and twisted in front of the mirror trying to see her back. So very French, so chique, she thought, pouting her lips and lowering her eyelids at the mirror.

Strange, she had dreamed of her mother last night. A soft dream, but she couldn't remember any of it.

No matter. She rubbed her cheeks to pink up the color and fluffed her hair out, beginning to feel quite good about the evening. Not that it promised to be anything like the fun times this old house had seen in years past. It would be nothing like the weekend parties they used to hold, or the times when they all went down to the Charleston balls in May during Race Week. Of course she had been too young for that, but she had listened to the stories. Sadly, as soon as she was old enough to enjoy the revelry, the blasted war happened and everything fun stopped.

But there was nothing to be done about it. She would have to make do with this gathering of her aunt's quilting bee friends, which promised to be as boring as dust.

Surely, someone would have some worthwhile gossip. Her eyes twinkled. Like the time Leah Perry had caught General Beauregard's eye at one of her Charleston soirees. The General, it was rumored had, for a time, been a frequent visitor to the townhome. She giggled at the thought.

The heart throb soldier with eyes that flashed obsidian. Eyes no Southern woman was immune to. None could resist his charm, they said. What a scandal that would have been if the affair had had time to flourish.

Katie Rose struck a pose, as she practiced the charms and wiles she would use with the gathering downstairs. "Well, my, my, Mistress Leah. I'm so very glad you could come," she would gush. "What, no handsome soldier beau this evening? Hmmm. Well, I'm sure he's sore distressed to be out there in that *horrible* wilderness tonight." She smiled sweetly into the mirror waving a pretend fan. "And Miss Mary Josephine. How nice to see you. Why! That color green's mighty becoming on you. You should wear the blue next time, don't you think? Yes, definitely the blue. It takes years off you."

"Katie Rose!" Millie interrupted, planting her hands on her hips. "You best behave yousef. Y'hear me? Don' you go actin out, upsettin yo aints an da company."

"I'll be good, Millie." Katie Rose smiled and walked out of the room with a swish of her hips in the long, slender pink skirt.

Millie watched the girl descend the stairs and muttered. "If she don' look jus' lak her mama dis night."

The wind whistled through the eaves of the old house and, catching a chilly gust off the ocean, a downstairs door slammed. Inside the parlor it was warm, and a fire crackled in the grate as the women sipped their cherry libations. They chattered like magpies as they picked at small crab canapés and the dried peach slices rolled in sugar that Charles Asquith passed around.

Mr. Asquith was an Englishman of some stature, at least in his own mind. He used to be Winifred's butler but had, out of necessity, and the dearth of house servants, taken on the duties of waiter, carriage driver and at large helper when company came. It was all quite beneath his station, of course, not to mention his dignity, but when you had the sons of plantation owners digging ditches in the rice fields and their women growing their own vegetables in the sandy clay, he supposed he could stand it. At least until things got better.

"Ah, here comes Katie Rose," he muttered. Things were getting better already. A smile cracked his usually saturnine features. He watched as she made her entrance, with a demure smile on her lips that didn't fool Charles Asquith one bit. He stifled a chuckle knowing how quickly the evening could become exceedingly entertaining in Katie Rose's presence. How elegant the child looked this evening. How poised. And how utterly charming in her pale pink folds of silk. A rose at dawn.

She nodded to the assembly of puffed and powdered ladies of Pawley's Island.

"There you are, darling," Winifred Merriman took her niece's hand. "How lovely you look. I think you know everyone here?"

Katie Rose gave a little bob and held out her hand to Mistress Anna Page from the house next door; a war widow with sad eyes and a lisp. "Good evening, Mistress Anna. Are you well?" She was rewarded with a watery smile, as the woman, dressed all in black, turned her eyes away from the deeply scooped neckline in front of her.

"And Miss Ellie! When did you get back from Northern Carolina?" Katie Rose turned to Ross and Will's old tutor. A stern-looking woman, she had gone to live in Wilmington when war broke out to keep her sister company while her naval husband was at sea.

She took the teacher's hand. "I wasn't expecting to see you. Tell me," she asked. "Have you any news of our navy men?" Katie Rose searched the teacher's eyes.

"All sorts of rumors, child, most of them nonsense." She flicked her hand in dismissal. Slowly, her demeanor softened as she looked at the young woman in front of her. "Our navy has suffered most horribly, but thankfully we had word that Richard, my sister's husband, is safe—although he is a prisoner in those terrible barracks by the sea."

Katie Rose touched her hand sympathetically. "Did he ever speak of Ross?"

"The only thing I heard was that Ross escaped imprisonment when his ship was captured in Mobile Bay."

The girl's heart fell as her hopes of hearing something new were dashed.

"A canapé, Miss Merriman?" Charles Asquith stood at her elbow with the plate of snacks.

"Thank you. I'll take two," she said, grateful for the distraction as she picked up one and popped it into her mouth, followed by another—and another in rapid succession.

Too late, she remembered the dress. Here she was stuffing herself with canapés and at any moment the thing was likely to burst wide open. With her cheeks bulging, she turned, ready to make a dash for the kitchen and spit the canape out, when there was a tap on her shoulder.

"My! But you look so grown up this evening, Katherine Rose."

Leah Perry. A rush of violet-perfumed lace, a little stale, a little musty, enveloped Katie Rose as she swung around chewing frantically. A chunk of crab stuck in her throat making her eyes water. She flushed bright pink thinking that this must be what a snake felt like when it stuffed itself. Swallowing hard, she held out her hand.

"Mistress Leah," she managed a slight curtsy, blinking hard and hoping her nose wasn't going to run. "That is a lovely dress you're wearing."

The mistress of Edenton ran her two hands over the flair of her skirt, eyeing the slim lines of the pale pink gown in front of her.

"How sweet!" she cooed placing a hand on Katie's Rose's arm. "I always loved that old French style you're wearing. It must be years since I last saw it."

"It was Mama's." Katie Rose straightened her shoulders, daring Leah Perry to continue.

"Yes, I can see that," she said pointedly. "Those necklines were something of a trademark of hers." Her mouth curved in a one-sided smile. "Before I forget, Sadie Jones gave me a note to give you. Your Aunt Trudy has it."

A small bell tinkled from the dining room, and the aroma of baked ham and hot corn muffins wafted from the kitchen as the cook opened the door.

"I believe that's Millie calling us to dinner," Katie Rose said sweetly. "I can smell the almond cream cakes baking. Can you, Mistress Leah? Oh dear, I forgot! You're watching your waistline, I heard."

Leah Perry straightened her shoulders, tucked in her chin and huffed, "Well! I declare!" as the girl turned away with a swish of silk and headed toward her aunt who was ushering guests into the dining room.

Looking beyond the women, Katie Rose saw a neatly folded note lying on the mantle and holding her skirt up, showing a pale expanse of bare leg, she hurried over to pick it up.

Her name was neatly written on the front of it in Sadie's script. Katie Rose tore it open and began to read.

Her eyes opened wide as they scanned the childish lettering and then her hand flew to her heart. As if from far away, she heard the voices of their guests as they entered the dining room. Her ears started to ring, and a wave of unsteadiness swept over her. She put a hand out to hold on to the mantle.

And that was all she remembered before she crumpled to the oak floor.

She felt her mother's hand on her brow; warm, softly stroking the hair out of her eyes the way she did when she was a child. "Mama," she cried. From far away she heard another voice calling her.

The voice called her name again, "Katie Rose!"

She opened her eyes and realized that she was lying on the couch. Aunt Winn was standing behind the sofa, fluttering a fan in front of her face and saying her name, and Leah Perry was waving salts under her nose while the rest of the company hovered around her clucking like mother hens.

She twisted her head away from the salts coughing feebly as the ammonia fumes threatened to choke her. She tried to raise herself on one elbow.

"Lie back down, Katie Rose." Leah Perry commanded putting a hand on her shoulder to hold her down.

"No! I must get up!"

"Leah's right, darling girl." That was Aunt Trudy.

"You'll only get dizzy if you move too quickly."

"Mama," she whispered.

"It's Aunt Trudy, dear."

"Mama was here. I know she was."

"What is she saying?" Leah asked.

"Hush, darling, it's just us here," Aunt Winn said.

Katie Rose lay back down on the pillow. Her eyes opened wide as recollection returned. "I dreamed of her last night. We were standing on the beach watching Rossie riding toward us." She lifted herself up again and swung her legs over the side of the couch. "He'll be here soon. Sadie said so." She looked wildly around the room her eyes darting from one dumbfounded face to another. "He's coming home. Sadie Jones wrote to me saying he's coming home!"

Her head began to swim, and she lay back down as Leah Perry loomed over her and began waving those wretched salts around again. Katie Rose pushed them away. "I'm alright," she said irritably. "Really I am."

The mistress of Edenton drew herself up to her imposing height and breadth, adjusting her corset as she did so. "*Really!* I must have a word with William. That Sadie Jones is just too much. Filling your head with fantastic untruths. It's quite untenable—I shall see to it that he puts a stop to this at once."

"That's not so. And no you won't!" Katie Rose cried.

Trudy drew in a sharp breath and was about to say something, but the young woman was not finished.

"Sadie knows things that other people don't. She's the most truthful person I know."

A noise somewhere between a snort and a choke blurted out of Charlie Asquith at about the same time as two buttons flew off Katie Rose's bodice. But she appeared not to notice them, or hear the small gasps of breath that issued forth from the female gathering.

"Well! Well, I never!" Leah muttered.

"Well, now you have!" The girl said sharply and turned toward her aunts, "I *must* see Sadie Jones. If not tonight then in the morning. Please, please let me go to Willowgreen." She looked pleadingly at Trudy's and Winifred's unhappy faces. "Charlie will take me."

"We'll talk about it in the morning, dear," Winifred said.

"*Surely,* Winifred, you're not going to allow her to go chasing after some hokus pokus story that old woman has concocted," Leah remarked, and might have evoked a stern reply from her hostess, who was becoming increasingly vexed with her guest's presumptions, but for the fact that the butler stepped in.

"That won't be a problem at all, Ma'am," he announced as he bent his head toward Winifred's in thinly disguised conspiracy. "I can take her in the morning and combine the trip with a stop at the market. With your permission, I would be delighted to take Miss Merriman to Willowgreen."

"Well—" Winifred faltered.

"What absolute nonsense!" Leah chimed in.

"But for now, Miss Merriman," the houseman turned pointedly to his employer, "dinner is served." Charles Asquith stepped back with a barely concealed smirk, one hand behind his back and the other showing the way as he ushered the ladies into Fairhaven's dining room.

A joyful smile spread across Katie Rose's face as she ran lightly toward the bay window that looked out over the marshes. She pulled the deep blue velvet drapes aside. Ross was out there somewhere. She knew it.

PART 2

February 18, 1865

Twenty-Five

Dark Intruder

THE FIRE HAD died sometime during the night. At dawn, not quite awake, Ross felt the chill of the great room as he reached clumsily for the coat that had slipped down to his thighs while he slept. He cracked one eye open, saw that it was still dark outside, so closed it again. He groaned and pulled his legs up trying to get warm. The rain had stopped pounding against the windows, but he could hear the wind rattling the shutters as he tried to go back to sleep.

A charred log shifted in the fireplace and fell with a thump to the brick casing. Ross yawned. The wind moaned, and, just before the light sleep of early morning claimed him, he heard another log fall.

Or did it. Shrugging off the last waves of sleep he listened. It wasn't a log. He held his breath. The logs would have burned to ashes hours ago. Ross sat very still in the chair, fully alert. Looking toward the shutters daylight was starting to show between the cracks. As he watched, a loud snort shattered the silence.

He sat bolt upright in the near dark grabbing for his pistol on the floor beside him and waited. Was it a boar? No, he would smell a boar.

A low whistling sound came from somewhere in the room, and he leapt from his chair. Someone was in the house. He kicked his chair back, and as he did so, something sent the chair opposite him falling to the ground. A shadow lunged out of the dark, and, before he could bring his gun around, it grabbed him around the waist, pinning his arms at his sides. He twisted and turned, trying to free himself, not hearing the voice as it said his name. Not until that voice yelled out a second time did he stop for a second, stunned, and yelled, "Zacky! Dammit! Is that you?"

Zack, who outweighed Ross and stood three inches taller, had a fierce grip on his friend. "Yes, dammit! It's me. Trying to keep my ass from getting blown off." Came the muffled reply, as Ross struggled. "You hear me, Rossie Boy? Don' shoot—you jackass white boy! It's me."

Ross began to laugh. He laughed so hard tears rolled down his cheeks. He couldn't tell whether the reaction came from fear or relief, but he felt Zack's grip loosen. "Let go of me, you crazy fool."

Zack let go of Ross's arms, took a step back as Ross lunged for him, and the two men landed in a bear hug on the floor, laughing and shoving as they rolled on the grass mat. "Dammit. I could have killed you." Ross thumped his friend on the back. "What in the hell are you doing here?"

"Looking for you, man—" Zack panted. "'Bout time you get yourself back home." The two men stood up trying to catch their breath and Ross grabbed Zack in another rough hug.

"Damn! I've never been so pleased to see anyone in my entire life, but what the devil are you doing here?"

"Mama sent me," the Gullah man stood in front of Ross with his hands on his hips, smiling.

"Sadie Jones? How'd she know where I was?

Zack threw back his head and laughed. "You bin gone too long. Sadie Jones knows dese tings," he mimicked her, twirling his forefinger in the air the way she did when she wanted to make a point. "She said to fetch you home."

"But— how'd she know where to look?"

"She didn't. I figured this is where you'd be. Wasn't figuring you'd stay in Charleston. Met a Geechee boy last night, one of the brick makers, running from Boone Plantation, who told me Charleston's full of nothing but ghosts. Said an ammunition depot exploded yesterday killing hundreds of people trying to leave. Women, children—didn't spare anyone."

Zack ran his hand over his face hiding the fear he felt. "I'm wondering if my sister Mollie was one of them," he said.

"Oh, man. I saw that explosion from the boat." They were quiet for a moment. "How'd you get here?"

"Blue Boy and me, we left early yesterday. Got here in rain pouring down thick as buttermilk. I remembered where the stable was so I found him some oats and let him sleep."

Blue Boy, the big white ambler his father had bought at auction when Ross was a boy. He became Ross's favorite. Some called him a medicine horse. All Ross knew was that he was as strong as an ox with twice the endurance.

And that was just the sort of medicine he needed. He clapped Zack on the shoulder. "Good man, Zacky. He'll carry both of us. When did you eat last?"

"I found your leftovers in the kitchen. You didn't learn to cook from Sadie Jones, that's for sure." He grinned as Ross aimed a punch at his arm. "I got some of your dumplins, poured some gravy and greens on top and was so hungry I ate 'em all. Oh, and your honey's gone."

"You ate all the honey, Geechee boy?"

"You know it, white boy. But there's two dumplins left and a sweet potato. And a loaf of cornbread in my saddle from Mama. We're in high cotton, boy."

Ross looked around. "Let's get what we need and get going. There's clothes lying everywhere. Find something dry that fits. I'll look for guns and ammo."

What a day it was turning out to be. The sun wasn't up yet but, as Sadie would say, it was going to be a fine sunshiny day. Come rain or shine.

They needed to leave if they hoped to be close to home by the next morning. It would be slow going. As strong as he was, Blue would be carrying two men until, and if, they found a second horse. They would have to rest him and find food for themselves. Even with fortune and another horse riding with them, it would be more like late afternoon or evening before they reached Willowgreen.

"How was the King's Highway?" Ross called up the stairs to where Zack was rummaging through discarded clothes by the light of an oil lamp

"Didn't see much of it," came the muffled reply. "I stayed in the forest mostly, but the parts I did ride weren't bad." His face appeared "The road is built pretty high in places,"

Ross said. "I'm hoping it's not washed out anywhere."

"We can try it, but they're saying there're Yankees and thieves all over the place." Zack walked down the stairs carrying an armful of clothes. "Thing is, if there's a horse to be found we'll find it somewhere 'round those small towns and farmlands that the road runs through."

"Yankees don't bother me." Ross tapped the pistol on his side. "And if the road gets too bad, we can head through the woods and stay to the high ground. No guns upstairs? "

"Nope." Zack looked pensive. "That swamp water's going to be high. You should'a seen the rain coming down last night. Oh, man." Zack chuckled. "Me an' Blue got wet as rats in a downspout."

Ross handed him a mackintosh. "Wear this. It'll help if it starts up again." They had a long, hard trip ahead on a wet corduroy road, but, with the thought of Katie Rose waiting for him at the end of it, he was in a hurry to get going. Thieves and bandits be damned.

Twenty-Six

"Trouble Gonna Fall"

"LAWSY! DAT STORM made a mess of de yard." Sadie informed ginger cat as she stepped outside the kitchen. It was still dark, so she couldn't see much, but leaves and branches littered the hard-packed clay, and big, black cauldons lay every which way. "Dat was some wind. Mmm, *mmm*! De chilluns swing done wound clear 'round de tree trunk," she sniffed the air. "And de storm ain't over yet."

The rain had stopped for now, but black clouds rode low over the road to town and she could hear thunder rumbling over the ocean. "And de rivah he high." Sadie knew that because she could hear it roaring between its banks, gathering fallen trees and broken boughs as it rolled downstream. "Oooeee! He high!"

She raised her eyes to the sky where the first light of day struggled to seep through the clouds. "Uhn,uhn," she shook her head. "Dat river's fixin' to jump de banks."

"Morning, Sadie." Will stepped out of the main house and watched Daniel come around the corner bringing the horse and buggy he would be driving down to Georgetown and the Waccamaw plantations.

"You leavin'?"

"Might as well, the rain's stopped for now."

"Well, you cain't be goin nowhere 'til you eat," she told him and not waiting for his answer, she picked up her skirt and walked back into the kitchen house.

Will followed her inside. It was no use telling her he wasn't hungry. She'd feed him anyway, and arguing with Sadie was a waste time.

"Here, sit in mah chair. I jest put a log in da stove." She scooped a cup full of hot rice, and molasses into a blue ceramic bowl and handed it to him.

"What for you riding out dis mo'nin, Willie Boy? Dat storm ain't done yet."

"People need medicine," Will said. "Somebody's got to take it to them."

"Mah bones tellin' me dere's a wuss storm coming. Sky's awful black down yonder where you goin'." She flicked a moth off the countertop and changed the subject. "You go see de baby down yonder on de Street?"

"Yes, he's a sick boy. He can't breathe. That's why he's that funny color," he said.

Sadie nodded. "He gonna die?"

Will stood up and put his bowl on the counter. "We're doing everything we can, but he's in God's hands now." He put a hand on her shoulder. "And don't worry about me. If the weather gets too bad, I'll turn around."

"Ain't no tellin what gonna happen in a storm."

With that, he left the kitchen house and climbed aboard his buggy. Picking up the reins, he asked, "Think Rossie's coming home today?" He gave her that little cock-eyed smile of his.

She grunted and chomped down on her gums. "Mebbe dis night, mebbe t'morrow mo'nin," she said.

"I hope you're right, Sadie. I need him, and Pa's not getting any younger." With that, Will left her with a wave of his hand and a cornbread loaf on the seat beside him.

 He missed his brother and had feared for him all the time he was away at sea. It would be the happiest day of their lives to see Ross come riding down the driveway. Especially Katie Rose. She had been waiting far too long, never knowing when, or even if, he was coming home. If only Sadie was right.

Will urged the horse into a trot, trying to escape his feelings. He had loved Katie Rose since he was a boy. He could still remember how the sun trickled through the oak leaves, dappling her shoulders, speckling her hair with gold when they were both too young to wonder about such things.

The truth was that both Will and Ross had loved her since they were children. He had always known that Ross was her favorite, and somehow he knew that when she was old enough, it was Ross she would choose.

And that was that. They both loved Ross and nothing would ever change that, not even the ache in his heart for Katie Rose.

Sadie hadn't slept well. The night had brought dark thoughts that smothered her dreams, making her toss and turn until after midnight. And the wind and the rain beating on the roof had kept her awake watching the lightning flash outside her window.

But she had a full day's work ahead of her, starting with the big black cauldron of soapy water for the household wash, so a nap would have to wait.

"Mebbe Moses he light de fire for de wash tub afore another storm come." She muttered and went back outside. He would be here any minute now for his cup of buttermilk.

She wondered where Zack was. "He musta found Rossie by now." She mused, praying they hadn't been caught out in the open last night. It was a fearful bad night to be out. Sadie's fears came back as she thought about them out there with only one horse between them.

It was starting to get light. A watery dawn, shot with pink rays glimmered in the east and she could hear the turtle doves cooing in the pines that grew along the path to The Street. Straining her eyes, she looked for Moses, and as she looked away from the piney woods, something white flashed past her and through the open kitchen door.

"What dat?" she cried out in alarm. There was a white bird in the house. She knew that from the flapping of wings and the panicked bumping off the inside walls.

"Dis not good." She shook her head, dislodging her head wrap and holding her hands to her mouth. Wide-eyed with horror, she backed away from the house. "Dis not good!" she cried. Her voice cracked as she saw Moses running down the path toward her. "Moses!" her frail voice wailed. "Moses! A bird be in mah house! White bird! Ohhh! What we goin' do."

Moses blasted past her through the open door and into the kitchen house. She could hear him yelling, "Out! git out!" He was opening shutters and she caught a glimpse of him flapping her dish cloth, this way and that, chasing the bird and stomping around.

The hullabaloo was more than the ginger cat could stand. He tore past the overseer and his dish cloth and was out of the door running for the woods before anyone could say anything.

Sadie stood in the courtyard whimpering. "Ketch dat bird, Moses.

Lawsy, dat not good, *mmmmm*! *Mmmm, mmm…* "

"He gone." Moses stood on the doorstep with the dishcloth hanging limply from his hand. "He ain't goin' trouble you no more he. Ah done shooed him. Come, Mama," he said, using the familiar Gullah term for older women. "You don' worry no more." Moses took her by the arm and ushered her back inside the house.

"Moses, Moses, You know what dat means. A white bird in mah house."

"I knows what 'em say, but you knows what Marse Doc say about such tings. He say not true, so you don' worry. We ain't goin' worry none 'bout no white bird. Why dat cat didn't grab him?"

"He scairt. Like me. Where'd he go, Moses?"

He gently sat her down in her chair, retrieved her head wrap, and handed it to her. "Ahm goin find yo' cat, Mama, and you fix mah milk jest like always."

She swayed back and forth in her chair and raised her hand as he left. "Trouble gonna fall," she keened. Sadie's eyes got round and her voice got high. "Ain't goin' fall on de ground! Goin' fall on somebody."

Twenty-Seven

Marooned

BANDS OF STORMS raged all night. They swept in from the Southeast, battering the island and coastal swamps with high tides and tearing winds. They rushed up the coast, shrouded in a malignant mass of dark gray fog and purple cloud. Torrential rain stabbed the ground as their fury built. Thunder boomed and lightning whistled into the marshes, as the gales gathered steam and drove northward, ripping trees from the sandy soil, laying bare their roots. Roof shingles lay scattered on the ground in front of the houses that dotted the shore.

Katie Rose tossed and turned all night. Sleep evaded her; her mind raced, her imagination flew on quicksilver wings from one place to another. Would Ross stop by Riverbend to look for her? Or would he ride to Willowgreen first, and then to Fairhaven? Did he know she was here? She had written him and told him—but did he get her letter? Would he ride a train? Or a horse? And was his heart still as full of love for her as hers overflowed with love for him?

When she finally fell asleep, her dreams were peopled with images of faces melting into blowing sand. Faces she didn't know, faces that swirled and bobbed among the dunes as the pale-yellow dawn broke over the flattened salt grasses of the marsh.

She awoke to the sound of Millie's voice and the sight of her pale brown face poking around the bedroom door.

"You gonna sleep all day, honey girl?" she called softly in the singsong tones of her native people.

"What time is it?" Katie Rose pushed herself up on the pillows rubbing her eyes.

"Why, it's past noon."

"Oh, no."

"An' Miss Winnie say dey goin' have lunch soon."

How could she have slept so long? "Oh, Millie. Ross is coming. I must get up."

"An don' you keep de ladies waiting. Dey already in a fluff. Y'hear?" The housekeeper rolled her eyes and exited, closing the door behind her.

The ladies were still here. Drat! That meant that she would have to wait until they left before Charlie could take her to Willowgreen.

Nobody had any idea when Ross would be here. Why, he could be on his way here this very minute. Sadie would know. Which is why she had to get to Willowgreen as soon as possible.

She glanced out of her bedroom window. It was a dark day. Indigo clouds hung over the island, and rain drove hard against the windowpanes. Every so often the massive hulk of Fairhaven shuddered in a wayward gust.

Katie Rose crossed the floor to the armoire and flung the doors open. Grabbing a deep green and blue plaid skirt with a frilly white blouse and black cotton sash off its peg, she threw it on the bed and ran to the bathroom to wash her face.

"Katie Rose?" Trudy called.

"Coming," she answered. She stepped into the skirt and pulled the blouse over her head. Grabbing a tarnished silver-backed hairbrush she ran the bristles through her hair. Then picking a peppermint leaf from a dish in the bathroom she popped it into her mouth, chewing quickly as she ran down the stairs.

Katie Rose could hear the chatter of ladies' voices as Winn escorted them into the dining room. She stopped briefly at the foot of the stairs, straightened her bodice, fluffing the frills, and swallowed hard, forcing the mint leaf down her throat.

A rose-patterned platter, holding neatly arranged slices of last night's honey ham, stood on the dining room table beside a matching bowl of spiced and pickled peaches. Millie placed a basket of warm, rice cakes and fig preserves beside Winn, and Charles poured East India tea into an unmatched set of bone china cups. They were all that remained of several sets, most of which had broken over the years.

"I trust you all slept well," Leah Perry remarked in a baleful tone calculated to concern her hostess. "I didn't sleep a wink."

"Was it the storm, dear?" Trudy asked. "I'm so sorry."

Katie Rose shot her aunt a look. "The storm wasn't any of your doing, Aunt Trudy. I'm sure Mistress Leah will feel much better after she's had her tea." She smiled at their guest. "I find that a brisk cup of tea does wonders for any sort of malaise or distemper, don't you?"

"Tea, m'lady?" Charles reached for Leah's tea cup and saucer. Holding it aloft, he poured the amber liquid from a height certain to make Winifred shudder and take a deep breath.

"Yes, thank you," Leah Perry's eyes widened as she leaned as far back in her chair as she could. "Watch what you're doing, man!" she snapped.

"Oh, he's very good at pouring tea," Katie Rose piped up. "He once served tea to a Maharaja at Lord Clive's country home in England. Didn't you, Charlie?"

Keeping a straight face, Charles inclined his head in Leah's direction, pulled his shoulders back, put his nose in the air, and made his way back to the kitchen.

"What about you, dear? Did you sleep well?" Anna Page, the war widow, asked Katie Rose. "No ill effects from last night's little spell, I hope?"

"Oh, that." With a dismissive wave of her hand, Katie Rose helped herself to a slice of ham. "Nothing serious, Miss Anna. But I was much too excited to sleep," she smiled, placing the ham on her plate. "Can you imagine! It's been over a year since Ross left."

"All I can say, young lady, is don't get your hopes up." Leah Perry had rallied from her lack of sleep.

"More tea, anyone?" Trudy interjected hurriedly. "Leah, you must tell us how you cure your hams at Edenton," she gushed. "I declare, this is the tastiest we've had all year." The dining room door slammed as a gust of wind whisked through the house. "Pork's getting harder and harder to find these days, isn't it, Winn."

"Indeed. Every spare morsel's going to our troops, I've heard." Her sister picked up the thread. "But we can't complain. Our coast has been blessedly spared the worst effects of the war. We can thank our soldiers and sailors for having the wit to stop the Yankee ships coming up the rivers from Winyah Bay. But this is the last of our East India tea, so I hope you enjoy every drop." She gave a tiny smile. "And don't let's forget the thousands who have so very little."

They were quiet for a moment. Tea was a luxury indeed, brought in by ships running the blockades from the West Indian islands.

"Yes, we are truly blessed," Anna Page replied softly. "I've heard they're practically starving in Mississippi and Georgia—with Atlanta burnt to the ground, and all their crops salted."

"Vicksburg and Natchez, too," Miss Ellie added.

"Even our troops are hungry." Trudy dabbed her eyes. "Damn this war!"

"Trudy!" Leah looked askance

"I agree," Miss Ellie blurted out. "Damn this war! Thousands dead, countless maimed."

Aunt Winifred glanced around. "We all agree," she said, in an effort to gain control of the conversation, Katie Rose suspected. "There are people on the streets begging for food, I hear, while others are dying of starvation."

Everyone shook their heads sadly. The Yankee naval blockade of Southern ports had all but devastated the food supply.

"Well, our plantations are contributing all they can to the cities of Georgetown and Charleston." Miss Leah interjected.

"Indeed they are," the war widow Anna Page said.

"Except for slave runaways, Georgetown and Horry Counties have been spared the worst of it, that's true." Leah said, helping herself to another slice of ham.

"The old way of life is over," Winifred said. "The plantations can't function without the slaves—"

"Don't say that!" Leah cried. "The South will rise! You'll see. The men will come home, and everything will go back to normal!"

"No, it won't," Katie Rose said. "Only the blindest members of our society believe that our way of life in the South will survive this war. In the meantime, we must all do what we can to help." If only they knew.

"Yes, dear, and we're doing what we can," Trudy replied.

"Every one of us!" Charles said as he wielded his tray of muffins over their heads, shooting a sidelong glance at Katie Rose.

"Do be careful with that thing, man!" Leah remarked, visibly put out. "I must say, Winifred, for a young woman, Katie Rose is very outspoken. Something young men of marriageable age don't care for," she sniffed.

Katie Rose caught the look shot at her by Aunt Trudy and decided to ignore Leah's remark. Charlie had that all-knowing look again. She glared at him as he retreated through the kitchen room door. Did he know about her morning's ride? What had that fisherman seen?

The lunchtime chatter resumed along a lighter vein. Just as the conversation was getting interesting, Katie Rose thought. She knew what they were thinking. It was best not to think about the war too much.

After all, the sun would still come up tomorrow no matter what they thought. And in the meantime, the few field hands that were left would grow vegetables and tend the chickens and pigs. They would survive this war.

Katie Rose stared morosely out of her bedroom window on Fairhaven's third floor. From here, on a clear day, she could see the marshes all the way to the south end of the Island. This afternoon, however, she had to strain her eyes to see the boardwalk not a hundred feet from where she stood. The rain had been coming down in torrents for hours, soaking the island's crushed shell roads, making them practically impassable. No one was going to be travelling either in or out of Pawley's Island. The South Causeway, which someone had the wit to build back in 1746 linking the Island to the mainland, must be underwater by now. And that meant that Winn and Trudy's friends, currently involved in a game of whist in the library, were stuck here for another night. More importantly, it meant that she and

Charlie would not be going to Willowgreen until this blasted storm blew itself out.

She could see that the marshes had risen drastically during the day, covering their banks and coming over the road in places. The boardwalk would be swamped at any moment. Already, the walk-up steps were covered in water, and the salt grass tops could hardly be seen above the flood.

"It's no use, we're marooned," she whispered despairingly. When she asked Charlie if he thought someone could take them over in a boat he had thrown his head back and laughed much too loudly for a gentleman.

"Excuse me, Miss," he said, "but it's unlikely a boatman could find anywhere to deposit you even if he got you off the island. The whole place is swamped."

It was hopeless. Katie Rose gazed out of the window wondering if Ross was caught in the storm. Was he out there somewhere trying desperately to reach her?

She looked out at the ocean but all she could see was the gazebo, a ghostly white circle, sitting stoically in the mist among the oaks. Turning away she looked out of the marsh side bedroom window. The chapel bells were ringing out for Evensong.

She leaned her head against the casing and gasped. There it was again. The figure she saw last evening. She backed away from the window and before she could get a good look at him, he turned and disappeared into the mist. Someone was watching the house.

Twenty-Eight

The Corduroy Road

SADDLED UP ON Blue Boy, with Ross taking the reins, the two men left the Ramsey house at day break.

A pall of smoke hung over the harbor and the surrounding land as they rode down the long driveway headed for Mount Pleasant Village. The pungent smell of wet charcoaled wood from the Charleston explosion was strong.

A dead dog lay half in and half out of the gutter and a stray cat miaowed from the doorstep of an abandoned home. They rode on in silence, one behind the other. The rain had stopped but the village streets of the seaside town glistened with moisture, and the gutters ran full. The men made their way through the town to the trader's route or, as it was called, The King's Highway.

An eerie silence hung in the fog that cloaked the houses huddled beside the streets. No lamplight shone from the windows, no smoke rose from the chimneys. The wet sand squelched under the gelding's hooves, and he stumbled once as he stepped into a rut.

"Easy, boy," Ross guided him to the middle of the road. He ruffled the flattened tuft of brown hair between his ears. "Can't have you coming up lame before we're even out of the gate," he said.

"Scary place," Zack said quietly. "There ain't a soul around. Yesterday, there were at least a few folks here and there."

"Better hope there're no Yankees holed up in any of the houses. Look over there Zack, the sky's lightening at the edge of town." Ross picked up the pace, and they trotted past the old Brick Yard and the turn-off to Oakland Plantation.

Soon, dense stands of long leaf pine, and oak hung with dripping moss, closed in around them on either side of the road. Its earthen passage, beaten down in earlier times by SeeWee traders, and further eroded by the ruts of coach wheels, was deep in storm water up over the horse's ankles. The road, which forged its way all the way up the eastern seaboard to Boston, was awash in places.

Once inside the forest, Ross dismounted and handed the reins to Zack. "Here, Gullah man. You know this route better than I do," he conceded as they switched places on the horse's back and continued the trek.

They soon entered the cypress woods, and the road became even more treacherous. The knobby knees of half-buried roots added ankle-twisting hazards to the journey forcing them to scour the ground as they rode.

Above the damp fall of the horse's hooves, they could hear large droplets of last night's rain falling from the trees, pitting the road. The sun, although they couldn't see it through the clouds, was high now and giving off just enough light, in spite of the forest gloom, to guide their way.

By noon they were out of the densest part of the woods, and riding into the clearing of the tiny town of Awendaw. They had encountered no one along the way, and there didn't seem to be anyone here either.

"And that's good." Ross said. "There could be a lot of folks roaming around we don't want to meet."

"Unh,unh," Zack grunted.

A few small dwellings and tiny shops in various stages of disrepair, lined the main street. Roof shingles lay scattered on the road and shutters swung on their hinges, as they passed. The result of little care, and last night's storm.

"Ol' Wappetaw Church's down the road a ways," Zack said. "Let's rest Blue there and take a look around."

Ross gazed down the empty street. The small buildings looked deserted. "If this is the main street, it's as empty as a blue bird house in January," he said. There was no movement anywhere.

Zack guided the horse down the road, looking to left and right.

Something creaked, and a door opened onto the street. A short, stout man stood on the doorstep with his hands on his hips. He wore a dirty striped shirt that hung outside pants held up by suspenders and swayed slightly as he reached out to steady himself against the pillar.

"Howdy!" he said, "where you headed?"

"Murrells Inlet. North Georgetown County," Ross called back. "Everyone left?"

"Gone. Packed up and skedaddled when they heard Sherman's coming." The man scratched his belly. "Rumors flying ever'where. Some say Columbia's on fire. No one knows fer sure what's goin' on. Mass confusion," he chuckled, hiccupped and steadied himself again. "Some say our troops are burning the cotton bales as they leave. Say the prison's bin emptied, and they're murdering and ransacking everywhere." He spat over his shoulder into the dirt. "Gang of thieves came through here yesterday. Tore the place up some."

"Chaos," Ross said.

"Ain't that a navy coat you wearing, son?" The man tucked his thumbs through his suspenders and walked unsteadily out into the street. "Usta be a navy man myself—'till I ran a skiff up on some rocks. Make that three—hic. Navy dint take too kindly to that." He came to a halt a couple of yards in front of them.

Home brew fumes assailed Ross's nostrils. "Ross Stanley. Lieutenant Commander Confederate States Navy." He tipped his cap. "I'm riding to Wilmington to re-join my ship."

"Commander, huh," the man stared at them through bloodshot eyes. "I heard there's not much left of the fleet. What happened? Y'all commanders couldn't hold off a passel of Blue Bellies?" He pointed to Zack. "And the slave? He gonna join the navy too?"

The man doubled over and laughed, nearly losing his balance. "Well, if that ain't a sight. Nigger man gonna join the navy. First time someone fires a shotgun he gonna haul his black ass so fast his feet ain't gonna touch the ground." He threw back his head and laughed again.

Ross felt Zack stiffen in the saddle in front of him and had to steel himself against the revulsion he felt for this man who smelled of sweat, bad liquor and unwashed clothing.

"Nigger's in the Navy. Never saw that kinda shit in my day," the man continued. He removed a flask from his back pocket and took a slug.

"Well, brace yourself." Ross's voice was deceptively soft. "You'll be seeing a lot more of that in days to come. In the meantime, don't worry about my man here, or his ass, *or* the Confederate Navy. And get *your* ass out of my way."

The man blinked and took another swig from his bottle.

"Now!" Ross raised his voice. "Get yourself and your rotgut whiskey out of my way." He pulled his pistol out of its holster and fired once into the air. Blue shifted and tossed his head.

Startled, the man staggered backwards against a hitching post, clutching at air as he fell to the ground.

Ross nodded in his direction, prodded Zack in the back and said, "This place stinks. Let's go, Zack."

"Yassa, Massa Rossie! Ah be gittin' ma black ass back on da road raht now. Sho nuff!" Zack replied loudly, urging the horse into a trot, jolting Ross as he did so. "Right after I get down and throw his ass into the swamp!"

"Not worth it," Ross said. "Where's the church?"

Zack gave the horse his head and galloped down the street, splashing water in his wake, leaving the drunk weaving his way back into his house.

Fifteen minutes later they reached the small white church, and found that it, too, was deserted. "Another ghost town," Ross said.

They lead Blue around the back of the building, out of sight of the road, and tethered him to a black iron post near a watering trough. Sitting down on the steps by the back door, they watched him drink.

Zack opened the bag holding Sadie's cornbread, broke it in two, and handed Ross a piece. "Sometimes I just want to hurl those folk into the swamp on the end of my pitchfork."

"Just a washed-up drunk." Ross put a hand on Zack's shoulder and grinned. "I can see I trained you all wrong. You got too uppity by far. OUCH!" He rubbed his arm where Zack's punch landed. "I'd have helped you—" he said. "But then we'd be late getting home."

They sat there in silence eating and staring out into the fields behind the church.

"Lookie there!" Zack reached down and scooped up a handful of red berries growing around the steps.

"Raspberries." Ross took one.

"Sour raspberries—it's too early for them." Zack screwed his mouth up. "Woah! That's bad." He raised a hand to shield his eyes from the glare of the struggling sun and turned to stare into the woods. "What was that?"

Blue suddenly raised his head from the grass and whinnied. He tossed his mane and snorted.

"What's going on?" Ross reached for his gun.

"Over there, in that clump of willows." Zack stepped away from the steps and pointed toward the trees as an answering whinny rose from the woods. "The boy's found him a friend. You can take your hand off your pistol." He stood grinning with his hands on his hips.

"A horse, by God." Ross was on his feet staring into the trees as the tangled vines and branches parted and a young roan mare pushed her way through to the edge of the tree line. She was dangling a rope, looped haphazardly around her neck, and she was shod. "A runaway. Looks like someone tried to grab her—the rope's frayed where she must have chewed herself free," Ross whispered as he and Zack moved toward her. Speaking softly, cajoling her they walked across the grass.

"She's part Arab," Zack said. The roan turned her head sideways with a high toss, her eyes showing white as the men approached. She whinnied again. "She's scared. We not gonna hurt you, girl," he said softly. "No one's gonna hurt you," he crooned, as Ross moved to her left flank.

"I'll distract her, you grab her." Ross said. The horse reared as she saw Ross's movement change. She tossed her head again, keeping her eyes on him.

"See that head toss? Look at the lines of her neck." Zack said. "Most likely Virginia bred. I heard they used to run them during Race Week in Charleston." He was getting closer to her right flank.

Blue whinnied loudly, pawing the ground and the mare reared

again. "Easy girl, that's just Blue, he won't hurt you," Ross whispered just as Zack reached out with both arms, lunged for her neck and held her fast.

"Got her." He hung on with all his strength, digging his heels into the ground as the mare bucked and reared in fright, trying to break loose. Choosing his moment, he leapt, just as her head came around. He clambered aboard her back, which sent her into a gallop around the clearing, just missing Ross, as she thundered past, hooves kicking up sand and gravel, her tail arched.

"*YeeHAW!*" Ross yelled, racing for his saddle bag. He hauled out the rope, bridle and reins he had taken from the Ramsey stables, and ran to the edge of the clearing. Getting his rope ready to throw, he let her go around once and waited. As he watched the horse, with Zack still aboard, he saw her veer sharply, then slow to a canter as the big man leaned forward, clinging to her mane.

"Hold on," Ross said under his breath, as they got closer.

Zack spoke to her, calming her as they continued to circle the clearing and it wasn't long before the mare slowed to a walk.

"Real scared," Zack called softly. "Hungry too, most likely, but she's not wild. Hand me that bridle next time around."

She reared as Ross approached with the bridle, but they managed to get it over her head and strapped down. She bucked once but Zack hung on.

"I got her," he said. "Gimme the feed bag."

It was several minutes before the mare calmed down, but when she did she took the first handful of oats he offered her. When she'd had a couple more, Zack led her to the trough and let her drink.

The road was slushy, and the horse's flanks were spattered with mud, but the sky had lightened for the moment.

Zack rode astride the young horse on a folded saddle blanket with Ross ahead of them on Blue. "Let's hope the rain holds off," Ross remarked.

"Yeah, but look behind us." Zack pointed to the clouds mounding behind them. The southern horizon was dark, and the occasional growl of thunder rattled the palmettos. "Let's hope we can stay ahead of it."

They came across more dead animals as they travelled north and the stench of bloated carcasses got worse in the warmth of the day. Flies buzzed and the odor of overflowing outhouses was strong. There were more people, too. Some were on foot, and some were on horseback. They passed a carriage in the ditch up to its axels in mud and circumvented a wormy oak that had fallen across the road. Branches lay strewn all over the track, slowing them down, but the old trader's path was still solid and that was something to be thankful for.

Two hours after leaving the church, the road turned southward. There were many more people now; farmers pulling wagons of dry hay, others pulling carts loaded with greens and milk jugs. Many of them, some with young children, hauled personal belongings.

As Ross and Zack drew close to the town of McClellanville, they passed a stand on the side of the road with a few half-full baskets of greens, apples and potatoes. There was a scribbled sign nailed to the post that said, "*CANT CARY THIS — HEP YORSEF.*"

"Family had to leave in a hurry." A horse and rider came up alongside them. "Tom Muncie's wife and son. They went north with a wagon train that left here last night." The newcomer was an old man, and he removed his hat as he approached. "Tom was kilt in Georgia last year," he paused and motioned toward the produce. "Go ahead! Don't leave it for the Yankees. We've bin hearin' about Columbia prisons bein' emptied. Barrels of liquor bin axed open and running through the gutters with folks running to catch it with their mugs. Most of the city's gone up in smoke, they say."

"What's the word on Sherman?" Ross asked, dismounting and going over to the stand.

"Nothing new since he left Columbia in flames. Which way you headed?"

"Murrells Inlet."

The old fellow scratched his chin through a grizzly tangle of beard and put his hat back on. "I's y'all, I'd head t'ards the Santee River. Take the south ferry." He pointed eastward with a bent forefinger. "Someone said this road's washed out higher up, near where the north ferry runs. River done jumped the bank. Y'all might want to stay on it for a while, then turn southeast when you get near the Hampton Plantation, and continue t'ard Georgetown, through the marsh, most likely."

Ross frowned. "Is there any kind of a trail once we leave the road?"

The man chuckled. "Deer trails, is about all—if they're not swamped. I's y'all that's what I'd do. Once you get acrost the Santee, turn north to Winyah bay," he paused. "I wouldna try and get back on the road, I's you. Yankees everywhere— thick as mosquitos. Stick to the woods where y'all can."

Zack dismounted and picked up two apples from a broken wooden basket on the table. He fed one to Blue and one to the mare. Then reached in, got two more and handed one to Ross.

"Well, y'all better get goin' if you wanna make the Bay afore dark. Looks like the weather ain't gonna be kind to y'all neither," he pointed to the sky. "But last I heard the ferry's still running."

"Yes, sir. Thank you." Ross stepped into the stirrup, swung

himself into the saddle and touched his cap.

Zack settled himself on the mare's back and inclined his head in the man's direction.

The old man raised his hand to his forehead in a half salute. "That a Navy coat you wearin' young fella?" he asked.

"Yes, sir."

"I's you, I'd take it off. You run into one or more o' them Yankees, they'll go hard on you. Their ships have been seen not far from Georgetown out on the bay. Whole line of soldiers rode through there yesterday."

Ross grinned. "You may be right, sir. Fact is if I go down, this grey coat goes down with me. Good day."

"Y'all boys take care."

"Thank you kindly, sir," Zack said, and they rode out into the street.

"What d'ya think?" Ross asked.

"I'm thinking he's right. And you're crazy as a loon. That's the most ignorant thing I ever heard you say!"

"What? About my coat?"

"Yeah. 'Bout your coat! The man's right. What're you thinking, sailor boy?"

"I'm thinking that this ship called the Confederacy is going down, my friend, and if it's going down, and I have to go down with her—I'll go down wearing this coat."

"Like I was saying—well, never mind. If you're gonna wear that coat, we'd best find a route where no Blue Belly soldier's gonna find us."

"The swamps." Ross said.

"Yeah. Nothin' but snakes and wild things, but there ain't gonna be no Yankee pickin' his way through all that mud and 'gators."

"Lead on, scout. Let's go." Ross said.

"Yeehaw!" Zack leaned forward and dug his heels into the horse's sides. "Move it, Arab Lady!" he cried, and the men galloped down the street.

A few miles outside of McClellanville the wind picked up. Ross glanced over his shoulder seeing the strong black line of clouds creeping closer now. "Make time while we can, Zack!" He shouted. "The weather's chasing us."

Twenty-Nine

Waccamaw in Flood

THE RAIN HAD stopped about mid-morning, but the Waccamaw continued rise.

Moses came up to the manor to say that the river was out of its banks and lapping at the edge of the road. "Ma 'pinion, by evening de fields be flooded em. Good ting we ain't planted no rice yet," he told William.

"You're right. We would have lost the whole crop if this deluge had come a month from now." The doctor said. "And there's more rain coming." He pointed to the southeast. Both men stared at high clouds scurrying northward and the black line of heavy weather swelling as it rode the dark gray sky.

"Be here raht 'bout dinner time," Moses said. "I best make sure ever'ting's tied down and da horses fed. Dey been squirrely all day. Jest a'pawin an' a hollerin'. One ting dey don' lak is a storm," he shook his big, grizzled head. "Nosir!" He turned to William. "You be needin a fire dis night, Marse Doc?"

"Yes. My old bones don't take as kindly to the damp as they once did. Thank you, Moses."

"Yes. You take care o' dose ol' bones, Sah. I best get started. Dat storm be moving fast." The overseer took his leave and lumbered back the way he had come, holding onto his hat.

Everything that wasn't tied down was starting to blow around, William noticed, as he stood on the back doorstep watching Moses run to the smoke house where they kept the dry wood. He disappeared inside, and the big cross-barred wooden door slammed behind him.

The smell of the approaching storm was much stronger than it had been yesterday. William drew in his breath. He could smell the steam that rose from the dark wet earth somewhere south of here, as he imagined the rain pelting down, leaving deep pits in the soil. This new onslaught must be the main thrust of the storm. Last night's was just a warning shot from the first bands that came ashore.

He was fairly sure Will would have made it down to Georgetown by late morning without running into any weather, but this new lot coming in would soon be right on top of the port town. And Pawley's Island was right in the path of the leading edge of the storm.

William hoped the young man wouldn't try to make it home tonight. He felt like asking Winston Perry to tap into one or more of the plantations that Will was visiting, places that also had telegraph machines, and see if he could get a bead on where he might be.

Then he chided himself for being an old fool. *Ahhhhgh!* Will was no dunderhead. He'd take shelter where and if he needed to. He must be getting soft in the head. Dratted old age creeping up on him like some malevolent fog!

Thirty

In the Path of the Storm.

WINIFRED AND TRUDY's friends left for the mainland late in the afternoon, as soon as Charles deemed the ground to be dry enough to hold their carriages. Mercifully, the rain had held off for a few hours, and the bridge had not disappeared under water as they feared it might.

Earlier, the boat builder's son had brought word from the mainland that the main street was passable. Speed, however, was of the utmost importance, as the brunt of the storm was on its way and expected to hit the island by nightfall. "Pa sent me out to let the island folk know about the roads," he told Charles. "This is my last stop, afore I head back to Murrells. Say, did you folks hear that the explosion at Fannies was set by someone from 'round here?"

"From where exactly?" The butler raised his eyebrows.

"Pawley's Island. One of them patrolmen saw someone ridin' away."

A flurry of packing ensued, reminding Katie Rose of a flock of hens running around in circles without a clue of what to do first. But at last, the quilts were folded, sewing baskets were stashed in the carriages and a second round of hugging and kissing bestowed. Soon, clutching jars of island honey, the ladies climbed aboard their various transports and left Fairhaven, waving from the fringed windows as they were borne out of sight.

"Wheeew." Charles muttered under his breath. "What a to-do."

Katie Rose giggled. "Talk about a tempest in a teacup."

"Quite so, Miss. Quite so. Eh, By any chance, did you happen to hear that the explosion at Fannie's was caused by a resident of the island?"

Katie Rose stopped cold in her tracks. "Of course not! How could I have heard such a thing? And you should not repeat gossip, Charlie."

"Quite so, Miss. Quite so." The butler said.

They went into the house together, with Charles holding the door open for her. She turned to look over her shoulder suddenly, dazzling him with her smile. "And now, Charlie, you must take me to Willowgreen."

He closed the door purposefully behind them, gave it a slight push and waited for the lock to click.

Katie Rose waited impatiently.

That was the trouble with living by the sea, every piece of wood warped sooner or later and things that didn't warp, rusted.

Charles gave it one more push and turned to look at her from under hooded eyes, with his hands clutched behind his back. "Absolutely not. Begging your pardon Miss, but no. I categorically will not take you to Willowgreen." He drew himself up and tucked his thumbs under the lapels of his coat. "I refuse to endanger life and limb by venturing out with a storm bearing down upon us." He turned on his heel and then stopped. "And don't get any ideas about taking yourself over there. The Waccamaw's cresting, and Mistress Leah will be lucky not to find herself knee deep in water before she reaches Edenton. So, no tomfool ideas, please."

"Oh, Charlie," she pleaded. "All you have to do is drop me off and go straight home. I'll stay there. You won't be endangering anyone's life or limbs!"

He was saved a reply as Winifred walked out to where they stood in the hall. "Stay where, may I ask?"

Katie Rose swung around to face her aunt. "I was just saying that if Charlie would drive me to Willowgreen, he could leave me there to wait for Ross, and go straight home."

"I've never heard such nonsense," Winifred raised an eyebrow and looked down her nose at the girl. "The impropriety of it! A young unmarried woman staying alone in a houseful of men. The very idea." She turned to leave. "Charles will not take you to Willowgreen."

The butler gave a tight little grin and beat a hasty retreat to the kitchen.

"But I'm practically related to Dr. Stanley! He'll be my father-in-law soon!"

"I know, dear. But we are bound to pay heed to the basics of social etiquette." Giving her niece a small smile, Winifred changed her tone. "I was just thinking, what a pity we didn't think about this when Leah was here. I'm sure she would have been delighted to invite you to stay at Edenton if she had known how much you wanted to be close to Willowgreen. She's such a good friend and a lovely hostess. I'm sure you agree."

Katie Rose blanched.

Watching the girl out of the corner of her eye, Winifred pressed the advantage. "What a shame we didn't think of it."

"But—"

"The answer's no, dear girl," Winifred said cheerily. "But compose yourself. I am quite sure, that if Ross Stanley is, in fact, coming home, Fairhaven will be one of his first stops. And I fully expect that he will call on us as soon as propriety allows. As a gentleman, and indeed, a naval officer, should." With that, Winifred picked up her hem and walked back into the parlor.

Katie Rose watched her go. The very idea. Staying at Leah Perry's!

The quiet chuckle coming from the butler's room did not escape her.

"Impropriety! *Ohh!*" She wrung her hands in frustration and turned sad eyes out across the marshes. She'd been outsmarted, but she hoped that her aunt was right about Ross making Fairhaven one of his first stops.

All she wanted at this moment was to speak to Sadie Jones. But it wasn't to be. Mist blew over the marsh. No birds sang and the salt grass waved back and forth. She could hear the pines creaking and soughing as the storm got closer. The sky was leaden; ominously heavy, threatening as the front swept northwards to pummel the coast.

A shiver ran down her spine as she remembered what Charlie said about the explosion. They knew that the one responsible was from the island. But, surely they would think it was a man. Wouldn't they?

Where was Ross? Was he out in the open, riding as hard as he could, trying to get home to her?

What if Sadie Jones was wrong?

Thirty-One

The Swamplands

ROSS SAT HIGH in the saddle scanning the watery landscape for high ground. A ridge, a mound, anything to get them out of this swamp.

They must have left the road two hours ago, by his reckoning, and the deer track they'd been following had disappeared under the deluge. Bands of rain, one after another, swept in, filling the marshes, erasing the landmarks as they rode. The rain poured down for an hour or more leaving the horses wading through muddy water up to their knees.

About thirty minutes earlier they had reached the south ferry crossing. Looking down from the high ridge, they could see the Santee in flood. Its waters frothed and swirled around uprooted shrubs and logs as they watched the ferryman maneuvering his craft across the waterway.

"Last crossing!" he called as he brought the barge alongside the dock. "Load 'em on."

Once aboard with the horses, Ross paid the captain and put what little was left of his money back in his pocket. He hoped it was enough to get them across Winyah Bay. If they ever got there, he thought wryly.

The weather was worsening as the heavy wooden craft ploughed toward the opposite bank, the currents pulling her this way and that. Steam belched from her stack, rising toward the blackening sky and her sturdy hull rolled like a barrel.

When they landed they found the ground waterlogged with no sign of the trail.

"We've landed too far downstream. Dang current pulled us south of the dock," the ferryman shouted from the wheelhouse. "Ride up a ways. The trail will be visible near the higher landing dock." And it was. An ear-popping clap of thunder shook the ground, rattling the palmettos on either side of the track. The young Arabian shied, almost throwing Zack, as her hind legs sank into the mud. "Woah!" He held tightly around the neck. "Easy, girl. Easy.' The mare tossed her mane and began to whinny, struggling to free her legs.

Zack leapt off her back and coaxed her forward until slowly she began to move, inches at a time, eyes rolling. "There you go. Easy now! You got it. You got it." One last tug, and she was free. Rain rolled off his hat almost blinding him. He kept his hand on the horse's back and, still talking, climbed back up and onto the makeshift saddle. "Okay, let's go 'fore the next bolt hits."

The frightened horse responded to Zack's voice and listened as he began to sing an old lullabye. Soon, she settled into an uneasy gait, keeping her eyes on the water as dead branches swirled around her legs.

"I know that song," Ross said.

"Your mama used to sing it to us."

It was getting dark on the trail. A gust of wind swept across the reeds, carrying the muddy scent of the marshes mixed with the fishy smell of the sea.

There was no telling what time it was. The sun was gone, swallowed by the clouds that blanketed the land as far as he could see. Ross doubted he could read his timepiece even if he could have found it under the layers of raincoat and jacket.

"Look! There's a ridge up ahead," he called out.

"Sure is. Looks like it runs for a pretty good ways over the marsh. Let's go."

The wind blew fiercely, flattening the palmetto fronds and shaking the cypress tops. Ross guided Blue toward the high ground, with Zack close behind. Sensing the change in terrain, both horses picked up their pace. It didn't take long to reach the ridge, and spurred on by a dagger of lightning, Blue's big hooves cleared the water fast, as he heaved his bulk and his rider onto the mound.

The mare shrieked as Zack, afraid she might balk, clapped his heels into her sides and propelled her out of the swamp.

"Solid ground!" he shouted. "Good horse. Good girl, settle down now." And just in time, as another roar of thunder ripped through the wetlands, sending the young horse racing along the stony ridge for all she was worth with Zack hanging on like a burr, clinging to her mane.

Ross grinned. "Sing, Zackie. Sing," he yelled, as he watched Zack, sliding on the blanket saddle, hanging onto the reins for his life. Finally, dodging the mare's head as she flung it from side to side, he righted himself.

Ross threw back his head and laughed until his sides hurt. "You need to calm that lady down, Boy!" he cantered toward them still laughing as Zack brought the horse under control. "That was good!"

"What's wrong with you, White Boy? You ain't never seen me jockey like that before?"

He sat there straight-faced and breathing hard, as Ross pulled himself together, trying to contain his laughter, as he looked at Zack's face. "You rode like a swarm of horse flies was after you." he roared with laughter again.

Zack began to laugh. bent double over the horse's neck he spluttered, "Been you, Rossie boy, you'd be in the swamp with 'gators snapping your ass."

Their laughter trailed away, and Ross wiped his eyes on the back of his dripping hand. "I've missed you, Zacky." He said somberly. "I haven't laughed like that for years."

"Me neither."

Another blast of thunder brought them back to their senses. The storm was almost overhead. The next lightning bolt followed within seconds, lighting up the marshes, cracking like a whip, as it hit the water.

"Jes' like Mardi Gras!" Zack yelled. "C'mon. It's right on top of us. We gotta find some shelter before we get killed out here."

The ridge held firm as they rode as fast as they dared through the gathering dark, knowing that soon they wouldn't be able to see where they were going. "Keep your eyes skinned for lights." Ross yelled over his shoulder.

How long they rode through the storm, neither of them knew. The minutes melted into the enveloping darkness and pouring rain as the track disappeared under the horse's hooves. Both men rode blindly, keeping their heads down, their eyes on the watery path praying that the ridge wouldn't suddenly disappear into the swamp.

An hour later, exhausted, they knew that very soon, shelter or no shelter, the horses would have to be rested. He leaned down and spoke into the white gelding's ear. "Good boy, Blue."

He slowed the pace realizing the terrain had changed again. The ridge had flattened out, and the vegetation had grown sparse. Only a few dead and twisted oaks spiked the darkness as they passed. All around them, the ground was covered in flattened grass. It looked as though a giant steam roller had passed by.

Zack rode up alongside Ross. "You know what this is?" he asked.

"Nope."

"That's where the bay came up last night—and then receded."

"Winyah Bay?"

"Think so, the timing's 'bout right and, this here's flood-flattened grass."

Of course. This was how the land around the rice fields looked when the Waccamaw flooded. Georgetown was up ahead. "Let's go."

"There's a light!" Zack yelled. And before Ross could answer, a loud male voice boomed out across the grassland

"Who goes there? Say your name!"

"Yankee boy wouldn't be out here," Zack hissed.

"Lieutenant Commander Ross Stanley, United States Confederate Navy! And my man Isaac Jones." Ross shouted back.

A tall, bearded man on horseback rode out of the gloom, holding a lantern up to his face in one hand, and a loaded shot gun in the other. "What in God's name you doing out in this storm?" he shouted.

"Riding to Murrells Inlet, sir. Do you know of any shelter around here? We have to rest the horses and get out of the weather."

"Follow me. Confederate Navy, you said?"

"Yes, sir."

"Straight up ahead, let's go. Ayah! The weather's worsening as we stand here jawin'. Let's get outta heah!"

The hairs rose on the back of Ross's neck. Something wasn't right.

Thirty-Two

An Ill Wind Blowing

BURIED BEHIND DARK clouds since yesterday, the sun slipped below the world, taking with it the turbulent day. And in the darkness left behind, the ancestral ghouls of Sadie's youth could roam. The unquiet dead, the evil ones came back, owning the darkness, they trolled for souls.

Sadie was afraid. She had been on edge all day following the white bird incident. Moses sent some of the women from the quarters to calm her down, and they sang with her, and rubbed her hands, but the cold dread in the pit of her stomach sat there like a rock.

She knew what she knew. "Ain't no good em tellin' me don' worry. Everyone knows dat white bird he a evil sign," she told the cat. "He a haint bird."

Sadie shivered and dragged her eyes away from the blackness behind the shutters. The images in her mind writhed like demons, as she sat in her chair beside the fire, listening to the rain on the roof and the creaking of the oaks.

"Dat wind be howlin like a evil haint," she muttered. "And wid all dis rain comin' down, for sho de riber goin' jump he banks," she told the ginger cat sitting on the stool beside her. He lay down, wrapped his tail around his head and went back to sleep.

"Yes," she told him. "And all my chilluns is out in da storm; Marse Willie, Zacky an' Rossie." The ginger cat grunted.

Someone was knocking on the door. Sadie froze.

The knock sounded again. "Who dat?" her voice sounded like a croak as she tried to raise herself on one arm.

"May I come in, Sadie Jones?"

She held her hand to her cheek. "You kin come," she called weakly.

Ducking to avoid hitting his head on the low door frame, William opened the door to the kitchen house and walked in. He placed his bottle of single malt Scotch on the table.

"I heard you might need a strengthening libation," he said. "So, you won't mind if I pour you a drink, will you." It was a statement, not an invitation, and he proceeded to rustle around in the overhead shelves looking for something to pour the stuff in. He settled for two pewter goblets.

Handing one to Sadie, he pulled up a stool, and said, "Tell me about this bird Moses says has got you in a tizzy."

She took the goblet from his hand, and her eyes got wide. "White bird done flew in mah house dis mo'nin'," she said flatly. "Dat no good. White bird fly in a body's house, den somebody gonna die." She took a long sip of the smoky liquid. And then another.

"Perish that thought, Sadie Jones. No one's going to die, but if someone dies, it will be because they're ill or have suffered an accident. You can be sure the bird didn't make it happen."

"You knows plenty, Marse Doc, Ah knows dat." She pushed herself forward and looked him squarely in the eye. "But Ah knows dat white bird him bring bad hoodoo and somebody gonna die." She held out her goblet for seconds. "I hope you got lottsa dis." She tapped the bottle. "We goin' need plenty good hoodoo dis night." Her voice had taken on the sing-song quality of the island creole.

William couldn't tell whether it was the whiskey or her superstitions that carted her off into some other dimension, but it didn't matter. He knew he couldn't dissuade her, so he poured her another drink instead. And one for himself.

When he left, she was nodding off in her chair. The room was warm from the earlier fire, but he picked up her shawl and draped it over her lap anyway, then made his way to the door.

He opened it quietly and was about to duck through it into the night when he heard her mutter from her rocking chair, "Dis a bad night."

In spite of himself, and his disdain for superstition, William thought of the baby on The Street whose heart was failing. He was close to death, and he might very well die.

He stopped and turned around with his hand on the doorknob, started to say something then realized she wasn't really speaking to him.

The rain had stopped and from somewhere deep in the cypress woods William heard an owl hooting. It was one of those big horned owls, the ones Sadie and the boys called 'Hootie owls.' He wondered if she had heard it.

As he stood there with his hand on the doorknob, the cat jumped up on her lap and began to purr. "Dere's a bad wind blowing, ginger cat." Sadie Jones whispered.

He stepped onto the breezeway, just as the owl hooted again.

She was asleep before the door closed behind the doctor and his half-empty bottle of whisky. It wasn't lost on him as he walked to the main house that two strong drinks of whiskey had gone a long way toward calming his own anxiety about Will, out there somewhere around Georgetown. And if Sadie was right, Ross and Zacky were out there, too.

"God only knows where any of them are," he muttered. The back door slammed shut behind him, as he entered the house. It was a bad night out there.

The owl hooted from far away. And another answered.

Thirty-Three

Winyah Bay-Georgetown County

A SINGLE LANTERN swung on a chain suspended from the rafters, casting jittery shadows on the walls of the log cabin on Winyah Bay. The wind, whistling through the gaps in the log walls, made the lantern's wick shiver, as Ross and Zack sat down at a heavy oak table in the center of the room.

"Where'd you fellas come from? Charleston?"

"Mount Pleasant," Ross replied.

"I heard in Georgetown late this afternoon that the arms depot by the wharf exploded."

"I heard it," Ross said.

"Heard tell the explosion could be heard for miles around," he said not appearing to hear Ross's reply. "One of those telegraph fiddlers picked it up on his machine. Also heard a band of Union soldiers was headed down yonder."

Ross and Zack exchanged a look. "We could smell the smoke when we left Mount Pleasant," Zack said.

"Cotton bales, fields, and the plantation homes will be next." The man said dourly. "It's a bad business."

He walked over to his stove and pulled three bowls down from a shelf above his head. "You fellas hungry? Cain't offer you much in the way of dinner, but you're welcome to share what I got.

Ross hesitated, then said, "You're very kind, sir. If it hadn't been for you we'd still be tramping around in the marsh." He removed his cap and put it on the table.

"Yes," Zack said. "And the horses thank you for the shelter and the food. We're all indebted to you."

"T'ain't much of a shelter—few planks nailed together and a roof, is all."

"More than they had, sir," Ross said, as he accepted a cypress root bowl full of soup. "Thank you."

Their host, a big burly man with red hair curling around his neck and ears, wearing a pair of patched brown pants and a yellow wool sweater, handed Zack a bowl and filled his own before sitting down to join them.

"This is the best tasting soup I've ever had," Zack raised the bowl to his lips and slurped a mouthful of the rich, meaty soup. "I bet this turtle came slap outta the Waccamaw."

The man chuckled. "That it did. Found him flappin' on the bank when I arrived to check the ferry. Don't get much fresher than that. Makes a wicked good soup."

"The ferry?" Ross shot a quick glance at Zack.

That's right. I bin runnin' that ol' tub since back in the '40s sometime." He chuckled again. "Won it off a fella when I bet my mule could beat his'n in a half-mile race down the strand."

"He bet his ferry?" A flash of lightning hit the ground nearby and thunder rattled the wooden door.

"Sure did. T'weren't much of a ferry," he said wiping his mouth on his sleeve. "And glad to be rid of it, he was. Rotten decking, broken rails and taking on water. Took my life savings to get her where she could run again. Bin runnin' ever since."

The lantern swung fiercely overhead, as the wind gusted under the door.

"We were headed for the ferry," Ross looked at Zack who was sitting across from him with his bowl halfway between the table and his mouth. "Can you take us across?"

The ferryman let out a guffaw and slapped the table. "Not tonight, no! Maybe sometime tomorrow, or whenever this So'easter blows itself out. Just afore dark I walked to the boat to check her lines and they was holdin' but the seas musta bin four feet high."

Ross felt his spirits drop. It could be days.

"We can wait," Zack said reading his friend's mind.

"Sunrise we'll walk out there and see what's going on," the man said. "Course, t'other thing is if I kin git you across Winyah, we hafta find a piece of dry land to drop you off on the peninsula. Only thing I know for sure is we gotta stay south of Georgetown. Night afore last, one of them Union ships carrying a bunch of marines was seen headin' for Georgetown. Place could be crawling with them by morning."

He picked up the bowls and stacked them on the counter next to a bucket of water. "We'll have to head for one of the inlets on the other side." He paused. "Won't know which one till we git there. And even if I can land you, you'll need to make your way up the peninsula a mile or two afore you start looking for the main road. I figure the Waccamaw's swallowed it up around heah."

They could hear water sloshing around as he rinsed the bowls out.

"Once you get to the other side, head north and you'll see where someone's bin clearin' part of the barony land for new housing. You might find shelter in one of the work huts they bin using."

"We'll be fine," Zack stood up and patted his stomach. "I sure do like your soup, Mistah!"

"Name's Nathaniel. And you're welcome. If I cain't help a fightin' man, what good am I?

"I have little money, sir. What will I owe you for the ride?"

Nathaniel looked at his palms. "I'll be needin' two fares and if you want to carry the horses aboard that'll be extra. No charge if they want to swim behind the boat."

Zack shot Ross a look. "I got some money."

"Tomorrow then," Ross said.

"You boys kin bed down in the loft. Plenty o' straw and it's dry up there."

Ross stood up and gave him a small bow. "Thank you. I expect we'll sleep well."

Climbing the ladder to the loft Zack hissed "Think he's one of the thieves they talked about? "What if the horses are gone when we wake up?"

"Nah, he just wants our money." Ross replied and flopped onto a pile of straw. "Might cut our throats, though, and get both." He yawned. "I gotta get some sleep."

Lying in the hayloft, with Zack already sound asleep beside him, Ross breathed deeply and thought about the next day. Katie Rose had written how she liked to sit in the gazebo and watch the ships. *"I stare down the beach, pretending I can see you walking toward me. And I cry when I realize it's just a day-dream."*

His thoughts went to Katie Rose. "Weep no more, my love," he whispered into the darkness. "If my throat's intact, and I have to pilot the ferry myself, I'll get us home!" The straw rustled as Zack turned over in his sleep.

Would he ride down the beach? Or up to Fairhaven's front door? Would she run down the stairs to meet him? He grinned into the darkness picturing her taking the sweeping steps two at a time, flying into his arms. There would be at least one of the aunts at the top of the steps holding a hand to her forehead, beseeching his Katie Rose to show more decorum. His grin grew wider.

Perhaps he would gallop along the beach and find her staring out to sea, waiting for him to come home. Would he gallop toward her as she raced down the sand to meet him? Would they fall to the beach in a lovers embrace on the deserted shore with no one to witness their love? No one but the sea, and the birds. Or a wave of seagulls, shielding them from intrusion as he held her in the deepest recesses of their love for each other.

Lying there in the loft, Ross could feel her flesh under his weathered hands, feel the soft curve of her breast against his chest, as her lips sought his as her fingers traced the lines of his face. An older face than the one she had last seen all those months ago, a more serious and sadder face than the one she remembered. He would take her wrist, as her fingertips softly touched his eyelids, and kiss the palm of her hand. Her body would arch to meet his, yielding to the thrust of his longing for her. It had been too many years without her.

He exhaled and relaxed his body into the musty smelling hay.

"I'm coming home, lovely lady." He thought about her hair like silver strands of silk, her eyes, deep pools of blue. Honey-colored skin, and her smile that said, "I love you, Ross." Was this a dream? Why were his eyes filled with tears?

His thoughts were jumbled as the long day gathered them into its shadow. The small white church in Awendaw crept into one corner of his mind, and the nerve-racking race along the ridge began to take its toll. "Katie Rose . . ." His thoughts spun out into wind, and the sound of his whisper kept getting further and further away.

An owl left its perch outside the shack and flew silently across the bay.

PART 3

February 19, 1865

Thirty-Four

The Shore at Daybreak

THIN RIBBONS OF the palest yellow and blue lay across the horizon trimming the purple night with the first tinges of dawn. Waves along the narrow shore lapped the edges of the beach, churning through the broken shells at the water's edge, before quietly retreating into the body of the ocean,

With all of their fury spent, the storms that blew so savagely out of the south, whipping the wet lands, flattening the marshes as they raged, had moved out during the darkest part of the night. High tides that had caused the ocean to swell and crash in never-ending crescendo were calm this early morning.

Seagulls speckled the beaches of Pawley's island, hunting for treasures of the night amid foam-flecked seaweed and broken wood. A battered crab, broken mussels, and tiny fish became tidbits, cast on the sand by the angry sea.

The tide had turned, and the waves, broke crystal white, like fat curls of bright metal shavings on a silversmith's floor.

As the new day crowned, and mother-of-pearl winked pale pink and silver in its light, Fairhaven slumbered in deep shadows. A single candle burned in an upstairs window, its wick flickering orange and green as it melted into a pool of wax that spilled over its saucer onto the sill.

A dream had awakened Katie Rose sometime after midnight. It was a happy dream played out, in sepia tones, among the clumps of salt grass in the marsh.

Lying on her pillows, listening to the rain, she tried to bring it back into the tangible fullness that had permeated her sleep.

Ross was in the dream, his arms reaching for her, as the bobolinks played among the reeds. An invisible wind blew his black, curly hair around his face, and flecks of sand peppered the stubble of his beard. He was trying to tell her something, but she couldn't hear the words. The marsh was strangely silent as she walked toward him. And then he smiled, and she heard, "I'm coming home."

Katie Rose climbed out of bed almost afraid to hope. She had prayed for his homecoming for so long. Was it finally happening? Walking to the window, she lit another candle, one of a stash she had hoarded since the day he left.

Katie Rose gazed into the darkness. Her body was filled with longing for the man she had promised to marry. Sadie Jones said he's on his way. And now this dream. The tall steeple of All Saints church rose stark and white against the purple sky. It was where she would marry Ross one day.

On that day of days she would wear her mother's wedding dress that was packed away in the cedar chest in Aunt Winn's attic. Millie would make it fit properly and stitch the tiny seed pearls from a broken necklace of Violet's to the bodice.

Katie Rose hugged her knees to her chest. The sun would be shining on her wedding day, as brightly as their love for each other. She just knew it. Wrens on the fences would sing, and the marsh birds would trill. The watered silk of Mama's gown would glow in the candlelight of the chapel, and there would be flowers on the altar and white ribbons on the pews. She would wear gardenias in her hair and carry the palest pink and white wild roses. Her veil, a cloud of pearl-studded tulle would be of the palest lavender to match the sash around her waist.

Happiness flooded her. The deep indigo of the night was receding, leaving the sky vibrant with translucent lavender and rose as the sun's halo tipped the horizon. A soft smile tilted the corners of her mouth as she watched the dawn turn into day.

Closing her eye she pictured Ross waiting for her beside the altar, his eyes filled with love for her, and a sob escaped her lips. What a wonderful day it would be.

Katie Rose went back to bed and fell asleep, listening to the waves breaking on the shore, the sound of them mingling with ripples of pearl-studded tulle and lace.

Thirty-Five

The White Bird's Prophecy

A ROOSTER CROWED from the barnyard and another answered as daylight filtered through the trees, uncovering the ravages of the storm.

Dark green and cold from the rains, the Waccamaw tumbled beside River Road winding through the willow woods, cutting its path to Winyah Bay. Sometime during the night, it had crested, overflowing its banks, covering the rice fields and the road with muddy water.

Sadie Jones lay on her back, her hands crossed on her chest, snoring. This was unusual for her.

A heavy thump on the foot of her bed made her start in her sleep. Small footsteps moved carefully up to the pillow and stopped at her head. A 'brrup', from ginger cat, broke the quiet of her room, and a small ginger paw tapped her on the cheek.

Sadie opened one eye and tried to raise herself on her arm. But the effort was too much, and she fell back on the pillow. She lifted one hand to her aching head. "Lawsy. It's daylight out there!" She remarked slowly turning her head to the shutters. "Be still an ah'll feed you," she said and tried again to raise herself. This time it worked and, very carefully, holding her hand over her eyes, the old woman brought herself to a sitting position on the side of her bed.

She had no idea what time it was when she struggled out of her rocking chair and went to bed. "Dat hoodoo Marse Doc brung is like to kill me, pussy cat. Oueee!"

It was a good thing Marse Doc had built her a new bedroom leading off the kitchen. "Wid ma haid beatin like a hammer ain't no way dis ol' woman be able to get down dose stairs dis mo'nin." She put her hand up to her bare head. "Where mah night cap?" She wandered into the kitchen and took the cat bowl down from the shelf. "Fact is, it prob'ly don' matter none. Ah might be daid by evenin' ifn dis haid don' quit hurtin'."

There was no sign of Moses yet, and she figured he must be tending the flooded fields. But as she was thinking about that, someone knocked on the kitchen door. ding down gingerly, she placed the cat food on the floor under the table. "Who dere," she called weakly.

The door swung open, and a small boy stood outside chewing on the end of his shirt.

"Mama said tell yo de baby done died in de night," he said.

"Take dat shirt outta yo mouf, boy. What baby?" Sadie asked, squinching up her face.

"Jenny's. She be mah mama."

Sadie frowned and brushed her hands on her apron. "Oh." She crinkled her eyes trying to see the child more clearly. "You Jenny's boy?"

"Yas'm, Gogo. Mah name be Toto."

She remembered now. "Dat be da one Marse Doc call de Blue Baby," she muttered. "You go tell your mama Miss Sadie Jones gonna tell Marse Doc and Marse Willie."

"Yas'm, I tells her." And with that, the child scampered off down the path.

"Hmmph! Ah clean forgot Willie's gone." As she made her way to the bedroom to get dressed the realization hit her that her headache had mysteriously vanished.

The white bird's prophecy had been right. The sick baby died. "De po' baby Marse Doc say is gonna die." And that meant Zacky, Rossie, and Marse Willie were safe. She felt lighter than she had felt since yesterday before that bird had come flapping through the house.

And if she heard the owls in the woods last night, she had forgotten all about it.

Thirty-Six

Troubled Waters

THE HORSES WERE saddled and waiting patiently under a full moon, pale and round as a biscuit, as the men loaded up their scant belongings. The sky was clear, the wind had moved out carrying the rain inland. All that remained was a soft breeze.

Ross breathed in deeply. His nostrils flared at the stink of dead fish that lay stranded and putrefying among the grasses. His face split into a smile. It was going to be a sunshiny day.

Zack threw the saddle blanket over the mare, climbed up, and seated himself easily behind her withers. Picking up the reins, he waited for the ferryman's signal to follow.

In the distance they could hear the roar of the rivers running into the bay, which, their host said, was only a half mile from where they stood. "You'd a kept going in the dark last night you'd a walked right into to it."He chuckled.

What was the man waiting for, Ross wondered impatiently.

The big grizzled fellow in his overalls slowly mounted and settled himself aboard his horse. His eyes scanned the dark water in the distance for a while and finally he said, "Ready to go? Reckon there's enough light to see the path."

"Ready." Ross replied.

Brambles crowded both sides of the flooded trail and, small fish jumped out of their way, swimming rapidly through the shallows, as they pressed forward.

The sound of rushing water became louder as they neared the bay and Ross heard Zack muttering close behind him. "The water's high. You think he'll take us across?"

"If he doesn't, we'll hog tie him and take ourselves across," Ross replied.

"You full of jesting," Zack grumbled. "You ever drive a ferryboat, Commander ?"

Ross grinned. "Nah, but there's a first time for everything. Stick with me, Isaac Jones."

"There she is," The boat man pointed straight ahead into the wispy rays of dawn that provided just enough light to see the outline of a wooden jetty jutting out into the bay.

"Hot darn. There it is." Zack rose up in his saddle to get a better view of the bulky vessel, still solidly moored to the thick cypress pilings at the end of the jetty.

"Looks like she rode the storm okay," Nathaniel said.

"Looks like it." Ross eyed the ferry, an old rice barge with a wheel house, and what looked like a sturdy deck astern. It seemed solid enough.

The man cackled. "Yes! The old girl's a pissah, that's for sure!" He dismounted, stepping in water up to his knees and waded over to the jetty.

"What about the bay?" Ross shouted, looking out over the ruffled water as it heaved and slapped against the pier.

"I've seen worse," Nathaniel yelled back. "This old lady's

handled some high water in her time." He waded onto the pier.

"The horses can't swim in this," Ross said to Zack. He looked out over the water to where waves were breaking far out into the middle of the bay. "As tired as they are, they'll be swamped."

"Get yourselves and the horses boarded." The ferry captain was halfway down the pier.

"Sir?" Ross called. He jumped up onto the swaying wooden slats.

The man stopped and turned around.

"How much do we owe you?" Ross held out his hand with all the money he and Zack had between them.

The ferryman took the money and counted it. "This heah will get you and the negro on the ferry. If the horses ride, that'll be extra."

"I fear that's all I've got."

"No money, no horses. They'll have to swim."

Ross stared at him. There was more than enough money in his hand for all of them. "You got a knife?" he asked.

The boatman pulled a wicked-looking hunting knife out of its leather holster and handed it to him. "What you gonna do?"

He watched carefully as Ross cut three gold buttons off the front of his jacket. Three gold buttons with a small black anchor imprinted on each. He handed them to the captain. "These will get you further than any money I can give you. Take them."

"Where'd they make these?" he rolled them over in his hand.

"Boston."

"Three more." The captain thrust out his other hand.

"Wait!" Zack rode up beside him. "That's robbery!"

"Of course it is." Nailing the man with a hard look, Ross cut three more of the buttons off the coat saying quietly "Get the horses on board, Zack."

"Yes!"

"Now, Zack!" Ross never took his eyes off the ferryman, nor did he give him the buttons, nor did he return his knife.

"Give me those!" The man held out his hand for the buttons. "And the knife."

"When the horses are on board and when you've landed us safely on the other side you'll get your knife. And the buttons."

They left him standing there and walked back down the jetty to load the horses.

"They ain't gonna like climbing onto this plank one bit," Zack mumbled.

"I know. Let's get them to the end of the pier where the water's shallow."

It took them the best part of an hour but finally, with a lot of shoving and cajoling, both animals were safely on the wooden deck of the ferry.

"That durn filly kicks like a June bug on a string. We're all covered in mud." Zack brushed his sleeve across his face and spat over the side of the barge.

With the big propellers churning up mud and debris, the sullen captain backed the barge away from the pier.

Standing beside the horses, the two men exchanged a look. "What got into him?" Zack asked.

Ross shrugged. "Our world's changing. Everyone's scared right now, not knowing what's going to happen to them." He gazed out over the bay. "So much for *'If I can't help a fighting man, what good am I!'*"

Zack snorted in disgust. "The world's changing alright. White and black folks out there fighting like fools, while fires putting folk outta their homes. Whites fleeing, looking for relatives to stay with, black folk being told to leave their homes—sent out on the roads looking for food and shelter anywhere they can find it because they've got no place to go. Is this the freedom y'all fought for?"

"Things will get better Zack. Emancipation's almost here. I heard talk these last few weeks that in December Congress passed an amendment abolishing slavery." He put his arm around Zack's shoulder. "That means you, Zackie my man. Look for the opportunities that are coming and take them. The world's changing."

"My world's just fine where I live."

"The plantations are done," Ross said. "We're finished. We all have to change, and it won't be easy."

"What in the world did you fight for?"

"For a lot of people I love who believed in the cause—people who believed in the old ways and were willing to die for those beliefs. I guess I wasn't thinking of you." He stared down at the swirling water, its currents wildly pushing and pulling the barge in one direction and then another. "Jefferson Davis tried to tell us it was a mistake."

"Your Pa agreed with President Davis. What about you, did you believe in the cause?"

Ross laughed without mirth. "You bet. I was in the navy. Young and bound for glory! My blood was raging and needed an outlet," he said wryly, "All we got was killing, and more killing. I was wrong."

They stood in silence for a moment feeling the roll of the ferry in the confusion of currents.

Zack persisted. "But you were willing to spill that blood."

"Once I was. Even now, I'll fight to the end if need be. Not for any cause, but for the men who died defending something they believed in—and a way of life we all loved."

"That's just plain crazy. You say yourself this war's over. Why don't you come home? It's time."

"Nah. Gotta finish what we started."

"You're not making a lick of sense."

Leaning on the rails, Ross had a faraway look in his eyes. "I've looked into a dead soldier's eyes and thought, 'Why him? Why am I still here?' We keep fighting because he can't. Just one thing, Zack, if anything happens to me—if a stray bullet or something gets me, tell Pa and Katie Rose how much I love them. And Will, and Sadie Jones—Moses too." Ross let his hand rest on Zack's shoulder. "You know, I love you—"

"You kin stop that loopy talk right now, I ain't listening."

But he was, Ross knew. Ross was struggling with his loyalty to a cause he no longer believed in. And it wasn't because he was on the losing side.

Thirty-Seven

A Time to Kill

S ADIE JONES SHUFFLED across the kitchen feeling good about the world as she began the ritual of fixing breakfast. "Just Marse Doc, me and Tansy dis mo'nin," she muttered. We still gots corn meal and syrup for pancakes and we in a good place. Sho are. Too many folks ain't gots nothin' dis day but we in a good place."

The lack of food all around them troubled Sadie. Every day, it seemed, more beggars came to the kitchen door. The plantations, who still had viable gardens, carted what they could in the way of home-grown grain and vegetables into the markets around Georgetown and Horry counties.

"Yes, we in a good place. And ah'm fixin to cook up a mess a red beans and rice wid de last of de sausage Miss Leah sent. Mebbe later we make rice puddin'. You like dat."

Sadie's headache had vanished. She opened the door and stood with her hands on her hips smiling and breathing in the rain-freshened air. "Yes, Lawsy, I tank you for dis day!"

Suddenly she frowned. She could feel the earth vibrating under her feet and heard the drum beat of horse's hooves coming down the driveway toward the manor house. At the same time, a shadow fell across her. She turned abruptly to see Moses standing beside her watching to see who was coming.

"What for yo wan' scare Ol' Sadie lak dat?" she scolded. "Come a' creepin in here like a weasel. Who dat comin'?"

"It's Marse Willie," the overseer exclaimed. "He musta gotten done wid his doctoring."

Sadie shaded her eyes with one hand and watched as Will steered the horse and buggy into the courtyard.

He saw them standing in the kitchen doorway and waved as he brought the vehicle to a stop and got out.

"Glad that trip's over." He stretched. "How's it going?" he asked, unhitching the horse as Moses walked over to take care of it. He bent down to rub his bad leg. "I feel as though we just waded across the Atlantic. There's water everywhere, and it's still rising." He grinned at them. "What you got to eat, Mama Sadie? I'm hungry as a bear."

Sadie gave him her biggest smile and squeezed him around the waist. She liked it when Will called her Mama Sadie. "You quit dat! I ain't even started dinner yet!"

"And I'm going to need some of that bad-smelling salve you mix up for my aches and pains."

"Dat Ah got. Git you inside and Ah fetch it to you." She picked up her skirt and went into the kitchen.

"I've got news for you," he said, ducking his head through the door.

"'Fore you tells me news, you best git yousef in de house and tell Marse Doc you home. He bin frettin all night waitin' on you. We's all frettin waitin on you an Zacky an' Rossie."

"Yes, Ma'am!'

"And den you git back here and tell me what you gonna tell me."

Thirty-Eight

No Man's Friend Creek

AS CHOPPY AS Winyah Bay was when they left the south shore, out here in the middle, where the PeeDee and Waccamaw rivers met the sea, they were chugging through treacherously rough water. Churning and roiling, the dark greens of the Waccamaw, streaked with red mud, mingled with the black sediment of the PeeDee to create a witch's brew of swirling water, moss, and broken limbs. Strong eddies swirled on every side of the barge, swinging her from left to right, but somehow she managed to stay her course.

"We gonna get bounced around some 'till we get through this convergence," the ferry man shouted from the wheelhouse. "Let's hope the props don't get tangled up in all this junk."

Ross gave him the thumbs up that they had heard.

"This thing rolls like a pig," he grimaced at Zack who hung onto the railing with one hand and the mare's reins with the other.

"I'm just hoping this barrel stays right side up 'till we get our asses on dry land!" Zack shouted back.

"It will," Ross peered out across the bay to the opposite shore. "But we're going to have a time finding dry land. Nothing but salt marsh around here—far as you can see." Dense fog draped like a tablecloth over the approaching shore, and, as they drew closer, its tentacles enveloped the ferry.

Navigating the angry tangle of rivers and the incoming sea slowed them down. At times, it felt as though they were dead in the water. At other times, the craft plunged into troughs, hoisting its stern aloft, its propellers growling as they churned thin air. But finally the waters calmed down enough to allow them to press forward, leaving Ross with renewed respect for the captain and his handling of the barge.

"We're out of it." Came the shout from the wheel house.

"You can let go now." Ross grinned at Zack clinging to the rail like a clam. "Looks like he's heading for that inlet up yonder. I'm going up to check."

Ross made his way to the wheelhouse where the barge captain was tamping down his pipe. "Superb seamanship," he said to the ferryman. Guess you earned those buttons."

The man snorted. "Bin at it since afore you were born, sailor," he replied spitting into a spittoon beside his chair. "Durn tobacco's wet," he grumbled. "See that creek up theah? That's the closest I can get to Hobcaw Rd. If you head due north you'll cross it—if you can find your way through the marsh. I can only go so far, you understand."

"I understand. How deep is the water?"

"When the rivers ain't in flood, it's hardly over your knees. Right now, I don't know. You'll find out," he gave a humorless grin. "This creek is the shallowest of any around and like I said, it's close to Hobcaw Road, the road that will take you to the highway. It's where the Barony land is."

Ross didn't like the plan, but the man knew this coastline and it was the only option they had. He stood beside him, watching as he maneuvered the ungainly vessel into the creek. Staring over the side Ross watched the submerged grass waving under the barge. "How far up can you go?"

"Not much further. Soon I'll have to find a place to turn around."

By Ross's reckoning there was still four feet of water under them. He walked back to where Zack was holding both horses.

"We may have to swim," he said.

"What're you talking 'bout?"

"He's going to drop us in the marsh. He can't get the ferry up any further."

They waited and watched in silence as the boat pushed its way deeper into the creek. They could see nothing on either side of the channel except for a glassy sheet of water with the occasional spikes of palmetto piecing the surface and a few dead trees.

"Turning! Hold on!" the captain shouted, and within minutes, he had the ungainly barge rocked about and facing back the way they came.

Zack stared out over the water. "There's a coupla high places on this side. Look like old rice field embankments maybe," he said.

"If we can make those, we'll be okay," Ross said.

"Gonna wedge the back of the ship close to that bank over yonder and throw that plank out," the ferryman yelled pointing to a slatted wooden plank leaning up against the side of the boat. "You boys get on the horses and ride them off. This is the best I can do," he added.

"Let's go, Zack. Water's about three feet deep here—horses can wade through this to the ridge."

The barge captain opened a gate at the stern of the ferry and heaved the plank out. It hit the shallow water near the bank with a splash. He stamped on it with his boot. "Should hold, it's on firm ground. You never know around here what you've got underfoot."

Ross handed the man the extra buttons and his knife. "Thank you for the ride."

"Hmmph." He rammed the money into his pocket. "Don't trust no one, do ya, boy?"

"Not when they're trying to rob me." Ross paused, "And not when I hear Boston in your speech, sir."

The man stared at him with a blank look on his face. "I'll be damned." He changed the subject. "When you get to that ridge, follow it north a ways, then look for anothah ridge going off to the left." He pointed away from the barge. "Keep going 'bout two miles or so on that and you'll get to Hobcaw Road. Then go to the right. That'll get you where you're going."

"Got it."

The boatman turned away and spat over the side of the rail. "I'll be damned," he muttered.

Ross climbed onto Blue's back, leading Zack, praying the Arabian didn't get hysterical on them. He guided the white horse down the plank.

The gelding snorted as his hooves hit the creek bottom and he started toward the bank. Ross let out a sigh of relief. "Little over three feet," he called.

The mare hesitated at the head of the gangplank, tossed her head, then listening to Zack's voice, she followed Blue into the water.

Ross turned to the captain and tipped his fingers to his cap.

The ferryman hauled his plank back on board, looked back at Ross and said, "Just one thing, this waterway is called 'No Man's Friend Creek."

Thirty-Nine

Black Magic

WILL FOUND HIS father mixing concoctions in his office. "Morning, Pa!" He removed his hat and hung it on a hook behind the door.

"Ah, Will!" The old doctor turned to greet him, smiling over the tops of his spectacles. "By the looks of you, dare I ask how was the trip?"

"Hellish, awful ride. The buggy bogged down once or twice, and the horse was up to his knees in running water at times. It's a miracle we got through without having to spend another night. It's good to be out of there."

"Where did you stay last night?"

"I ran into someone I knew in the mercantile on Front Street. He offered me a bed for the night,"

William shook the mixture vigorously. "What was his name? Drat! This stuff is sticky!"

"Jack. Jack Shakleford. A Virginia Shakelford.

What's in that bottle?"

"Turpentine cough mixture." William set the medicine down on the counter. "Shackelford, huh?"

"Yes. They graciously took me in. Treated me kindly. But no one's happy. The rice mill's wrecked. Grain's piling up on the docks and wagons, growing mold. It can't be shipped, and in any case, it's got nowhere to go. Two nights ago, my host's store was ransacked. The apothecary was cleaned out, too. We talked about the difficulty of practicing medicine and getting supplies. He just laughed, saying it's nigh impossible. The occupation's supposed to be over, but the damn Yanks keep coming."

"It's a terrible war, son. All wars are. Would that it had never begun, but the few who raised their voices for compromise were drowned out." William shook his head. "Ah! That's got it." He turned his medicine bottle upside down and watched the liquid flowing freely, then placed it in his bag. "It's for the child down the road who can't shake a stubborn bout of bronchitis. Sadie wants to heat pine resin for her to inhale. It can't hurt, but you can overdo this turpentine mix. What else?"

"I reached everyone on the list, but the talk's all about the stream of refugees from down south. And the US navy was seen carrying a boat load of soldiers up the river to Georgetown."

"Well, I'm glad you're out of there. How's old Merriman doing down on the Wando River?"

It amused Will to hear his father refer to his friend as 'Old' Merriman. Katie Rose's father had to be ten years younger than William. "Worried. He's picking up a confetti mix of rumors about where the Yankees are going. Some say they're headed to Richmond, others say there's a branch of them heading back to Charleston. If that's true, his place will be right in their path."

"Hmmph."

"Well, I need a bath and clean clothes." Will turned to go. "How is Fairhaven weathering the storm? And Katie Rose? Have you heard anything?"

"Not yet. They must be fine, or someone would have sent word." William stepped back from his work table with a half-grin on his face. "The Duchess of Edenton went across to the island to stitch quilts or something. I'm sure she'll be busting with all the latest gossip when she gets back."

Will smiled. "Zack's not back yet, Sadie says."

"Holed up somewhere, I imagine." He clapped Will on the shoulder. "If the rumors are true regarding the troop movements, the Merriman's could lose everything. Not that the indigo plantations are doing much these days, but still, it's not a good thought."

"Word in Georgetown is that is that the days of indigo growing are over. The Chinese are taking over."

William frowned and reached for a box of empty bottles to fill with his homemade cough syrup. "Course, if by some dreadful happenstance, Riverbend should get burned out from under them, Jack will still be all right. Like us, he converted most of his money into English pounds, some months ago." He thumped a cork top into the bottle in his hand. "I wonder if the Yankees still have their horses penned up in St. George's Church? Damn shame that. The building must be ruined."

Will closed the door to his father's office behind him and walked through the breezeway to the kitchen house. He could hear childish voices coming from the oak grove and cupping his hands around his mouth, he called for Daniel. He came on the run, closely followed by three of the children all clamoring for the older boy's attention.

"Yes, Marse Willie," he was out of breath and wet with perspiration from a game of tag. "Quit dat!" He swatted at one of the youngsters. "Quit pullin' on me, boy!"

"Daniel, bring some hot water upstairs, please? I stink worse than a wet raccoon!"

The children shrieked with laughter and held their noses, pointing at him, and it wasn't long before their taunting cries of, 'Wet coon! wet coon!' brought Sadie Jones out of the kitchen flapping her dish towel.

"Ya'll take off, y'hear! Shoo! Raht dis minit," she shouted at them, swatting left and right. "Daniel, you do wat Marse Willie say!"

"Yes'm," he replied and walked into the kitchen to where a cauldron of hot water stayed warm on the back burner for just such things as someone needing a bath.

As soon as he was gone, Sadie turned on Will. "So. What news you got fer me, Marse Doc Willie?"

"Marcel Dubois is dead." He watched the old woman's face. It told him nothing. She stood stock still, staring straight ahead.

"Did you hear me? I said, that murdering overseer from down yonder—"

"Ah knows what you said. Dooby daid. How he daid?"

"Someone shoved him off one of the lookout platforms in the rice fields and he landed on a spike of dead wood. Pierced him right through the throat. They found him the next day in the mud, but no one's fessin' up."

"Hmm." Sadie Jones turned away from Will and made her way back into the house without another word.

"Did I hear you talking to Sadie Jones?" William asked as his son came back into the house.

"Yup. Strange old bird, isn't she."

"You can say that again. What now?"

"I gave her some news I thought she'd want to hear and got absolutely no reaction!"

"What was it? Something about her daughter?" They all worried about Mollie who had run off to Charleston as soon as she was old enough. "It must be four or five years since she left."

"No. The night before I got to the plantation, Marcel Dubois was found facedown in a canal. Pushed off a viewing platform. He died impaled on a piece of dead wood through his throat."

"Hmmph," William walked into his library running his hand over his chin. "A fitting end. She should be pleased."

"You would think so. But, nothing."

Walking across the room, the doctor stopped in midstride and turned to look at Will. "That's because she thinks his demise was caused by a spell she put on him."

"I thought she'd stopped all that nonsense."

"She told me, he 'needed one,'" William said. "So she probably gave him one. No use arguing with her. It's ingrained in her. She believes it, and that's that."

He let himself down easily into his chair, wincing as he did so.

"Your back's bothering you."

"Son, at my age, everything's bothering me." He smiled wryly then frowned. "God only knows what whirrs around in that head of hers. Sometimes, I think she's as mad as a hatter."

Will shrugged. "I thought she'd welcome the news."

"She does. In fact, I doubt anyone's mourning that murderous lout. I never figured out whether his master knew what he was doing or not."

"Hmmm."

"Dubois kept the laborers in check, and that's what the masters want. On the other hand, the slaves may have been too afraid to say anything, so it's possible the man didn't know. Nasty way to go, though." He chuckled. "Better keep on Sadie's good side. God only knows what she's liable to stir into our supper if she takes a mind to."

With great difficulty, Sadie Jones knelt down and pulled a box out from under her bed. Then, standing up, hanging onto the bed post, she carried it into the kitchen and placed it on the table. She shuffled over to the firebox, selected a log, and threw it into the hot coals inside the stove.

Wiping her hands on her apron, she lifted the lid on the box and stared at the cloth and straw doll lying inside. A needle pierced its neck as it lay there on its back with its sightless black seed eyes staring into nothingness.

Picking it up, she walked to the stove, opened the door, and threw it into the flames.

Forty

The Land Between the Waters

RIDING HIGH ON the ridge between the flowing creek and the rivers on one side and the ocean on the other, the men could see for miles. Miles of salt grass grew on either side of the ridges, their bright green tips, brushed gold by the morning sun. It was a brilliantly sunny day, with no hint of what was to come before the sun set.

What a difference the daylight makes, Ross thought. "Look over yonder, Zack, a tree line. Reckon that could be the Hobcaw Road?"

"Could be. He said there's a ridge that goes off to the left that should take us to it."

"We might see signs of that settlement he was talking about too. I think all of this land we're on belongs to the Hobcaw Barony—big, soggy tract of land in the marshes. I s'pose there could be a home place up in there if anyone's crazy enough to live here."

"There's a village. I heard Mama and Moses talk about people they know who live there." Zack said.

The creek was wide along this stretch of the ridge. The tide was coming in and wide arcs of water rippled upstream, pushing up from the bay, lapping around the base of the embankment they were on. A loon cackled among the reeds, and a couple of wood ducks fluttered over the waterway as they passed. A heron croaked, and somewhere a wren was singing.

"Listen, Zack. The birds. It sounds like a symphony."

"I never heard a symphony, but if it sounds like this, I hope I will someday."

"You will."

They followed the ridge in almost unbroken silence for nearly an hour. Zack rode up ahead scouting the trail. Both men were quiet, savoring the sunshine, the sea breezes, and the smells and sounds of the marshes.

Off in the distance a pair of storks trod purposefully along a sand bank in the middle of the creek and a gaggle of geese preened in the sun, ridding themselves of insects.

Ross grinned as he watched them. He knew how they felt. His clothes were stiff with mud and muck, his boots were damp, and pinched his feet, and his wool jacket scratched his arms.

All around them the scent of sea lavender filled the air. A vague memory of his mother seeped into his mind, as he remembered the small china bowls of lavender oils Sadie placed beside her bed. To calm her, she said.

Funny. Ross hadn't thought about that in years. For a few moments, he let his mind go to the lock box of old memories where hot summer afternoons spent rowing on the river with Will, playing chess and riding around the plantation with his father were stored. Baked lemon puddings belonged among that stash of memories, too.

Sadness crept in around the edges of his thoughts. Their world was changed forever by this war. But his thoughts of home were warm, and before dark this evening he would be in the embrace of the old manor house and the love of his people. He was going home to a place where he could forget about the horrors of the last four years; to the place where his heart might find its youth again. Together, he and Katie Rose could put away the lost years and rebuild their lives. He leaned forward and spoke into Big Blue's ear. "Yes sir, Blue, home to Willowgreen. And a warm bath for me then dinner with Pa and Will and maybe one of Sadie Jones venison stews," he chuckled. "And you to the stables for a soaking and a rub down." The gelding snorted in reply. "Tomorrow we'll saddle up again, and head for Pawley's Island and Katie Rose."

Two red-tailed hawks swooped low across the ridge, interrupting his thoughts. Ross shaded his eyes and watched them climb high into the sky. Veering, diving, skimming the tops of the grasses, they soared above the creek in a graceful ballet of feathers.

So intrigued with the birds, so warmed by the sun and his thoughts, he never noticed the long brown water snake winding across the trail toward them. Without warning it struck Blue's foreleg. The horse shied, whinnying in panic as the snake became tangled around his leg. He reared, frantically waving both forelegs high in the air and throwing Ross off his back, catapulting him into the creek.

Ross landed with a yell and a loud splash as his body hit the water hard about fifteen feet from the embankment.

His yell and the loud splash startled Zack who turned around and stared, then burst into laughter. He watched Ross scrambling to find a foot hold, churning up clouds of mud and thrashing his arms.

"Ross! You alright, my man?" he yelled, with a wide grin on his face. He waited for him to strike out for the shore. When he didn't, Zack swung his horse around and galloped back along the ridge. "Are you alright?" he shouted again as he drew level with the place where Ross was struggling to stay afloat.

"Quicksand got me!" Ross managed to spit out "I'm stuck. Get something to pull me out."

"Don't worry, I'll get you!" Zack finally realized what was happening and looked around frantically for a branch he could throw out, a thick vine—anything. "I'm going to get you. Don't struggle, man, stay still."

Off to one side of the creek a dead tree was partly submerged, and Zack leapt into the marsh and heaved on one of its branches sticking up through the water. Tugging and twisting until he thought his arm would break, it finally snapped off. He hauled it up the ridge and went scrambling down the bank. Then extending it out as far as he could, tried to reach Ross.

"Hurry!"

"I'm goin' to get you, Ross. Here, catch!" The branch fell short of its target by about a foot. Zack waded into the water.

"Stay there, Zack." Ross spluttered. The water was over Ross's shoulders, splashing into his mouth as he felt his legs being sucked down, aided by the weight of his boots. He ducked under the brine, trying desperately to loosen them and one of the boot laces broke as he pulled it tighter still. He tried again, but the motion dragged him deeper. He forced his hands inside the boot to dislodge it from his foot, but the suction of the mud and sand held it tight.

"Stay still, Ross. Dammit! Don't move. I'm going to find a vine."

"Get the rope from my bag," Ross shouted. He watched Zack scramble up the bank, loosen the snap on the saddle bag and take out the two ropes. The one the mare had dragged in and the other from the Ramsey stables.

Zack tied them together and then to the branch. He held the other end in one hand and threw the log like a spear toward Ross. "Catch!" he yelled.

Ross watched it fall within inches of his reach. Stretching until he thought he would break a blood vessel, he reached as far as he could choking on the water, spitting leaf mulch. His struggle made him sink further into the mud. Surely, there was a bottom to this muck. This pluff and quicksand usually only covered a few feet at worst. Underneath it there should be solid ground.

A swell slapped up against his head as he took a deep breath and tried to reach the end of the branch again to no avail, coughing up green water.

Sweating now, Zack hauled the log back in and tried again. Again it fell short. Ross was deeper now and his reach was shorter. Zack watched as his friend, straining with everything he had against the sucking sand, reached out again and again he fell back, unable to grasp it.

"No time," Ross yelled, spitting muck out of his mouth. "I'm in a stump hole. Get Blue."

Ross closed his eyes and tried to catch his breath. When he opened them, he saw Zack climbing up the bank.

Zack threw one end of the rope over the horse's back, looped it around both shoulders and tied it in a knot around his chest. He led the horse down to the water and arched the rope across the stream to where Ross was.

"Not enough," Zack muttered. "Here it comes again!" he shouted. But the ropes were just too short.

"Won't reach." Ross sounded hoarse.

Zack was already removing the reins from around Blue's neck and tying them to the end of the rope. Sweat blistered his forehead and ran into his eyes. He could hear Ross coughing as he eased the horse closer to the water. "Hold on, Rossie boy! I'm gonna get you."

Zack closed his big hand around the coiled rope and stepping back onto solid ground, he planted both feet, and aiming as close to

Ross as he could, he flung the line out across the water.

This time it worked. Ross raised his hand, grabbed the end of the reins, held on, and his voice tense, he shouted, "Got it!"

Not wasting any time, Zack climbed onto Blue's back, settled into the saddle, and speaking into the horse's ear, he said, "You gonna pull, Blue. Y'hear me?"

The gelding's feet slipped in the mud. Zack backed him up a few steps to firmer ground. "Okay Blue, *PULL!*" The line tightened. The horse dug his hooves in, put his head down, and heaved.

"Not moving," Ross spluttered. He could hear the edge of panic in his voice.

Zack backed the horse up another few inches. "Okay, Blue. Now PULL!" He shouted.

The big horse raised his head, the great muscles in his shoulders and flanks tightened as the animal planted his hooves again and pulled. *"More! MORE! C'mon*, Blue!" Zack yelled, digging his heels into the horse's sides, begging him, *"PUULL!"*

Listening to Zack, the thought flashed through Ross's head that the only pair of spurs they had between them were tightly secured to his boots. And they were helping to drag him under. Cold water lapped at the base of his skull and cascaded down inside his collar and under his coat.

A nasty thought snaked through his mind. "Tide's coming in!" he shouted and the panic in his voice was clear.

"We got ya. Let's go, buddy." Leaning back in the saddle, Zack urged Blue on. "Again, Blue! Com'on big boy!"

The horse pulled. Muscles bulging, nostrils flaring, he heaved.

"It's no use!" Ross shouted, spitting water. The muscles in his arms burned. With an enormous effort he tied the rope to his belt. "No use." He coughed as a wave drowned his words.

"Stop that crap talk!" Zack leapt off the horse. "I'm coming, Ross. Hold on." He shouted, wading through the grass that wound around his legs, he kicked off, and began to swim.

"Get back! Get BACK you fool! We can't both die." And still Zack swam out into the creek.

Ross screamed, "Get back you jackass man! Someone has to tell them what happened." The last part of his sentence was swamped by the rising tide. "Don't die for me, Zacky—don't die for me, brother. Go back."

With tears flowing down his cheeks, mixing with the yellow-green swamp that coiled around him like a tangle of water snakes, Zack swam with all his might back to the bank and once more, dripping wet, and trailing grass, he flung himself on Blue's back.

"Okay. Pull Blue! PUULL big horse, PUULL! C'mon Now! LET'S GO!" he screamed, choking on his tears, spitting mud, he dug his heels into Blue's flanks reared back, and yelled, "Hold on Ross! Hold on!"

Ross thought his torso was being pulled apart.

The horse snorted, whinnied once, and dug in. Lowering his body, with his ears folded against the sides of his head, he put his full weight behind the struggle and pulled.

"You got it Big Fella. You got it. Okay, now Puul!" Zack panted. "Again!"

Pouring all his strength into his back and shoulders, with the bridle tearing at his neck, the horse shrieked, and pulled with everything he had. Sweat blackened his hair, and foam coated the inside of his mouth. He dug his feet deeper into the dirt and pulled.

Something snapped.

Like a rifle shot zinging across the creek, the torn reins whipped through the air and Zack went hurtling off the horse and landed on the bank on his back. His head hit a half-buried rock in the sand, and he lost consciousness. And the tide kept rising.

Ross watched the scene on the bank unfold as if in slow motion. He saw Zack lying on the grass not moving and he knew they were done. Throwing back his head, he let out a long drawn out wail. *"Zaaaaaakieee!"* A lost sound torn from somewhere inside him.

And then adrenalin took over. He worked himself into exhaustion, twisting and turning in the water, slinging his upper body to left and right. He tried not to move his hips and legs, but the drag on his lower body was just too much. His head was underwater now as he tried to hold his face up to the sky.

"Oh God! Oh, God." The water rose and he felt something nuzzle his arm. With his panic rampant, Ross grabbed for it and felt the gelding's big head, and his mouth trying to clamp over his forearm.

"Blue—" he breathed, and felt himself go limp as exhaustion overtook him. He sensed the horse heaving him, his great body thrashing, his hooves slipping in the sand. Blue hauled with all his might, but the animal could find no foothold.

Something tore, and Ross found himself floating, suspended in the greasy yellow creek as the water closed over his head.

Strangely, where there should have been terror, Ross felt only peace. The water was suddenly warm and clear and as he looked up toward the surface, his mother's face looked back at him. Elizabeth's auburn hair floated around her face on an invisible breeze and her eyes were filled with love.

"Mama . . ." Ross said her name, but he wasn't aware of having spoken the words. As he looked into her eyes she smiled, and he could feel the warmth of her love, deeper than anything he had ever

known. She was so beautiful. Her lips moved, and he felt his name ripple through the light around her. It was the first time he noticed the light. It dazzled him, and he had to close his eyes.

The last thing Ross heard were church bells ringing somewhere faraway. They were the bells of All Saints Chapel where he and Katie Rose were to be married.

Forty-One

Going Home

H E MUST HAVE been unconscious for hours. Zack lay on the side of the embankment where he had fallen, taking stock of his surroundings. His thinking was muddled and something was stinging his neck. As he raised his hand to rub the place, a cloud of flies took off. He looked at his hand and saw that it was covered with drying blood. And he remembered.

"Ross!" he yelled, staggering to his feet, clutching at tufts of grass to keep his balance. A sharp pain stabbed through the back of his head, making his eyes swim as a wave of dizziness almost toppled him. He retched until, with nothing left in his stomach, he could retch no more.

Raising his hand, he felt the back of his head and found a two-inch-long, deep gash. He saw the bloodied rock lying on the ground, and he looked out over the creek.

There was no sign of Ross. The water was calm and clear. Not a ripple. Zack fell to his knees, put his head in his hands and screamed Ross's name. Tears rolled down his cheeks as he cried, calling for his friend over and over again. But no one answered.

"Rossie!" Sobs shook his big body as he ran to the water's edge, dove in and swam to where he'd last seen Ross. Diving below the surface, frantically clawing the weed, he felt for Ross—but there was nothing. Four times, he scrambled below the surface and came up empty-handed. Finally, with black spots swimming across his vision, Zack headed back to the bank.

Lying face-down on the grass, he grasped the ground in anguish, filled with a pain so deep he couldn't name it. Ross was gone. The word was the emptiest sound he had ever heard and, mercifully, he lost consciousness again.

How long he lay there he didn't know, but at some point Zack got up slowly and walked to the edge of the creek. The frayed reins were floating among the reeds beside him.

Sudden rage filled him with a blinding red miasma of agony and he fell to his knees, arms raised to the sky screaming, "It's my doin'! It's my doin' Ross! I didn't save you! I didn't save you! AAWWW! I want to die." And he wept. He sobbed until his head felt as though it was going to split wide open. He wept until his eyes were almost swollen shut, but at last, the storm inside Zack subsided. Slowly the sobs quieted and he heard Ross's voice saying. *"Don't die for me Zacky! Don't die for me brother—go back."*

He sat back on his knees in silence remembering the time near the old broken bridge at Willowgreen when Rossie's Mama died. He had told Ross he would do anything for him. He would die for him. Fresh tears cascaded silently down his face. He sat quietly staring at the creek as the words came back. *"Don't die for me, Zacky. Tell them what happened."*

Zack stood up, waded into the creek and stopped. "Nothing," he whispered. Like the emptiness in his heart, there was nothing there. "I'll go now, Ross," he whispered. "I'll tell them what happened."

He turned and walked slowly up to the top of the ridge.

He had to get Moses. Moses would know what to do.

He could see the young roan standing beside a dead oak a few feet away. She saw him and ambled over to where he stood. He put his cheek close to hers and scratched her ear distractedly with tears flowing silently. She nuzzled his neck and whinnied softly. It was then that Zack realized that Blue was missing.

Turning from the mare he walked along the ridge calling his name. He waited for Blue's answering snort, but it didn't come. He looked up and down the ridge and whistled. He waited. He whistled again, and there was still no sign of him.

"Blue!" His shout sent another dagger of pain through his head. He walked along the creek. Above the high tide mark, he could still see the deep grooves made by the big horse's hooves when they were trying to save Ross—there were no hoof marks showing where he might have galloped up the bank. He groaned and looked across the creek. Had Blue tried to swim the creek? There was no flattened grass, no prints that he could see. Had he perished too? Zack called him again. Nothing. He had to get home. Had to get home and find Moses.

He climbed back up the bank, picked up the blanket he had been using as a saddle, and climbed gingerly aboard the Arabian to begin the long ride home. With no saddle and no reins, he wound the blanket around the mare's neck, tied it around his waist, and one of his arms to hold him steady. He wound his fingers through her mane, lowered his cheek to her neck and said, "Let's go, let's go home."

Zack lost consciousness about fifty yards down the ridge. The last thing he saw was a hand-painted sign at a fork in the trail that pointed the way to Hobcaw Road, the King's Highway and home. So close . . .

Forty-Two

Spirit Horse

TWILIGHT CREPT AROUND the edges of the plantation. Long shadows striped the sandy clay of the swept yard. It was still too early for crickets but, as darkness fell, small birds found their nests and settled down for the night. It was the end of a pretty day, and the playful voices of children drifted from The Street where their mothers cooked the evening meal.

Sadie Jones sat in the doorway of the kitchen house listening to the sounds of evening. She had fish and hush puppies frying gently on the wood stove and a sweet potato pudding firming in the oven. Marse Doc's table was set, and in a few minutes, everything would be ready to take into the manor house.

She breathed in the fresh air, savoring its clean scent. It was a golden evening to be sure. The only thing that worried her was not setting a place for Rossie. She started to, but something stopped her. There was still no sign of Zack and Rossie. Willie said they might be sheltering from the storm.

"It's time they be gettin' home," she muttered to herself and walked back inside to check on dinner.

The aroma of fried fish filled the air as Sadie removed them from the stove and placed them in a shallow basket lined with newspaper to drain. Marse Doc always saved his newspapers for the fish. He taught her how to make rice vinegar, too. And although she had balked at the idea of sprinkling it on her fried fish, she tried it a few times and liked it.

She could hear Moses stomping the mud off his shoes as he came up the path from the fields to collect the pies she'd baked for the families. She intended to tell him that his boy, Daniel, had caught enough fish for everyone today.

She turned around expecting to see Willowgreen's overseer walking through the door. He wasn't there, so she shuffled outside to see what was keeping him.

Standing beside Daniel, in the courtyard, Moses stared down the driveway, and as Sadie looked, she could see something in the distance. It was too blurred for her to make out, but she could hear horse's hooves scuffing the clay road. "Who dat comin'?" she called.

"A horse," Moses said without turning around. But, as recognition set in, he ran, followed by Daniel, toward the riderless gelding. Blue limped down the driveway, covered in dried mud and dragging a lasso-like, rope from his belly. "Blue—dat you?"

The horse raised its head at the sound and quickened his crippled gait as Moses approached.

"Where's Zack?" Moses shouted, as if the horse might answer. Cold fear crawled up his neck making his scalp tingle. He reached the horse, caught the rope in one hand and looked down at Blue's left front hoof. "Foot's dripping blood," he said

"Dere's a piece of wood caught up in dat cut," Daniel bent down, and stared at the hoof. "It cut bad."

"C'mon, Boy." Moses began to walk the horse to the yard.

Something was very wrong. Where was Zack?

"Marse Willie!" he yelled. Fear curdled in the pit of his stomach. "Marse Doc! Daniel, fetch de doctor."

"Dat Blue?" Sadie stood stock still peering down the driveway.

"Yas'm."

"Wat he do wid Zacky. Where Zacky?"

"We gonna find out, don' you worry none. Marse Willie!" he shouted again. "Ah'm goin' look for Zack. Don' you fret now," Moses put an arm around Sadie's shoulders and tried to lead her back inside the house.

"No! Ah'm waitin for my boy!" She brushed his hand off her shoulder.

"Moses?" Will hobbled down the front steps. "What's going on? What's wrong with Blue?"

"He done come home by his sef." Daniel said. "He hurt bad."

Will picked up his pace, walking as quickly as he could and reached the horse.

Daniel squatted down beside the animal. "Cain't see much o' nothin on account all de mud, but dere's a wood piece in he foot and he shoe done dragged loose. He bleedin' bad."

"Dat horse walked a long ways," Moses said, pointing to the horse's badly damaged soft pad beneath the hoof.

Will looked at the Blue. His white fur was stiff with mud and his mane was tangled with weed and grass. The saddle hung around his belly, the bridle was cock-eyed, and there was some sort of rigged harness hanging loosely around his neck and shoulders. "Let's get him into the yard," Will put his hand on the harness-like rope. "Let's go, Big Boy." He got a soft snort in reply as Moses lead him away.

"Toto," he called to one of the children who stood in the grove watching. "Get me a shoeing stool. And ask Miss Sadie to fill a bucket with boiled water and bring me a bag of salt," he instructed him. "And a sponge."

Sadie Jones, who had stood there silently watching, was already on her way to the kitchen with the boy in tow.

"What's all the shouting about?" William stood in the breezeway taking in the action.

"The gelding's come home without Zack—and he's in a mess," Will called. "I'm going to take a look at his hoof. The shoe's dragging, and from the amount of blood, I'd say the soft tissue's pretty badly injured. Looks like the frog's split but there's so much mud I can't see anything."

Moses cut the reins off and unbuckled the saddle from around the horse's belly as the child returned with the stool.

Daniel moved in closer. "What 'frog', Marse Willie?" Without waiting for an answer, he pointed to the horse. "Lookee here. He got big rub places from de rope. 'Round he shoulders and belly. Dere be blood some places and de hair done rubbed off."

Will glanced at the rope burns and shook his head. "Frog, Daniel, is what they call the soft part of the hoof. What happened to you, Boy?" He muttered, pulling the stool up close to the horse. "Where's that boy!" He shouted. "Oh, there you are." Toto stood behind him with the bucket of water. "Pass me a sponge—please." He plunged the sea sponge into the water and gave it to Daniel. "Sponge the blood and muck out of the cuts," he said and turned his attention to the basin that held his clinchers and hoof nippers.

Blue whinnied softly as Moses held the hoof up for Daniel to clean. "Dis here's a frog," Daniel informed Toto, pointing to the soft tissue.

Blue whimpered as Will pulled the last nail out of the shoe and drizzled water over his hoof to get a better look at the injury.

"You're right," William leaned in for a better look. "The hoof's badly hurt."

"Lookee here." Moses pointed to a bulbous swelling on the horse's ankle.

Will glanced at the two-pronged puncture wound.

"Snake bite," Daniel said.

"It is." Will said. "Blue probably shied and threw Zack. Someone needs to go look for him."

"Ah'm goin' ride out now. Someting bad done happened," Moses muttered.

William could see that Sadie Jones legs were cramping, and she was trembling.

She looked around for something to hold onto and found Toto at her side. "I tink you best hep me to ma chair," she told him as he put a hand under her elbow.

"Don' you worry none, Miss Sadie. Ah'm goin' bring dat boy home." Moses called after her.

Will waited until the old lady was out of earshot and said. "How are you going to find him in the dark?"

"Ah knows dese parts. Ah gots to go, Marse Willie." the big man said. "When you finish, Ah be getting' dis horse to da stable, den ah go find em."

"Get going. Daniel can help me here."

Moses hesitated, watching the young doctor. Holding the horse's head steady, Will examined the tear in his mouth. He bent down and picked up the tattered reins. "These reins got caught on something, and Blue either struggled to get away, or he was pulling something—" He ran his hand over the horse's belly. "Someone rigged a makeshift harness."

William looked at the hoof that Daniel had washed clean. The exposed split went through to the soft tissue. "How he managed to put any weight on this at all is beyond me. I wonder how far he's come?"

"Only ting we know is that he weren't movin' fast." Moses said. Maybe travellin' since mornin'."

A wave of anger swept over William. This whole thing was triggered by a ridiculous whim of Sadie's. And now Zack could be lying out there in the dark somewhere, unconscious. Or dead.

The doctor put his hand on the horse's neck. "You found your way home, big boy," he said softly. "That's what matters. But where's Zack?"

"Will, you and the boy tend to the horse," his father said. "I'm going to get my bag and ride out with Moses to find Zack."

"It's getting dark, Pa. And the water's still high."

"I know. Moses get the horses saddled up."

"Yassir! Daniel, hold dis foot."

William put a hand on the horse's back. "Good boy, Blue."

The horse lifted his head, bared his teeth, and snorted, making William forget what he was going to do.

What was that? Something glinted inside the horse's mouth. Holding the bit in one hand, William closed his other hand around the lower jaw and pulled it open.

Blue struggled, trying to shake his head loose, but William held fast. There was something wedged between two of the horse's teeth. Digging into his coat pocket, he pulled out a knife, inserted the blade between the teeth and forced the object out.

It hit the ground and William bent down to retrieve it. He rubbed the dust off it on his sleeve and turned it over. It was one of the gold metal buttons from the cuff of a naval officer's coat.

The blood in William's veins turned to ice. He stared unseeingly down the driveway into the dusk, as the truth dawned on him. Ross was out there, too. Holy God in Heaven. His son.

"Sadie was right," he muttered. Shoving the button into his pocket, he turned on his heel and strode toward the kitchen house.

The old woman was sitting in her chair, holding the cat on her lap chanting softly, rocking to and fro.

"Moses and I are going out to find Zack," he told her. "In the meantime, mix up that ointment you use for cuts and such—the one you mix with honey and nettles, and take it to Will." That should keep her busy.

She stopped chanting and shooed the cat off her lap. "Yes. Ah goes do it, an' you go fetch my boy an'—" She was going to say "and Rossie," but the words wouldn't form.

William walked briskly to the manor.

Sadie rose shakily from her chair and began taking things down from her medicine cabinet. Her hands moved by themselves. Her mind was removed. It felt as though something outside of her was directing them from one jar to another, from one root to the next. And although there was nobody there but the cat, she had the strongest feeling that someone was standing beside her. The feeling was as soft and sweet and warm as the honey candy she used to make for him when he was a little boy.

Sadie Jones' eyes filled with tears.

Late dusk lay like a pall over the courtyard and by the time. Will finished applying Sadie's sticky salve to stem the bleeding in Blue's foot, it was dark. "Daniel, fetch some bandages from Marse Doc. And hurry!" he said.

"Yassir!" The boy ran to the house and was back in minutes.

Will held out his hand for a bandage and began to wind it around and over the horse's injured hoof, crisscrossing it and tightening it, pulling the split together.

He could feel the boy's eyes on him, watching his every move. "Tomorrow you can help me remove this, and we'll drive three screws into his hoof to hold it together."

"Yassir," Daniel said.

As Will worked in the dim light, he saw Moses coming through the grove with the two horses, carrying a couple of lanterns. Good. He was going to need light if he was to stitch up the cut on Blue's neck and the ragged tear in his mouth.

Moses took one of lamps and set it down on the clay beside Will.

"All set, Moses?" The doctor, medicine bag in hand, came striding toward the saddled horses.

"Yassir! Ah's ready."

Will signaled to Daniel to give his father a hand up onto his horse.

But Daniel wasn't watching. He was staring down the driveway. "Somun's coming!" he shouted.

They all turned in the direction of road. Will listened to the sound of fast approaching hoof beats on the hard-packed clay. There was no moon and he had to strain his eyes to see the shadowy form of the horse and rider approaching fast.

"Lawsy! Zacky!" The shout burst from Moses as he dropped the reins and began to run. "Zacky!" He yelled again.

There was no answering cry.

No one recognized the horse that cantered into the courtyard. Foam frothed around the animal's mouth. Its coat shimmered with sweat and the mane was matted with burrs and cobwebs and leaves.

Zack slumped over its neck, on a tattered blanket, with his hands still wound in the horse's mane.

"Whoa! Whoa!" Moses cried. Waving his hands he reached for the mare as she slowed, keeping about ten yards distant. "Woah, dere! Woah! Zacky, kin y'hear me?"

Will heard the alarm in Moses voice, as he grabbed the horse and began to reach for Zack. "Hold it!" His voice bellowed out.

"He's unconscious," William shouted. "Daniel, *very carefully*, help your father get him off the horse and onto the cot in my office."

He watched as they unwound Zack's hands from the mane, disentangling him from the blanket which looked as though it was the only thing holding him on the horse's back. There was a deep gash on the back of his head matted with bloody dust. "Carefully! Is he breathing?"

"Yassir." Daniel put his ear to Zack's mouth. "He breathin'—but jes a little."

With his bag in hand, William walked behind them, as they carried the unconscious man into the house. His thoughts raced, as he tried to make sense of what was going on. The commotion in the courtyard attracted the workers and their families who stood in the grove making no sound, taking in the scene in front of them.

"Toto!" Will shouted. "Get Zack's horse to the stables. Let her drink then rub her down!"

"Yassir! Marse Willie!" The youngster came running and, as he approached, the mare reared. "Eeeee!" he cried, taking a step backward, throwing his hands in the air.

"Whoa!" Will reached for her. "I'll be damned. It's an Arabian. Easy, now." Where did Zack find her? "How on earth did she found her way to Willowgreen," He muttered.

The boy shrugged

"She's scared, Toto. Talk to her softly, and she'll go with you. I've got to go and help the doctor."

Having situated Zack, Daniel left the house and ran back to where Will stood holding Blue's reins.

"We're done here, Daniel. Help Toto take the horses to the barn. Real easy. Put Blue in a separate stall with plenty of straw and help Toto with the mare."

He watched as the older boy put his hand on Blue's mane and urged him forward, calling softly for the roan to follow. Seeing her balk, Will gave her a firm shove, which was all she needed to leap toward Blue. "She'll follow now."

Then, she did something he'd never seen before. Nuzzling Daniel out of the way, she pushed herself in close to Blue and nudged him gently.

"You see dat, Marse Willie?" the boy said.

Will nodded. One lame step at a time, Blue began to limp alongside the mare. Every time the big horse stopped, the mare nudged him. "She's guiding him."

Whether it was Blue's scent—or something else, that had led her to Willowgreen, they would never know.

Will walked across the courtyard and knocked on Sadie's door. A trembling voice from inside told him to come in.

"Sadie?" He poked his head through the half-open door. "Zacky's here."

She gave a little cry.

He took a step inside the house and pulled the cat's stool over to where she sat. "He's in the house with Pa—"

"Ah gots to go to he." She grabbed the arms of her chair and tried to push herself up.

Will reached for her. "I think you should wait. Let Pa come and talk to you."

"An' ah tink you crazy as a loon. Ahm goin' see Zacky!"

"He's sleeping," Will tried lamely.

"Den Ah goes wake he up. We gots to know what happened to Rossie. Hep me up, boy."

She grabbed her shawl off the back of the chair and shuffled past him on her way out.

Will closed the door behind them. Short of wrestling the old woman to the ground, there was no way to stop Sadie Jones from leaving.

Two horses and Zack were home, but no Ross.

The back door swung open and Moses ran out of the manor house brushing past them on his way to the horses.

"What's going on?" Will called after him.

"Doc he give me a letter take over Edenton—ax Marse Perry call de men an' we goin' find Rossie," Moses shouted over his shoulder as he mounted one of the horses and thundered out of the courtyard.

Forty-Three

By Morning's Light

THE MEN OF the Waccamaw, Murrells Inlet, and Pawley's Island, some too old to fight, others wounded, gathered in Willowgreen's courtyard at daybreak. Their women came with them, busying themselves in the kitchen, making hot cider and handing out buckwheat cakes with honey.

Inside the manor house, Sadie Jones opened her eyes in the gloom of the doctor's office. Will and Tansy, the house maid, had prepared a pallet for her to lie on and placed it beside Zack who lay on the cot deep in coma.

Will had slept in the library, and the doctor had gone upstairs, but both were up now. They walked out to the courtyard together to greet the search party.

Sadie sat up and listened. Something had awakened her. She turned her head to look at Zack. He lay very still. Sadie didn't know how anyone could be that deep asleep and not be dead. And then she heard, "Mama." It was less than a whisper.

"Zacky?" She croaked and, hanging onto the side of the cot, she pulled herself up to look at him. "You 'wake, boy?"

"Water," was all he said. He spoke so softly she hardly heard him. Tears rolled down her cheeks as she called out as loudly as she could. "Willie! Zacky. Willie! Zacky he waked up!"

She heard footsteps walking purposefully through the house. "Willie!" she cried again as one of the women poked her head through the door with an alarmed look on her face.

"Wha—!"

"Git Marse Doc. And Willie. Hurry!

The woman ran out of the house and Sadie could hear her calling for William.

Daniel, who had been helping with the horses, came at a run, and was in the dispensary before the old woman could pull herself up off the pallet.

"Zacky!" the youngster exclaimed leaning over the cot. He put a hand on his shoulder. "Don' you move, now." Daniel sat on the floor beside Zack. "Be still," he told him. "I hep you."

He turned as William strode into the room. "He wakin', up Marse Doc," he said and stood back to let the doctor pass.

"Moses, bring that lamp." William called over his shoulder, only to discover the big Gullah man was right behind him, holding the lantern up over his head.

"Open your eyes Zack," he said. He knelt beside him, holding his head toward the light. "Can you hear me?"

"Water." was the immediate response. He turned his head toward his mother.

"Rossie, Mama . . ." his eyes filled with tears. "He gone." His chest began to heave, and wrenching sobs shook his frame as he reached out for her, and she took his hand in both of hers.

"Quiet, boy." William put his hand on Zack's shoulder. "Be still." The pain he felt at hearing Zack's words struck deep into his core like an ax.

"Quicksand. He fell in a stump hole. Deep hole—kept sinkin'." He pulled his hand away and turned to the wall. "I tried, Mama. Blue pulled, and we tried and tried to get him out, but the waters 'em risin' over he head." The sobs came unabated as Zack reverted to his Gullah English telling them the story of falling off Blue's back. "An' when I waked—Blue he gone an' Rossie too."

In a daze, William stood up and walked outside with Moses supporting him.

The sun crested pale and silver over the courtyard while the men and women stood in devastated silence as Moses told them what Zack had said.

One of the men from down river stepped forward and took the Doctor's arm. "We'll find him, Doc." He looked around and caught sight of Will leaning against the door frame of the dispensary with a hand over his eyes.

"Will! Take your Pa inside. Josephine!" he called for his wife, "You and the womenfolk stay here with the Doc and Will," he turned back to William. "You stay here, Doc. Me and the boys will search the marshes until we find him. Moses will go with us."

The old man turned to his son. "We have to go to Fairhaven—Katie Rose. We have to tell her."

"Yes, we will, Pa. Let's go inside first," Will took his father's arm. He had never seen his father so stricken. "We'll get Winston Perry to telegraph Merriman. She'll need her Pa here." He urged him toward the door.

"How soon do you think he can be here?"

"Probably sometime tonight if we get word to him right away."

William nodded, and leaning on his son's arm, they walked into the manor house together.

Will stood on the threshold of Edenton's ornately carved front door, knocked, and waited. He could hear footsteps hurrying across the marble floor. In seconds the door was flung open by Leah who stood there staring at him in shock. Her cheeks were flushed, her cap was missing, and her hair was in disarray, making Will realize that it was still very early in the morning.

"Mistress Leah, Ma'am—" he started to say.

"Will! Something's wrong! Something's happened to the doctor."

"No, Ma'am—"

"Then what? It's not even six o'clock."

"It's my brother," he said, tears filling his eyes. "Is Major Perry up? I must speak to him."

"Yes, yes," she blustered. "Come in, dear boy. Then you must tell me what's going on."

"Last night we sent word that Ross was missing and we asked for the Major's help in getting the word out for a search party."

"Oh! I wasn't told! Why wasn't I told? Oh, dear! Winston!" She called loudly down the hallway. "Will Stanley is here."

Will knew exactly why Leah hadn't been told. She would have been on their doorstep last night with God knows how many members of the Ladies Guild, well-meaning he supposed, all of them, but totally confusing the situation.

He closed his eyes, a wave of dizziness assailing him. He hadn't slept, fatigue was setting in, and that couldn't happen. There was still far too much to do. He couldn't afford to rest. His father needed him. He realized with a jolting feeling, that in one miserable half hour, their roles had been unalterably reversed.

It was up to him now to take control. Where his father had always been the leader, the patriarch—the decision maker in the family, Will was now faced with the reality that all that had changed. As resilient as William Stanley had always been, Will knew that he might never recover from the tragedy this day had brought.

"Will! My boy!" Winston Perry wheeled himself into the parlor in his nightshirt and a shawl he had hastily thrown around his shoulders. "Did the men show up?"

"Yes, sir. Thank you. In the meantime, sir, we've had some terrible news."

"Here! Sit down. Leah, get the boy some brandy."

"No, no. I'll be fine." Will shook his head. "My father asked if you would be so kind as to get hold of James Merriman and ask him to be here as soon as he can."

"James Merr—?"

"Katie Rose's father at Riverbend," Will interrupted. "We have to tell her that Ross has met with an accident—and is dead." He could hardly get the words out, but he drew himself up, and said, "and her father should be with her when she finds out."

There was a stunned silence in the room until Leah Perry caught Will up in her arms and began to sob. "You poor, poor boy!"

Winston Perry cleared his throat loudly. "Yes, yes. Of course. I'll get hold of him right away. I assume he must be told the details?"

Will nodded unable to speak.

Leah stepped back, mopped her eyes and braced her shoulders. "Yes. Well, there are things to be done. And you mustn't worry about a thing, dear Will. Winston and I will be over to see to everything— all the arrangements—just as soon as he contacts James Merriman. Oh dear," she groped for the armchair behind her and dissolved into tears. Give your dear father our love. And that poor girl. Yes. We shall all go over to the island together!"

In as short a time as necessity and good manners allowed, Will beat a hurried retreat, and with Leah's pledges of help and copious quantities of food ringing in his ears, he rode home.

PART 4

February 27, 1865

Forty-Four

Journaling . . .

I CAN'T REMEMBER *what day this is.* Katie Rose wrote. *All I know is that it's been seven days since that dreadful afternoon when Doctor Stanley arrived with Will and Papa to give me the news of Ross's death.*

Oh, God, I can hardly say that word, let alone write it. The finality of the sound of that word is too hard to bear. I still can't believe what's happened. Oh, God! *My heart's broken. It feels as though it's been wrenched from my body and trampled into the ground.*

I can't live without you, Ross. There's no life for me without you, my love. My soul . . . my pen is wet with tears, the paper's damp and smudged with ink. Where are you, my love?

All they told me was that you were thrown from your horse. Blue was scared by a snake, they said. How does it happen that one minute you're galloping through the marsh lands—and the next you're gone. You're gone, Ross, gone from me forever. I can't believe it. My throat is raw, my eyes sting, but I have to keep telling myself that you're gone, to bring me back from that twilight place, that well of disbelief that has me suspended between worlds. Here one moment and gone the next. What does it mean . . . I don't even know if my words are making any sense . . . Perhaps I've gone mad.

Papa came from Riverbend, he held me in the rocking chair on the porch while I cried and cried. He doesn't know what to do. No one does. Aunt Trudy walks around talking to herself. Doctor Stanley gave them some sort of calming medicine to give me. I spat it out and gave it to her. They say they want me to sleep, to forget this horrible time. I can't forget! I don't want to forget. What are they thinking?

Last night I felt someone sitting on my bed. When I opened my eyes, I saw Aunt Winn silently weeping and holding her prayer book in her lap. No one knows what to do. Except me. I just want to run out into the ocean and keep running until the sand under my feet disappears, and so do I.

I open my hand and stare at the gold and black Navy button Doctor Stanley gave me. He said it was from Ross's coat sleeve. He found it jammed between Blue's teeth. They think Blue tried to drag him out of the creek. They said Blue's mouth was cut and bruised. My hand is cut and bruised from holding the button so tightly.

It's dark outside the window. In spite of the oil lamp, my room is darker. My heart is filled with darkness.

I heard today that they've stopped the search for Ross because another storm is coming in. Oh, God! Let me die.

Forty-Five

The Kitchen House

S ADIE DIDN'T KNOW what day it was. The only time she slept was after she'd taken the dose of laudanum that Will gave her every day. Her days and nights all ran together. Whenever she awoke, she thought she saw Toto sitting on the stool beside her.

She leaned her head back on the head rest of her rocking chair and began to mutter to herself and the cat, who sat straight up staring at her.

"Ah usta wonder what dey mean by being 'dog tired'. Dat's wat I am, I guess. But ah cain't worry none 'bout dat fer now. Ah'm so dog tired. Let me sleep, Lawsy, let me sleep."

"Yass'm. You sleep, Gogo." The little boy said. "Marse Doc say I gotts ta see dat you sleep."

She would sleep. Because there were too many things she couldn't think about right now. "All of em runnin' around in mah haid like horse flies in a jar," she murmured. "Marse Doc says Zacky bin sleeping a lot. Say dats what he need. But ah knows ma boy. He cain't sleep on account he tinkin 'bout Rossie. An' I kin see from Marse Doc's face when he come to see me, he ain't sleepin none neither. He look like a old man."

"Yas'm, Gogo."

It was raining. It seemed to Sadie that it rained a lot these days. Often, she thought she was in the middle of a dream. "Mebbe someday Ah wakes up from dis dream. Lawd knows what in dat bottle Marse Willie keep givin me. But it sho' is strong hoodoo. It hide de worl away so Ah cain't tink about it no more," she sighed. She thought they were still out there looking for Ross. "But Ah knows he's gone," she said. Sadie closed her eyes, too tired to think.

"Dere jes one ting I don' know, Kitty cat," she reached over and tried to touch the cat. "Who dat come fer Rossie boy? De white bird? De hooty owl? Or de spell ah puts on Dooby?" Her forehead furrowed in pain at the thought, tears rolled down her cheeks, and the ginger cat began to purr.

"When Ah ax Marse doc 'bout dat he jes' say, it cain't be all dose tings so it must be none o' dem. Moses he say he tink angels com after Rossie. What kinda angel dat be? But sumpin took ma boy."

"Yas'm." Toto said.

Sadie Jones didn't know how long she slept, or what day it was. When she woke up the sun was throwing long shadows over the yard. She walked unsteadily to the kitchen door to see what all the noise was about.

Loud voices had woken her, and the sound of children squealing, and their mother's voices trying to calm them. Will called from the porch, wanting to know what was going on.

Squinting into the twilight, Sadie could make out the figures of a man and a woman. They were talking to Moses who was helping the woman off the horse they had ridden in on.

She watched the woman d over and smooth her skirts. The man

removed his hat, as he listened to what Moses was saying.

What was it about the woman? Sadie's eyesight was too bad to be sure.

Will joined them and stood there with his arms crossed, listening intently to what the man was saying. And then Will said something to him, and the stranger put his arm up to cover his eyes. Sadie could see his big shoulders shaking, as he reached out to clasp Will's arm with his free hand.

The woman had her hand to her mouth. She raised her head and saw Sadie standing in the doorway of the kitchen house. "Mama!" she cried.

With her arms flailing, Mollie ran across the courtyard to her mother.

"Mama!" The young woman fell at Sadie's feet and clasped her hand, covering it with kisses. "It's me, Mama!"

"Mollie. You home." The old woman's voice wavered as she pointed to the man who was walking toward them. "Dat your husband he?"

"No, Ma'am." The girl stood up. Her purple and yellow striped dress was torn and scorched around the hem and the sleeves were covered in soot. "He foun me hidin from de fires aft somun put a beatin on me. 'Em big fires in Chastin, an' ah ain't gots nowhere to go so he brung me home, him. He a good man, Mama."

Sadie walked slowly to where the newcomer stood with his hat in his hand.

He inclined his head in Sadie's direction and said, "Mah name be Simeon, Ma'am. I sailed wid Commander Ross Stanley dese four years long. He told me when he left de fort to come find him if ah cain't find my folks. He said, 'Ax fer Sadie Jones—dats *Miss Sadie Jones*.' And then I found dis woman," he gestured toward Mollie, "and when he say he live here, and Miss Sadie Jones he mama, I brung her home."

That evening, dinner was marked by long silences. Neither William nor his son had any appetite for the crab gumbo and cornbread that Mollie and Sadie had made.

They talked about the arrival of Simeon and his close ties to Ross. They could now string the events of the last few months of Ross's life together and that eased the pain somewhat.

"Seems like a good man," Will ventured. "He's certainly done Mollie a great kindness by rescuing her from the Charleston calamity and bringing her home."

"Let's hope she stays, son. Sadie needs her." William said. "That girl will always yearn for greener pastures." He paused. "But, back to the fellow Simeon. Can we find work for him around here? I think that's what Ross wanted."

"We might well be able to use him," Will said. "Moses has been teaching Daniel carpentry skills and I think he'll encourage him to move to Charleston to find work." He paused. "But I'd like the boy to help me on my rounds. He's bright and he's showing some interest in medicine. So, Moses will need help—if he doesn't decide to go."

"Hmmm."

Will knew it was hard for the doctor to think of losing Moses. But Moses wasn't getting any younger. He deserved his chance. Another long silence descended over the dinner hour.

"Zack told me of a conversation he had with Ross who told him there would be new opportunities for him too when this is all over," Will said.

"Well, if the 13th Amendment holds up, Zack will be a free man. What does he want to do?"

"He wants to teach school."

"Where can a black man teach school, for God's sake?"

"A lot of ex-slaves will be looking for an education now, and people will be there to teach them. I think, Pa, there're going to be schools opening for them everywhere soon."

"Never!"

Will let the comment pass. "It's being kept quiet, but I've heard that Miss Ellie is opening one of the first black schools in Wilmington."

"Good heavens!" William rubbed his chin. Big changes were coming. What happened to standards? It was hard for an old man to process. He was silent for a long time and then he said, "Would she be willing to train Zack, do you think?"

"She might."

"Well, talk to Moses and see what he thinks about giving this chap, Simeon a job. Then invite Miss Ellie to tea. Not right away. Maybe next week."

"Yes, sir." Will hid a small smile behind his napkin. The old doctor had proved once again that he could adapt. Even when things went horribly wrong. New ideas had always been part of his life, and that would never change.

"How is Katherine Rose?" William asked.

Will shook his head. "Not doing well." he sighed. "She seems to have lost any desire to live. I'm seeing her tomorrow."

Forty-Six

Katie Rose
(I think it's March 1865)

*T*he gazebo is cold this morning, and the ocean is as gray as I feel. As though a cold, wet blanket is wrapped around my heart. The clouds are as dark as a witch's veil.

Writing in my journal is the only thing that helps these days. So I write.

They didn't find Ross. I heard Charlie telling Aunt Winn that there's no hope. And tomorrow everyone will be at All Saints Chapel for a memorial service.

Sadie Jones won't be there. When Aunt Winn and Millie went to see Doctor Stanley and Will, they said that Sadie sleeps a lot these days. The doctor doesn't think she can last. The shock's been too much, and she's too old. Zacky's getting better. They say he's up and doing chores.

Aunt Trudy says I don't have to go to the service. I'm glad. Funny. Tomorrow might have been my wedding day.

The paper's wet again. My hand's slipping on the pen, and I can't see. Everyone say the sun is shining but my world is dark.

Forty-Seven

... To Have and to Hold.

ZACK STOPPED THE carriage at the bottom of Fairhaven's broad steps. Will stepped out onto the driveway in his pinstripe vest, dark trousers and tails, holding a gold-topped cane,

"Pull over and wait for me, Zack. I doubt this will take long." He smoothed his coat and gazed up the stairs. "Pick me up if I come rolling down the steps on the end of Merriman's boot."

Zack gave a little smile. "That won't happen."

"I hope you're right. Here I go."

"You okay with those steps?"

"I'll make it." And with his hat in hand, the young doctor climbed the wide stairway to the front door.

Today was the day they were holding the memorial for Ross. A sad day. Will glanced toward the church yard as he climbed, noting the line of carriages on the road, all heading for the church. The whole town must be here, he thought. A wave of emotion washed through him as he cleared his throat and rang the doorbell.

"Hello, Charles," he said as the butler opened the door.

"How are you, sir ?"

"Stupid question, Asquith. "I've had better days.

"To be sure, sir." He took Will's hat. "It's a bloody awful day if you ask me. The whole thing makes me feel quite sick. My condolences to you, Dr. Stanley. I can't for the life of me imagine how you're holding up."

"Thank you. The human spirit is an amazingly resilient thing. Merriman's expecting me, I hope?"

"In the parlor, sir. The ladies are already in the chapel and Miss Katie Rose is upstairs resting." The houseman reached out and put a hand on Will's arm. "How is your father holding up?"

"Reasonably well, thank you. We've just dropped him off at the chapel—in the capable hands of Mrs. Perry."

The corner of Charles's mouth twitched, and he had to refrain from rolling his eyes. "Yes, sir. A most capable woman, as you say."

"Pa was talking to Winston Perry when we left him. He wanted to know more about the ship that was blown up in Winyah bay a couple of weeks ago. The *Harvest Moon*?"

"To be sure, sir. Some chap by the name of Duggert sent a barrel full of gun powder rolling into the bay, and she was struck amidships. Mr. Perry will know the details from that telegraph machine of his."

"I'm glad Pa's showing some interest in things finally. Have you heard any more speculation on who blew up Miss Fannie's place?"

"Someone saw a youth riding away from the scene, that's all I know." Charles held out his hand to allow Will to pass and pointed him toward the parlor.

"There you are, Will!" James Merriman came out to greet him and ushered him inside.

"Will that be all, sir?" The butler asked.

"That's it, Charles, thank you. Come in Will, have a seat."

"This won't take long, sir" Will leaned his cane against the chair arm. "If you don't mind, I think I'll stand."

Katie Rose's father waited.

"I know this couldn't come at a worse time, but I have something on my mind that I would like to discuss with you." Will cleared his throat. "Understanding that you'll be leaving soon after the memorial, I decided not to wait."

"How can I help you, Will?" James Merriman put a hand on the mantle and waited.

"Sometime in the not too distant future," Will said, "when Katie Rose has had all the time she needs to heal from this tragedy, I would like to ask your permission to broach the question of marriage to her." He paused. "I know that physically I suffer from a slight impediment, but I can offer her as much, or more security than most, as a doctor's wife, my wife, sir, and her position as Mistress of Willowgreen."

"Is that all?" Jack Merriman asked.

Will was taken aback. "Forgive me, I don't understand—"

"Do you love her?"

"With all my heart, sir." The words flew out of him. They had always been there, but no one had ever asked before.

"That's all I need to know. Love, after all, is the greatest security." He paused. "You know, better than most, what a handful my daughter can be. So, if you can handle that, you have my blessing to plead your suit."

"I don't know how to thank you." It was true. Never in his wildest aspirations had Will imagined himself in this situation. It would have been preposterous for one thing, and impossible to contemplate, anyway. But things had changed.

Oh, how they had changed.

Sensing his consternation, James put his hand on Will's arm and said, "No need to thank me. Like your father, you're a scholar and a gentleman." Now it was his turn to clear his throat. "I hope you will wait until we get back from Europe." He turned toward the window and crossed his arms. "Word came today that we've lost Riverbend. The house was destroyed, burned to the ground by Union soldiers, the day I left."

"I had no idea—"

"We are homeless for the time being so the European trip makes infinite sense at this time. I don't wish to impose on my sister's kindness or her home for too long, so, we will leave a week from today. We'll be away for three months. I feel that should give Katherine Rose plenty of time to recover from this dreadful thing that's befallen all of us."

"Yes, sir. I'll give her all the time she needs," he hesitated. "I'm sorry about Riverbend."

"Huh! Bricks and mortar, Will. We shall bounce back. Rebuild if we can, and if not, we shall start anew like everybody else. Heaven knows, we've been spared more than most during this blasted fight, leaving us much to be thankful for. Not least of all your family's friendship." James Merriman hooked his thumbs in his lapels and stared at Will.

"You're one of the unsung heroes, Will. You've taken life by the horns and you've proved your worth in a noble profession. So it is settled."

With that, he handed Will his cane, and they walked toward the door. "It's time to go. Will you ride to the chapel with me or is your driver outside?"

"Zack's waiting for me, sir, but thank you." He took his hat from Charles who was standing at the top of the steps. "Thank you, sir, from the bottom of my heart." He bowed toward James Merriman and shook his hand.

Will took the steps cautiously, as Zack waited below. He wished he could gallop down these stairs, take them two at a time! As pleased as he was at the outcome of his conversation with James Merriman, notwithstanding his news about Riverbend, Will wanted to throw his hat in the air and jump for joy.

His greatest challenge, he knew well, still lay ahead. Katie Rose must be healed and wooed. "With God's help and with time, it will happen," he whispered. Tears filled his eyes as he stepped into the waiting carriage, and for a moment he didn't trust himself to speak as he remembered the main reason he was here today.

Inside the chapel, the organ played softly, as Zack let him out of the carriage at the front door. A single bell tolled mournfully across the island.

Forty-Eight

All Saints Chapel

KATIE ROSE STARED at her journal lying on the window sill, closed it carefully, and placed it under her pillow.

From her upstairs bedroom window, she watched the carriages coming down the sandy road. She could see the church, right white in the afternoon sun, and Charlie and Moses showing people where to park.

Everyone was dressed in dark colors. A stream of indigo, she thought. Millie had come in to check on her before she left for the service, and she was all in black. So were the aunts.

Someone was knocking on her door. She didn't want to answer it.

The knock came again, and she heard, "It's me, Papa. May I come in?"

Getting up from the window seat, Katie Rose crossed the room and opened the door. He had his top hat in his hands, and he was wearing a grey silk vest and tails. Such a handsome man, she thought. "Hello, Papa."

She turned and went back to the window. She sat down. He looked so sad.

"My darling girl." He held out his hands helplessly, noting how pale she was. "I know there's nothing to say that will make you smile but, oh how I miss that lovely smile!" There were tears in his eyes.

"Don't cry, Papa," she whispered. Her own tears started to flow as he raised her from the window seat and held her in his arms.

As her sobs abated, he released her and holding her arms, he stepped back and said, "When all these rituals are over, I want to take you to Europe on a long trip." He cleared his throat hard and was silent for a moment. "The Alpine breezes, the music of Vienna, the warmth of Rome." Then he smiled. "And the gaiety of Paris. They will warm your heart, my darling, put a spring in your step, and help you to smile again. That, I promise you, Katherine Rose."

This was not the time to tell her about Riverbend. So, he turned away, put his hat back on, and closed the door softly behind him.

She could hear his footsteps going down the stairs. Poor Papa. Katie Rose looked out toward the church. Everyone had gone inside. After a few minutes, she watched the lonely figure of her father cross the sandy parking lot and turned away. She didn't hear the organ playing the soft, sad notes of the Te Deum, as the church door closed behind him.

Nor did she see the stranger in a frayed black suit and scuffed shoes standing in the shadow of the oaks beside the church.

The man under the oaks glanced down the empty road and decided that everyone who was coming to the memorial service was already here. And there was still no sign of the young lady. He was pleased. This family had enough sorrow to deal with without having their daughter questioned about her whereabouts on the morning Fannie's Inn exploded.

The patrolman opened a small black notebook and scribbled

across the front page of his notes: CASE CLOSED. Then he walked away from the church.

Forty-Nine

Until Death do us Part . . .

VIOLET'S WEDDING DRESS hung in the corner of the armoire.
Kate Rose reached inside, took it out, and laid it gently on the
bed.

"Ross will love it," she whispered.

Stepping out of the navy serge dress she wore, she left it in a
crumpled heap on the floor. Standing only in her shift, she picked up
the wedding dress and, almost reverently, she let it slide it over her
head and shoulders, feeling the soft silk folds fall across her breasts
and over her thighs as it swirled around her bare feet.

Katie Rose closed the armoire door and stared at herself in the
wavy mirror. Her cheeks were too pale. Her face was much too thin,
and dwarfed by the dark blue pools of her eyes made larger by the
smoky shadows beneath them.

She hooked the small buttons that went all the way down the
back—easy to do now that she had grown so thin in the last few
weeks—and picked up the deep lavender sash that went around her
waist.

She looked in the mirror again and imagined the pearl-studded veil made of the finest tulle in the palest shade of lavender. 'How beautiful you are, my Katie Rose!' he'll say.

The sand on the boardwalk that led to the gazebo was gritty and cold under her bare feet, as she walked out to the dunes. Katie Rose climbed the steep wooden steps to its peak, diminished by spring storms, its grains of sand swept away by high winds.

Overhead, the sky was darkening, eclipsing the sun as it sank rapidly toward the horizon warming the cold sea, painting the gray waves with gold. Standing on top of the dunes, she gazed unseeingly down at the beach. She hardly felt the soft watered silk blowing around her bare legs, and feet as she stared at the empty shore below. Rose-tinted sand sparkled in the rays of the dying sun, the seaward slope of the dune was bathed in shadow, and the sound of seabirds filled the air as Katie Rose ran lightly down the sandy mountain to the ocean.

Her footprints made pale, disappearing circles that vanished into the wet beach, as she approached the water. But she didn't notice. She heard neither the tinkle of seashells tumbling in the surf nor the rustle of waves breaking on the shore, swirling in a cold caress around her ankles.

The hem of Violet's wedding dress floated in the surf, rising above her knees as she walked. A tiny smile played around her slightly parted lips, as she walked easily through the surf.

"Soon, Ross," she whispered.

A gull swooped low, breaking the hushed sounds of evening with its raucous screech, as it dove, but she didn't notice. The sea was above her waist now, creeping coldly and steadily higher, its clammy fingers encircling and covering her breast as she sank deeper into the soft ocean floor. She felt cold and alone. Inexplicably, she wavered, casting a glance back at the beach, at the tall white house.

And, in that moment of hesitation, Katie Rose never saw the monster wave rolling in. High, and powerfully strong, it came out of some offshore depth, towered above her before it shivered, trembled, and broke with a roar that vibrated through the surrounding sea. She never heard herself cry out, as the wave sent her body tumbling, crashing to the hard sand surface that had been drained almost dry of seawater.

Seawater rushed out ahead of the wave, and was sucked high into its massive breast before its full bulk descended, crushing her frail body under its weight. Tons of water dragged her tumbling, relentlessly over and over, filling her eyes, her nose, her throat with water, and crashing along the crusty bottom, before finally throwing her limp and battered body onto the dimpled shore.

Fifty

The Shore

THE EVENING SKY was filled with the sounds of roosting birds. Katie Rose lay like a discarded china doll on the sand. Wind gusted off the ocean. Thunder rumbled, and, from somewhere far away, she heard the sound of hoof beats.

She raised her head. The breeze lifted her hair as she opened her eyes and stared through the twilight to see where the sound was coming from.

Where was she? And who was the horseman riding down the beach? Shrouded in mist, he drew closer with every second.

Rising effortlessly to her knees, she put one foot out to steady herself and stood up with her arms at her sides, staring into the distance. She felt so light. Her eyes were clear. She felt vibrantly alive. But—where was she? It was as though she wasn't there—and yet, she could feel and see.

Her gown clung to her thighs, its bodice hugged her slim form, as she gazed at the approaching horse and rider. He was closer now. A man of average build, dressed in gray, or was it the mist that rolled around him, that made it seem so—and around his horse—a tall horse, strong and fast. Closer still, she saw that the rider wore a cap, and a sword glinted at his side. His dark hair curled around his ears. And Katie Rose thought her heart would burst.

"Ross!" Lifting her skirt up above her knees, she ran to meet him with tears streaming from the corners of her eyes.

She stopped. For suddenly—she didn't know how—he was beside her. She hadn't seen him dismount. In fact, the horse was nowhere to be seen. Her hand went to her mouth.

"Oh Ross," she whispered. His face was tanned, his eyes were the color of stormy seas, and he smiled that smile that crinkled his eyes and filled her with the warmth of a summer's day. The way it always had. Her hand reached out tentatively to touch his face. His skin was warm to the touch.

He smiled down at her. Flecks of salt and sand speckled his face, and a feeling of exquisite gentleness filled the space around them. His arms reached for her. He held her face between his hands. His hands were warm—how could that be?

"Ross." Her tears fell as she turned her face to kiss his wrist. The warmth of his body, so close to hers, enveloped her. He was alive and more vibrant than he had ever been. She ran her hand over the rough material of his coat and the hard steel of his sword at his side as if to assure herself that he was really here.

His essence filled every part of her, and he raised her face to his and looked into her eyes. There was no sound, but she heard, *"Katie Rose,"* and its vibration, like warm honey, seeped into the deepest recesses of her spirit. His lips, so close, did not move but came down to meet hers in a kiss so gentle, it touched every part of her. She stood light and tremulous in his arms. The love that overflowed from that kiss rippled through her very soul, as she held him, never wanting to let him go. It was as though they had melted into one in some cosmic fusion. And that oneness was complete.

"They told me you were dead," she finally gasped.

"Does it feel that way to you?"

"You're alive," she breathed. She could only stare at him in wonder, as a sob left her lips. "You're alive."

Katie Rose found herself engulfed in the radiance of complete joy. Something far beyond earthly love infused her spirit. Feelings became waves of colors she hardly recognized. She felt herself immersed in the perfume of the sea that mingled with the scent of this man, strong and moving in her arms, in her heart and soul—beside her, in her, embracing and penetrating her spirit in the sweetest love she had ever known.

As she clung to him, from the depths of their embrace, a fountain of ecstasy showered every part of her being, drenching every cell. An ecstasy as capricious as blowing foam, melting into thin air, as gently as the first snow, possessed her. She felt his breath on her face.

"I love you, Katie Rose. I'll always love you. I must leave now and so must you. There's a storm coming in. Stay with them, they need you. We'll be together again."

She felt the words, although he never spoke them. His lips never moved. "Don't go!" she cried.

"I'll never leave you."

She felt him separate from her, leaving his elusive warmth and the indescribable joy and happiness that engulfed her. "Don't go," she cried again.

She thought his eyes were filled with tears as he moved away, or was it her own tears reflected in his eyes? Holding out her arms, she watched him fade into the fog that rolled in from the sea.

From a great distance, she heard his voice, *"We don't die, my darling. We don't die, my Katie Rose."*

Fifty-One

Fairhaven

"SHE'S SAYING SOMETHING! What's she saying? She's reaching for something." It was her father's voice, and then strong hands and arms lifted her. Cradled her as her head rolled forward onto Zack's chest, and she felt herself carried her up the beach.

She heard Doctor Stanley's voice saying, "She's alive!"

Someone else said, "Gently now. Let's hurry, the storm's coming fast."

And then there was nothing. Until she opened her eyes in Winifred's parlor and realized she was lying on the settee.

Her father sat beside her, still dressed in formal garb but with his winged collar in disarray and undone. He rubbed her hands, as cold as ice, between his. All of her felt as cold as ice in spite of the thick quilts that they had wrapped around her. A vivid flash of lightning stabbed the oak grove.

There's a storm coming, Ross had said.

The next time Katie Rose awoke, daylight was pouring in

through the shutters. She knew she was in her bedroom at Fairhaven because she could hear the birds in the marshes.

Her whole body ached as she lay there trying to remember what had happened. She tried moving her leg and the movement sent a ripple of pain through her hip. A sling held up her left hand and arm, and her shoulder ached. Her fingers touched a place on her cheekbone that was raw and stinging, as did a wide sand burn above the cast and a gash above her right elbow.

Slowly, her mind began to find its way through the jumble of unrest inside her head. Katie Rose vaguely remembered walking into the sea. But as hard as she tried she could remember nothing else. Her eyes filled with tears of frustration. She knew there was more. She just couldn't reach it. A sob rose in her chest, as she tried to force the memory through the fog.

Running her free hand under the covers, she realized that someone had removed her clothing, and that her rib cage was wrapped in bandages.

Mama's wedding dress hung over the back of a chair, limp and torn. What was it doing there? Who took it out of the armoire? And why was it torn?

Katie Rose squeezed her eyes shut and tried to remember. She opened them after a while and lay back on the pillows staring around the room. As she stared at the ceiling, something else began to seep through the fog hovering around the edges of her brain.

It felt like a *presence*. Warm and light and filled with the sound of the ocean, horse's hooves and the faint scent of Bay Rhum . . . Katie Rose held her breath and lay perfectly still. The light in the room turned misty blue and a shape began to form. It came closer and closer until it exploded in her mind like a thousand lights in a myriad of colors.

"I'm here," he said.

She couldn't see anyone, but she knew that it was Ross. His voice came from a million miles away, and yet—it was right beside her.

Katie Rose sat up abruptly, setting off small sharp pains all the way up the back of her neck through her chest and into her head. But she didn't care. She felt light and alive and relief filled her heart. Ross was back. The deep sadness evaporated like mist in the wind. The memory of the evening came back and just as suddenly, the soft blue light melted away and she was alone.

For the first time in weeks, she smiled.

She welcomed the shaft of sunshine coming through the open window. It lit up the polished oak floor and made the colors in the rag rug bright and gay.

"Ross was here again," she murmured, and could hardly believe what she was saying. She only knew it was true. She held her hands up to her face and winced in pain. "He's alive. He told me so."

The image began to move toward the back of her mind, making room for the realization, the certainty, of what had happened on the beach last night. She remembered lying on the sand and listening to hoof beats. She remembered the horse.

And she remembered, vividly, how their love for each other had broken through dimensions and filled them with a cascade of indescribable joy in each other's arms! What had he said? *"We don't die, my darling. We don't die Katie Rose."*

She had to tell someone. Something unbelievable had happened and her heart overflowed with excitement. Her shoulders slumped suddenly. Who would believe her?

There was a soft knock on her door, and someone turned the doorknob and peeked into her room.

"Aunt Tru?"

"Katie Rose! You're awake."

"What time is it? How long have I slept?"

"Why, it's almost two in the afternoon." Trudy came into the room and sat down beside her on the bed. "How are you feeling, darling girl? You gave us such a fright. Thank God, Millie went looking for you when she found you weren't in your room. Otherwise—" Trudy dabbed at her eyes with a damp, lace handkerchief.

"Oh Tru Pru, it's the strangest thing!" Katie Rose's eyes were bright with moisture and she was smiling as she lay back on the pillows. "I hurt all over—from head to toe—but I'm so happy. I saw Ross." She watched the concern on her aunt's face.

"What a lovely dream, darling," her aunt finally said, smoothing Katie Rose's hair back from her forehead. "You must be starving. I'm going to get Millie to bring up some hot water and have her stay with you and help you wash. Then I'll bring you some breakfast."

Katie Rose laughed softly. "But it's way past lunchtime."

"When you've eaten, Millie will help you back into bed— "

"But I want to get up."

"We mustn't rush things, dear. Will says the more rest you get the better. He's coming in about an hour to see how you're doing."

"Will's coming?"

"Yes, Old Doctor Stanley isn't making house calls these days. Leah told us the poor man stays shut in his office all day. Sadie Jones refuses to disturb him, and apparently Leah was quite put out about that."

"Good for Sadie. I must get up and go and see him. Poor Doctor Stanley. Oh, Aunt Tru, I've got the most wonderful things to tell Sadie. And Tru Pru—you should take off that black dress. Ross didn't die."

"There'll be time for visiting when you're well, dear." Trudy patted the bedclothes down, blinking rapidly. She plumped the pillows and stood up to leave. "I'm going to fetch Millie."

Really! The change that had come over Katie Rose was quite extraordinary, not to mention disturbing, she thought as she went downstairs. The girl was raving.

Fifty-Two

And So It Is

WILL WAS COMING to see her. She knew Will would believe her. She tried to hug her shoulders and groaned at the sharp pain that caused. But a smile lit up her face as she gingerly put her feet on the floor and cried out as pain shot through her leg. Her bandaged ankle must be sprained.

Aunt Trudy was wrong about it being a lovely dream. She knew a dream from the real thing. She knew she had been with Ross on the beach. Whatever anyone else thought.

When Will was shown into her room, Katie Rose was dressed and sitting in her armchair by the window. Her foot rested on a cushioned footstool, and Millie had plumped a cushion behind her neck, and draped a shawl around her shoulders.

Funny, she had never noticed how tall he was, even with his one bad leg shorter than the other. Will was as tall as his father. His auburn hair curled at the nape of his neck, and he wore a black cape that he shrugged off his shoulders and draped over the back of the chair he pulled up to face her.

"How are you, Kate?" He eyed the swelling in her ankle and in the hand protruding from the bandaged splints.

He was the only one who ever called her 'Kate'. The sound of his voice, so like Ross's, caught her off-guard and a sob caught in her throat. "Oh, Will,'' she raised her hand to her eyes and cried. "I can't believe this is happening."

He reached out and took both her hands in his. "I know, I know. My heart is broken too," he said softly.

She looked up at him through her tears. "Oh, Will—I'm so thoughtless, I've been thinking only of myself!"

He leaned back, releasing her hands. "Don't think like that. Is this ankle very painful?" He laid his hand gently on the bridge of her foot.

"It's alright unless I try to walk on it. In fact, my whole body is fine unless I try to move anything." She blinked the tears away.

"Well, you got tumbled and dumped on pretty badly out there. One rib is broken. Does your shoulder hurt when you move it?"

"Yes. Everything hurts when I move." She looked hard at him, sizing him up for what she was about to say. "Will—"

"You aunt said you slept nearly eighteen hours."

"Did I? Will—" She almost changed her mind, and then she thought of them as children. Ross was always the dare devil, Zack followed him everywhere, but it was Will, the quiet one, who listened. He was the one who waited for her when she couldn't keep up with the others. He was the sensitive one, Sadie Jones always said.

What would he think about what she was about to tell him?

He moved her arm up and down, and around, to see if there was any change in the motion of her shoulder. There were no squeals from his patient, and that was good. It was bruised, but nothing worse than that. He noticed too that the back of her neck was bruised with a grazed place covering the top of the other shoulder. But it too would heal, as would the breaks and cuts and bruises. She was lucky not to have broken her neck. "No headaches?" He asked.

She shook her head, still sizing him up.

"Good, I'll leave something with your aunt to help you sleep again tonight and something to take if you find yourself in pain." He began to scribble on a pad on his lap.

"Will, can I tell you something?"

"Of course," he said without lifting his head.

"It's about Ross." She pushed herself higher up the back of her chair. "Ouch!" she moaned as her chest hurt.

He was watching her. "What about Ross?" She could see the pain in his eyes at the mention of his brother's name.

"I saw him, Will. Just as surely as I can see you." There. She'd said it. Her face lit up, and her eyes sparkled as she proceeded to tell him what had happened. She told him about the rider, all in gray, the horse, the love that streamed from him. "He looked just the same as he always has. Solid. Not like some see-through, wispy ghost or anything. He was alive, Will, and on the beach beside me."

He stared at her for a few moments, seeing the excitement shining in her eyes, the flush in her cheeks. But neither gave him cause for alarm.

She smiled and reached for his hand. "You must believe me," she said, watching his face intently. "And do you know what he said?"

The young doctor shook his head.

"He said, '*We don't die.'* Not once but twice. *We don't die.*"

Will was quiet for what seemed like an hour to Katie Rose as she sat there holding her breath, staring at his face wondering if she had made a mistake.

Very gently, he took her hand in his and said, "I believe you, Kate."

"Thank God. Not many people would. It sounds as though I'm making it up—but I'm not."

"I know you're not." He smiled and changed the subject. "Your Papa says you're going to Europe?"

"Yes." She looked down at her hands with a serious look on her face. "It's for Papa, really. I'm going to be alright now that I know that Ross is alright. It's Papa who needs the trip, not me."

Will reached for his cape and picked up his black bag, happy with his assessment that she wasn't raving, as Trudy had told him.

"Well, I think you'll be ready to make the trip, before long." He smiled at her. "And you'll have a wonderful time." He reached for his cane. "I'll be back before you leave just to make sure, and we'll all be here when you get back." He bent down and kissed her on the cheek, straightened up, and was about to leave when there was a knock on the door.

"Come in," Katie Rose called.

The door opened and Trudy poked her head in. She was smiling. "There's someone here to see you," she cooed as she pushed the door open to show the small, wizened old woman carrying a sweet grass basket full of pralines.

"Sadie Jones!" she cried joyfully. "You came."

Will gave the women a small bow and discreetly left the room as Sadie trundled in.

She was almost happy, he mused, standing at the top of the stairs looking down. Katie Rose was almost happy. And no sign of delirium that he could see. There was nothing the matter with her mind. Of that he was sure.

The strange thing was, as they carried Katie Rose to the house that evening, he looked down the beach, noting the thickening fog.

And as he watched it rolling across the shore, there appeared, shrouded in its mist, the figure of a man dressed all in gray, astride a horse.

He remembered wondering who on earth would be out riding in this weather. He watched as the mists swirled around the man, sometimes obscuring him, and once, he wondered if there might be two figures seated on the horse. It was insane, but he was almost sure that he saw the slight form of a young Gullah girl seated behind him.

The vision, as he called it, lasted only a few seconds, before someone on the beach yelled, "Let's get her inside!" and he had turned his attention back to Katie Rose.

Moments later, when he looked again, there was nothing there. And if it hadn't been for the faint scent of Bay Rhum floating on the mist, he might have believed he had imagined it.

Epilogue

From the Journal of Isaac Jones
(11 July 1868)

"THERE IS A time to live and a time to die. Miss Sadie Jones died on this day, in the summer of 1868, in or around her eightieth year." Zack wrote in the journal he started when he began his first teaching job in Miss Ellie's new school.

Later, with the money he saved in Mistress Elizabeth's bank, he would build his own school room at Willowgreen.

"Doc Stanley, Will and Katie Rose, the new Mistress of Willowgreen, Moses and Mollie and I were beside Mama at the end. The day before she died, mine and Tansy's son was born. And Mollie told her that she and Simeon are going to jump the broomstick when he gets back from his stint in the US Navy. Mama smiled.

We said 'Goodbye' when her time to live ended on a fine sunshiny morning in July.

Isaac Jones
11 July 1868"

THE END

Acknowledgements

Thank you, Lee Brockington, historian and coordinator of Public Engagement of the Hobcaw Barony, for your encouragement, and for sharing with me your historical knowledge of the South Carolina coast, both actual and anecdotal. Important to note that, any mistakes, or license taken, in or around the descriptions and portrayals of any place or character in the novel, are the author's. Not Lee's. Thank you too, for the many contacts you referred me to. They were invaluable to my research, as were our long lunches at small cafes in Georgetown and Pawley's Island.

I could not have imagined the Colonial Kings Highway of the 1800's without the knowledge and expertise shared with me by Dennis Chastain, a wildlife writer, who spent two years exploring and uncovering its existence. Thank you, Dennis, for helping to guide my protagonist, Ross Stanley, and his childhood friend Zack Jones, along its treacherous passage.

Thank you, Dana Stokes for giving me some great information, and contacts.

To Corinne Taylor, thank you for your gracious acknowledgement of my fictitious portrayal of your historical Pelican Inn that inspired the big white beach house, Fairhaven, and my setting on Pawley's Island.

Robin Gabriel, Director of the beautiful Civil War home, now the Kaminski House Museum, thank you for your very helpful and interesting information.

I must acknowledge Brookgreen Gardens where I was able to

get a broad sense of plantation living. The tour of the slave quarters and the recordings of their voices along the way were especially useful and inspiring. And the Brookgreen bookstore where I bought several historical books and CDs that gave me a palpable sense of the Gullah language, their food, and folk medicine.

My special thanks go to Glen Cox, the pharmacist of Pawley's Island, who gave me a firsthand and detailed account of his own encounter with The Gray Man. The Ghost of Pawley's Island.

To my Lake Writer's Group: My thanks, appreciation and admiration for your great ideas, your valuable observations and guidance along the way.

Special thanks go to Chuck Lumpkin of the Lake Writer's for the painstaking work he did formatting and, designing the manuscript. I am forever grateful to you for your unfailing patience and good nature.

And to my readers for taking on the blinding task of scrutinizing this manuscript in all its incarnations, thank you: Betsy Ashton, Judy Helms, Sue Coryell, Linda Kay Simmons, Pat Bechtler and Sue Patterson.

Justin McIntyre, Curator of the SC Maritime Museum, thank you for the great information you shared on the Grey Man.

To Larry Lehmann, without whose encouragement and sailing expertise I could never have sailed Ross Stanley across a stormy Charleston Harbor. Thank you.

CPSIA information can be obtained
at www.ICGtesting.com
Printed in the USA
LVHW040554210920
666618LV00013B/111